I0552348

Diplomatic Baggage

a Leathan Wilkey novel

Simon Cann

Coombe
Hill
Publishing

Published by Coombe Hill Publishing
33 Melrose Gardens
New Malden
Surrey KT3 3HQ
United Kingdom
coombehillpublishing.com

ISBN: 9781910398142 (paperback)
ISBN: 9781910398159 (ePub)

A big thank you to Cathleen Small for her editorial input.

10 September 2016

one

There was a torn piece of brown corrugated cardboard propped up, clearly intended to be seen. I couldn't read what was on it, but I was pretty sure what would be there: a short plea for help scrawled with a faltering ballpoint pen in pathetic spidery writing, the message ending "SVP."

S'il vous plaît.

Please.

Please help this man sitting in his makeshift home. Please help this man in his castle constructed from cardboard, wide stackable trays that are usually employed to transport food into stores, and weatherproofed with trash bags and old plastic sheets. Please help this man, sitting upright and wrapped in a blanket.

Please help this man, begging outside an apartment block on a residential street in Paris.

Please help this man, begging at night when every other beggar has left the streets.

Please help this man, sitting in the constant low-level drizzling rain. The constant drizzle that seemed to have been falling without pause since I woke up at 6 AM.

I looked closer. Beggars were a common sight on Paris streets. They usually chose to beg on the busy walkways, placing themselves so that you had to walk around them, or outside a store to highlight the contrast with your spending. Often they had an animal— usually a dog, but sometimes a cat—and occasionally when you saw them trying to sleep at night, you would see a child, maybe seven or eight years old, next to them.

In Paris.

Paris, the City of Light.

Paris, the center of the enlightenment.

Looking toward the homeless guy made me aware that there was more cash in my pocket than I was comfortable carrying. Usually, I wouldn't carry more than I was happy to lose—maybe 100 or 200 euros. I wouldn't want to lose that much, but if I did, it wouldn't be anything that I would remember after the second drink.

But now, I had at least 4,000 euros. It had started as 5,000 euros—ten bills of €500—but I had paid a few people, bought a few drinks, and offered some thanks. And, of course, I left 200 euros to cover the window. I wasn't sure how much I had paid in total—it wasn't that I needed to keep receipts—but since I'd broken two bills into smaller denominations, I knew I still had at least 4,000 euros, and now I was becoming aware of the risk of carrying that much cash.

The beggar's home was set against the outside wall of the apartment complex. A brutal, white, 1950s modernist concrete block, surrounded by a low white concrete wall with its concrete having been formed into geometric patterns. The low wall was then topped with a steel bar fence with triangular spikes running along the top at about eight feet high. In the dark and the rain, modernist Paris of the 1950s now had the feel of a totalitarian regime offering featureless housing to cheerful workers.

I didn't like the block—this was partly a personal preference that villages should be horizontal, not vertical, and partly a dislike of central planning—but that was my taste. And my taste had nothing to do with the question rattling around my head: How does a nineteen-year-old afford to live here?

This was Belleville. It was kind of downtrodden, but definitely not the worst part of Paris. Precisely where it lay on the socioeconomic spectrum was irrelevant—the fact remained, renting an apartment in Belleville would cost money, more than the average teenager could afford. Especially if the teenager was still in college, as this guy was.

If you gave me some sob story and said a kid was housed out in the banlieue—the sprawling human warehousing estates outside the city—then I might be able to accept that a teen could have an apartment. But here? In Belleville?

And why Belleville? Maybe he was a fan of Chinese food—I had passed a lot of Chinese restaurants as I walked up the hill. But to me, Belleville has always been the sort of place that people leave, and leave fast. Edith Piaf was famous for leaving and then regretting nothing. She only permanently returned to the 20th arrondissement to be buried. She didn't even return to die; someone had to take her dead body there to make her return.

I lost sight of the beggar as I turned the corner, following the side return of the caged compound. I was sure that the guy was making a call—or at least sure that he pulled out a phone.

I wasn't used to the idea of beggars having phones. I understood the necessity: If you're going to function in any way as a part of mainstream society, then you need to communicate. If you're going to apply for a job, then you need to be contactable. So I get that beggars have phones.

But phones need to be charged.

Most people charge their phones while they sleep. Or rather, *I* charge my phone while I sleep, and most people I know do similar, so I presume this is not wildly outrageous behavior. But if you're a beggar on the street at midnight, then when do you charge your phone? Shouldn't you be back at a hostel, or whatever, having a wash, getting some warm food, and letting your phone charge?

Around the corner, the brutal white frontage of the block gave way to an irregular surface. It was still flat, but sections came out to a different depth, giving some form of privacy between the apartments, and the windows were supplemented by narrow balconies, suggesting that the inhabitants of these hutches might be able to stand in the fresh air without leaving home.

Where the wall at the front was knee-high with the steel fence on top, this section of the wall was above my head and stepped higher still. As the wall got higher, the steel fence remained at its same height until the wall reached the height of the fence, when the fence stopped. Set into the wall under the highest section were windows with security bars fashioned from the same bars that made the fence. The lights behind the windows were off, removing any hint as to what happened inside.

After about thirty yards, there was the entrance to what was probably an underground parking lot. I paused—pondering—it was one way I could get in. But then I'd have to work my way through to the kid's apartment. And I didn't want to be in an enclosed space where I'd never been before.

Plus, there were easier ways to get in.

I could hang around near the front gate—which offered access to those who knew the code—and follow through when someone arrived or left.

Or simplest of all, I could climb the wall. There was a brown metal box—sturdy and locked—against the side wall. It had a utility company look about it: Maybe it was owned by the electricity company, maybe it belonged to the phone company. Whatever the case, it was a four-foot platform from which I could use the steel fence to pull myself up onto the wall and jump over.

I landed softly in a kids' playground in the corner of the compound.

Immediately it felt different. Warmer. Enclosed. And yet somehow sterile. I checked the time—three minutes past midnight. That meant I'd been awake for eighteen hours and three minutes, and on the move for all of those eighteen hours and three minutes, except for the time it took me to shave and throw on some clothes: the jeans I wore yesterday, a clean shirt, a pair of sneakers, and my leather jacket.

But now the day was coming to an end. I had finally arrived at the home of Pierre-Louis Dubois. Now it was simple: Get inside the block, find the right apartment, knock on the door, when the guy answered check that he was indeed Pierre-Louis Dubois, and leave.

With the knowledge of where the kid was, I could report back to Tolomush Okeyev, the diplomat who had hired me, tomorrow morning.

I looked around—the compound was empty. A few lights still blazed from apartment windows, and a few indistinct sounds echoed. I was aware of heavier breathing—my breathing—from the exertion of walking briskly up the hill and then vaulting over the wall. I took a few deep breaths, waiting for my heart to slow, then started following the path around the blocks.

The entrance to the block—like the front gate, which I had chosen to ignore—required an access code to be entered into the keypad placed to the right of the aluminum-framed glass door.

As I contemplated whether to kick the glass or look for another access—perhaps I was too hasty to dismiss the parking lot—I heard footsteps. A couple, maybe in their twenties—her younger than him. I ducked into the shadows across from the door and waited. The man looked hard at the keypad and slowly tapped four digits. There was a metallic click, and he reached across to open the door, following the woman.

I counted to three, listening as the stay of the closing door squealed, then ran forward, grabbing the door before it finally closed. The woman turned back. Her face, framed in dirty blond, frizzy hair, showed a look of shock, maybe agitation.

"Evening," I said. I was just another resident, right? I wasn't a threat.

She smiled nervously as the man said, "Hi." He had the sound of someone trying to sound confident. The movement of his eyes as they searched around the white-walled lobby—desperately looking for a way out—gave him away. The two showed the discomforted body language of two people who didn't want to be together. Two people who would probably start arguing the moment their front door closed. Two people embarrassed to be seen in this way, resenting the stranger who was intruding into their argument, which was brewing like a storm on the horizon.

The elevator pinged. Her face involuntarily twitched. I smiled, "It's alright. I'm taking the stairs—it's only one floor." Her whole body seemed to relax in her overly large green jacket.

And it was half true: I was going to use the stairs, but I didn't know how many floors it was. The truth was I didn't want to be stuck in a steel cage, if only for a few moments, with a couple who seemed to be embarrassed to be seen in public. But more importantly, I didn't want these two to remember me as the guy who didn't know where he was going.

I turned into the stairs, walking slowly until the elevator doors closed, when I stopped. As I heard the elevator start to move, I returned to the lobby and watched the floor count—looking for where the couple got out. Looking for the floor I should avoid if I could, if I wanted the small lie I had just told to hold up.

The count stopped at the fourth floor. I waited, watching. It didn't start again.

I took the stairs up to the first floor and cautiously stepped into the corridor outside the apartments. Like the lobby, the plaster walls had been covered in white emulsion, but the cement-colored tiles of the lobby floor had been replaced by a thin piece of cement colored carpet. Unlike the lobby, facing onto the corridor were doors—all painted with white gloss paint, the only personalization the numbering on the door. Some numbers were steel, some acrylic, some looked like a kid's design, and others seemed to be carved slate.

I checked the U-shaped corridor from one end to the other. Six front doors, one garbage chute, and several panels covering the pipes and cables for the services.

None of the front doors belonged to Pierre-Louis Dubois.

The second floor mirrored the first. The only noticeable differences were in the choice of metal, acrylic, slate, and kid designs to identify each apartment, and a different set of numbers. Where on the first floor, the six apartments were denoted by numbers beginning with 1, on the second floor the numbers began with 2. The apartment I was looking for began with a 4, so I returned to the stairs.

As I ascended from the second floor to the third, there was a sound. Loud. Slightly muffled. Yet unmistakable. I froze—looking up and when I saw nothing, looking down. It was difficult to be certain about the position other than to guess that the shot came from above.

When I had entered the block, it felt like the building had a low background hum. The noise of people—televisions and radios, water running, talking.

Now the block was silent.

two

One floor, probably two floors up, the door into the stairwell opened with a gentle sigh.

The silence was broken.

There was talking: soft, measured, unhurried…an attempt to be reassuring. "No, monsieur. The noise came from the floor above, not this one." A pause. The sound of an older female voice, her words indistinct but the reply clear. "I'm going to have a look, Madame. Lock yourself in your apartment. And you, monsieur."

There was the sound of footsteps on the tiled floor of the stairwell. It sounded like two sets of feet: one heavier than the other.

As the door bumped shut, the soft footsteps turned into two people running. Running down the stairs, seemingly taking two or three steps at a time. The momentum of descent being broken by the need to turn at the end of each half-flight of stairs.

White tennis shoes and blue jeans came into sight first, closely followed by faded red jeans. With three more steps, the first sprinter revealed his old denim jacket and the second showed a shapeless green jacket.

The first runner turned into the top of the next flight. The flight where I stood at the bottom—watching, waiting. Our eyes met, and there was a moment's hesitation as we recognized each other from our brief encounter in the entrance hall a few minutes earlier. The follower—her dirty, frizzy hair seeming to have become dirtier and frizzier—caught him up and, not noticing his hesitation, knocked into him.

This physical jolt seemed to translate into a mental jolt to action, and he launched himself from the top step. There was no attempt to take two steps at a time—he was taking the whole half-flight in one because he could cushion his landing.

On me.

And he had gravity on his side.

I wasn't sure what hurt most—where he came into contact with me, where I hit the wall and the handrail behind me, or how his momentum crumpled me to the ground. By the time I could begin to lift myself to a sitting position, I heard the door on the ground floor opening and the feet running out, their pace slowing to a non-suspicious walk.

I tried to catalog the pain as I started down the stairs. Nothing felt broken—not that walking down stairs is a substitute for medical diagnosis—but everything seemed to hurt. As I got to the door opening out from the ground floor lobby, I slipped off my jacket and dropped it to stop the swinging piece of aluminum-framed glass from closing, and took a few steps onto the path outside.

I scanned for a couple.

I scanned again. There were two people. Apart. By the wall, a man in jeans and a denim jacket was climbing over—leaving the way I had come in. And walking toward the gate, a woman in an overly bulky green jacket with faded red jeans. So this was how it was... He was there to shoot; she was there to carry the gun.

France, like every European country, outlawed carrying guns. This guy knew he might get picked up—a man on his own walking the streets at night immediately after a shooting would be a suspect for any passing cops. But knowing the sexism of the cops, she was unlikely to be noticed, and if anyone else tried their luck, well, she had a gun.

I jogged to the wall—I wasn't ready for a sprint, I wasn't ready to chase him. By landing on me, he had done enough to make sure he'd win a fight, but I wanted to get a look at where he went.

I stood on the wall, looking over to the drop below. He had turned and continued up the hill. I looked back to the woman, who was reaching the gate. She pushed the gate release button—the click of the lock echoing across the compound—opened the swinging metal bars, took two steps, and was gone.

I looked to the guy.

What guy? He had vanished, too.

three

I picked up my jacket—remembering it was probably not the smartest move to leave 4,000 euros propping a door open—and carrying it by its scruff, I returned to the stairs. I could have taken the elevator, but I didn't want the ping to announce my arrival to the alert neighbors. With each step I felt like I'd been in a fight, when in reality I'd been a mattress for some guy who had used gravity and momentum to beat me.

Looking through the door from the stairwell to the fourth floor corridor, all was still: The residents who had been concerned by the noise had apparently taken the advice to lock themselves in their apartments. I waited, catching my breath from the ascent, opened the door as far as necessary to get through, then closed it silently so as not to alert the neighbors, who were likely hyper-alert.

The corridor was a mirror of the floors below. I found the apartment, and after placing my ear to the door, I pushed. The wood moved in the frame, but the door didn't open. A glance behind, then I hefted the door with my shoulder. It swung open, slamming into the wall behind it, echoing through the corridor.

There was noise around—the other residents were alerted. I jumped into the apartment, shut the door—quietly this time—and peered back through the spyhole. An elderly man was tying a frayed dressing gown as he walked while talking to someone else at the other end of the passage. He shrugged—a shrug that only the French can pull off without irony—and continued walking, passing out of my sight.

Behind me, the short passageway in the apartment opened into a room. At the far end were a window and a door onto a balcony; at the closer end was a kitchenette wrapping around the corner. I guessed this was the main room of this small apartment, but it was lacking the furnishings I would expect: chairs, a television, maybe a table or some shelves.

The kitchenette had a few pieces—a charging base for a phone, some paper towels on a roll, an open bottle of beer, and in the sink were two paintbrushes that a decorator might use. That aside, the room was an empty white box with a wood laminate floor.

A white box, empty apart from the teenager propped against the wall, his breathing labored.

There was a phone next to him. A phone that matched the charger on the kitchen counter, but he'd probably want to wipe the blood off before he put it back onto charge. He held his hands to chest—bloody hands gripping against a gray T-shirt, which revealed paint-flecked arms. And coming from behind him, spreading across the laminate flooring as if flowing from his paint-specked sweatpants, blood.

I dropped my jacket, grabbed the roll of kitchen paper, and tore off a few sheets as I knelt by the kid. "I'm Leathan."

All his effort was dedicated to breathing. He was working hard for little return. "Are you Pierre-Louis?" I asked. "Pierre-Louis Dubois?"

He tried to speak, but struggled to communicate. I took the movement of his head as sufficient affirmation.

"Shall we try and put..." I looked at the few sheets of paper towel in my hand and nodded toward his chest. I felt I had to do something, but why was I focused on this wound? Sure, there was blood, and yes, he was holding the wound, but I knew that on his back—where the bullet left his body—the injury would be worse. The blood spreading across the floor that had now seeped into the knees of my jeans told me that.

The kid tried to talk.

"Shh," I said. "Just keep breathing."

He tried again. Weaker but more determined.

"Save your strength," I said. Who was I kidding? These were the last moments of this poor kid's life.

"Mari..." he said. At least I think he said—it was more an aspiration.

I laid a hand on his shoulder. Was this to be his confession? Was he going to name his killers?

"Marianne." He inhaled heavily and slowly, as if he were sucking oxygen through a pinprick. He exhaled in a single sharp burst, like a soul singer singing "huh." Slowly in, quickly out; with each exhalation, there was more blood spray and less air.

"Protect Marianne," he said.

He started to inhale more slowly. The sound of the inhalation got quieter; the force of his inhalation weakened and then stopped.

I was breathing; he wasn't.

four

It suddenly felt hot.

Very hot.

I had been on the move all day. Most of the day I had spent outside in the constant drizzle. It wasn't the sort of precipitation that really constitutes rain: It was just enough moisture in the air that—over a period of time—it soaked through everything I was wearing. Combining the damp with the wind, it was cold outside. But inside this apartment—this heated apartment—I was hot.

I released Pierre-Louis' shoulder and felt for a pulse at his neck.

He really was gone. "Who's Marianne?" I asked the dead body. "Why does she need protecting? Who do you want me to protect her from?"

The dead teenager didn't answer. He just slumped there with his hands clutched to his chest, his eyes staring.

I stood, trying not to stand in the puddle of blood around the kid. "Shit. Nineteen and dead," I heard myself mutter as I tore off some more sheets from the roll of paper towels and tried to wipe the blood from my hands. I tore a few more sheets and put them on the floor, then walked on them to clean the blood off my soles. It wouldn't fool a forensic analyst if they got my sneakers, but it would be enough to stop an obvious trail forming as I wandered around.

I tore off a few more sheets from the roll and tried to mop the blood on my knees. What was I doing? I was wasting time, and now there was a small heap of bloodied paper towels on the floor.

Bloodied paper towels with my DNA wiped on them and my fingerprints around the apartment. The apartment where a kid had been shot and had now died.

I gathered up the bloodied towels and went to the front door. The old man in his dressing gown wasn't in sight through the spy hole. Gingerly, I cracked the door—listening first, then stepping out. I was alone for the few seconds it took me to reach the garbage chute and dump the bloodied towels. Sure, the cops were almost certain to look here, but using the public garbage chute was enough to mix up any evidence.

I looked down at my shirt. When I put it on this morning, it had been a light-blue oxford shirt; now it was just a mess of coughed blood. It followed down the garbage chute.

As I got back inside, I tore off a few more sheets and took a moment to guess where I might have touched, then roughly wiped the door on the front and, after closing it, wiped the back. It wouldn't fool anyone, but it should be enough to smear any fingerprints.

The apartment was hot. Hot enough that the kid was happy in a T-shirt. Okay, he was dead now, but when he was alive, a T-shirt had been warm enough. I was topless, alive, and hot.

There was a key in the door to the balcony. Although to call it a balcony was to imply more than it was—wide window ledge would be a better description. I opened the door and stepped out, filling the space. I was prevented from moving further by the balustrade, two solid horizontal pieces of wood. The wind blew the drizzle in my direction—it seemed I had two options: too hot or cold with more dampness.

There were sirens. There are always sirens in Paris. At night it's usually a single siren that passes quickly. Now there were several sirens—at a distance but closing. Maybe Pierre-Louis had called with the bloodied phone. Maybe the neighbors. Or maybe they were just sirens that would pass in a few moments.

I went back, leaving the door open, and pulled out my phone. I squatted and took a few pictures of the dead kid. I needed some evidence that I had found him. I had been paid to look for him—and he was alive when I found him.

I took pictures of the kitchenette, then moved to the bathroom off the entrance corridor. It was unremarkable—a bath with a shower curtain, a toilet, and sink on which stood a toothbrush in a glass and some toothpaste.

Above the sink was a medicine cabinet. I opened it, hoping to find some painkillers. The cabinet was empty.

I photographed the room and moved on.

The first room off the main room was what property agents call the master bedroom. It was another white room with laminate flooring. The only reason I thought *bedroom* was the thin mattress with a sleeping bag. There was a pile of clothes—neatly folded, but stacked on the floor, there being no closets—and a small table. Keys, a mobile phone, and a wallet all sat atop an old-fashioned notebook held closed with an elastic loop and with papers sticking out. I took three photos of the room and one of the probable contents of the Pierre-Louis' pockets, which currently rested on the table, before heading to the last room.

The final room was tiny: I could stretch and reach the walls. Unlike the other rooms, these walls had been painted a pastel/lime green. I guessed the laminate floor stretched in here, but the floor was covered with newspaper, loosely spread to each corner.

On the newspaper was a workman's step—wide, about a foot or so off the ground and spattered with paint, supporting several tins of paint, all open. Orange, brown, red, dark green, and blue. A brush rested on each tin—a narrow brush, as if for detailing. On one wall someone had started painting animals. Crude, simplistic pictures, but endearing. A lion, recognizable by his mane, smiling. An elephant, or at least the outline of an elephant, squirting water. A seal with a ball on his nose.

I photographed the unfinished artwork, then picked up two empty paint cans. As I stepped into the main room, I could hear voices outside. There was banging on the door—three swift blows with the heel of a hand.

I put the paint back, picked my jacket off the floor, and ducked back into the bedroom, where I grabbed the contents of the table, stuffing the items into my jacket pockets as I walked to the balcony. As I stepped into the wind and drizzle, I closed the door behind me then looked down. Each of the four residential floors had a balcony.

I put on my jacket and stepped over the balustrade.

five

I stood on the outside of the balcony, gripping the balustrade. The moisture on the gloss paint reduced the friction, making it something akin to gripping a slab of ice.

On the ground there were people running around, people shouting, people directing, people ordering. Police and SAMU. Or was it SMUR? While I could speak the language, in the few months I had been in Paris, I hadn't got a detailed handle on the government infrastructure. SAMU, SMUR, seemed the same to me. Whatever it was, these were medical people: paramedics or doctors. I wanted to shout down to these ants running around four floors below me: "Go home. He's dead. There's nothing you can do."

My toes were on the balcony floor—the balcony on the other side of the balustrade. There was no lip—just a right angle where the paving slabs met the wall. No lip to grip as I tried to swing down to the balcony below. I had to hope I could stretch to the top balustrade below while holding the lower balustrade in front of me. Well, I had to hope I didn't fall. Hope that no one looked up and saw me. Hope that no one was on their balcony below looking out at the blue flashing lights and the dots of people scurrying around.

And once all that hope was done, then I could hope I could reach the next floor.

I took one last look into the room. Pierre-Louis was still against the wall: The lake of blood seemed not to be growing wider. At any moment, whoever it was that had been banging at the door—probably the cops—was going to force the door as easily as I had forced it.

The choice was simple—stay and try to explain that I hadn't murdered Pierre-Louis, or leave by the only route open to me. But still I was reticent. I was hurt, it was wet, and... And I don't know what. I was making excuses.

I reached down for the lower plank of the balustrade, pushing my ass out, then jumped—keeping hold of the plank and turning my head as my face crashed into the wall. My feet didn't reach the top plank of the balustrade on the floor below, but my legs swung freely.

And no one shouted, so hopefully there was no one on that narrow balcony.

There was another bang at the door—or at least there might have been; I was breathing too heavily to really notice, and my arms were moaning. I swung my legs, trying to build some momentum.

This descent was never, ever going to be elegant, and I would have preferred not to have had some guy jump on me a few minutes earlier. While from outside the compound, the block looked clean and crisp, up close the white render was rough. I felt the abrasion against the side of my face as I let myself drop, trying to curl under the edge and onto the balcony below.

I landed heavily. Awkwardly. But I landed and felt my hand go to my face.

The lights were out in the apartment. I contemplated whether anyone was in, and if they were, whether they would like to offer me a cup of coffee.

Probably not.

The next two descents were equally unpleasant, and as I reached the final balcony, one floor up from the ground, I stood, breathing heavily, able to better see the ants—primarily police, but several people without uniforms—as they walked to and from the entrance to the block where a few minutes ago I had encountered the couple I thought were about to argue.

Then there was no one—everyone had disappeared. I clambered over and jumped, trying to roll as I hit the path below. I felt my ankle twist and my foot slip as I landed heavily, falling more than rolling. I scrambled—half up, half stumbling—and moved farther up the block, dropping into a shadow before I reached down to massage my ankle that had just taken the weight of my landing.

Voices. Two police came out of the block but walked away.

I stood and headed to where I had seen the guy in denim clamber over the wall. I didn't feel a need to talk to the cops. I was paid to find the kid; I wasn't paid to tell the cops what I saw.

Over the wall I lowered myself onto the brown utility company box I had climbed from earlier. From the box, I looked the direction the guy in denim had walked several minutes before when Pierre-Louis had been alive.

I jumped and landed badly. Again.

six

Don't let the tourist propaganda fool you.

Paris au printemps—Paris in the springtime—*is* gorgeous. But Paris in the rain, even if it is springtime rain, is just plain tedious. It's worse than London. This is Paris caught between winter and early summer, and the wind is always bitter.

After being jumped on, finding Pierre-Louis, seeing him die, climbing down four floors—on the outside of the building— landing badly, climbing the wall to get out of the compound, and landing badly again, I was back on the street, following in the direction that I had seen the other guy walk. The guy who jumped on me, the guy who probably shot Pierre-Louis. And as I walked I was trying to get some warmth inside my damp jacket, which I wrapped tightly around my flesh, my bloodied shirt having gone down the garbage chute.

Paris is pretty much flat apart from two hills, of which Belleville is the higher. Pierre-Louis Dubois' apartment complex was on the hill. The hill continued up the side face of the block with the white concrete wall of the compound rising, always keeping its top above my head.

And the wall—like the compound, like the block inside— seemed interminable. I paused; at a guess I was halfway along the block. To guess again—and I couldn't really be sure I was seeing the end—the wall was a quarter of a mile long. A quarter of a mile of cast cement. A quarter of a mile, punctured by windows with bars and no lights behind, and by windows with heavy metal shutters, painted white, pulled down.

I kept walking. The road ended, turning into a pedestrian path, but the wall continued, and the block behind it continued. A quarter-mile wall is quite impressive. A quarter-mile single block of apartments, set over eight or maybe ten floors, is even more impressive.

Maybe I'm just an old romantic, but I think of apartment blocks as vertical villages. This monolith of white concrete wasn't so much as a vertical village as a whole city placed on its side. A whole city where, at the moment, at the most, only a few residents knew Pierre-Louis had been shot.

My mind was running in every direction as I carried on up the hill, but the basic fact remained: There was no sign of the guy who had probably shot Pierre-Louis. A broad footpath that had taken over when the road ran out gave way to a flight of stairs, which took me up to a road. A main road with a few cheap restaurants, grocers, and the occasional car passing.

And there was still no sign of the denim-clad probable assassin.

I looked down the stairs and back down the hill. At the foot there was the reflection of blue light. On the route I'd just followed, there were any number of storm drains and wheeled trash bins. I briefly considered, then ruled out, going to check the trash. But what would it do? Get my fingerprints on something? Waste my time when I was sure that the woman had taken the gun?

I turned left and left again. It was a risk staying in the area, but I wanted to circle back and see what was happening with the cops and the SAMU. And I figured any risk was small—the police would be preoccupied.

The road ran to the other side of the block. A narrow street which made its way between some housing blocks that had been built against the walls outside the monolithic white block, like peasants living outside the city walls.

The downward incline was welcome, but I soon felt the muscles at the back of my calves and thighs being pulled tight as I walked cautiously, aware that—while highly unlikely—there could be a killer around here who could recognize my face. I wanted to find the guy, but I wanted to see him before he saw me.

As the hill went down, the apartment blocks became higher, reaching sixteen floors, or perhaps twenty floors by the time I reached the main street. I wasn't in a mood to count.

I turned onto the main street and headed back up the hill I had already walked up once that evening, but this time I was walking toward blue flashing lights that hadn't been there when I first arrived.

There were four marked police cars and two other cars badly parked that I guessed were department-issue vehicles for the detectives. There was one white SAMU ambulance—a paramedic leaning next to it, talking animatedly to a woman who was taking notes. One of the detectives, I guessed. A small group of uniformed officers chatted while one of their number stood officiously by the gate to the apartment complex, which had now been propped open.

"Shit," I hissed under my breath. Something was missing. Or rather someone. The vagrant. The homeless guy who had seemed so out of place on a residential street at midnight. The vagrant I was sure had made a phone call just before the man and the woman arrived. He was gone. His makeshift castle was gone. Apart from a few crates stacked by the side of the road, there was no trace he had been there.

A homeless guy doesn't move in the middle of the night. Or did the cops spook him? And if they did spook him, why would he take his shelter? Wouldn't he just disappear and come back in a few hours?

No. He was the lookout. He called when the coast was clear.

On each side of the street, railings enclosed and protected, separating those on the inside from those on the outside. I wanted to be on the inside looking out, but that meant another metal fence with spikes on top, and another climb meant a whole heap of new opportunities to damage myself even more.

The entrance to an underground parking lot gave a break between the steel fences on my side. The lowered doors still prevented access, but the way the doors had been fitted—set back from the front face by about twelve inches—gave me somewhere I could sit. My ass—like the rest of me—was already wet; now it could be cold, too. But at least against the garage door, I was sheltered from some of the drizzle.

The cops hadn't noticed me—a murder was clearly far more important than some guy walking up the street. And how were they to know that I was the guy who had been there when the kid died? How were they to know that the same guy had taken the only possessions that seemed to be of any interest in the apartment?

I carried on watching the cops for a moment or two, then began to assess my state. My cheek felt tender where I had scraped it down the wall in my first balcony-to-balcony descent. Something at the back of my head hurt—I wasn't sure whether it happened when I was jumping from the bottom balcony, landing badly when I got down to the street, or whether it was from when the guy in denim launched himself on me in the stairwell.

I didn't dare look at my hands or try to assess bones, but as I lifted the right leg of my jeans, I found a gash six inches long. It wasn't deep, but it was unpleasant. I couldn't remember how I got that injury or reconstruct a scenario where I might have picked up that wound.

Having completed my personal inventory of pain, I reached into my pocket and pulled out the notebook I had recovered from the table in the bedroom.

I released the elastic strap and let it flop open. Notes. Notes in a notebook...huh. Handwritten notes. Lots of them. Short notes, crowded onto the page, each note written at a different time with a different writing implement—some in pencil, some in what looked like fountain pen, others clearly written by ballpoint, sometimes red, usually black, one or two green. And then occasionally, asterisks with notes inserted after the fact. Pointers to other places. It was like a bucket to collect a constant drip of ideas where someone had come along and tried to apply structure after the event.

It might have made sense to Pierre-Louis. It might have made sense to the shooter and the woman if they had thought to look. But it didn't make sense to me. I understood the words. I understood the sentences—or at least the fragments of sentences, more phrases rather than sentences. But there was a context here I didn't understand.

In between the pages, photos—some black-and-white and some color, newspaper clippings, receipts, photocopies, and pages torn from books. All inserted with a purpose. Some annotated, some referenced by notes. Notes that I didn't understand.

It made no sense to me, and without a good light and a magnifying glass, the photos were useless.

I put the notebook back in my pocket, pulled out the kid's phone, and flicked through his contacts. There was only one number I wanted, which I soon found, but before I called it, I wanted to have the person I was calling in my sight.

At this time of night the Metro was closed, and I didn't want to take a cab or a bus, so I had a walk ahead. I stood and headed down the hill.

seven

The walk from outside the apartment in Belleville took about an hour. By the time I arrived I felt drier, but I knew that was largely an illusion: All that had happened was I had warmed up the layer of moisture around me. I needed to take off my wet clothes, wash, and go to bed. But first, there were certain courtesies that were required of me.

I stood across the boulevard, looking up at the apartment. When I was here earlier, she had been reticent, nervous, cautious. And that was not unreasonable. If a complete stranger turned up at my door—somehow getting past the locked door from the street and the locked door into the stairs and elevators—and started asking questions about my son, then I would not be forthcoming. I would not have a reason to trust or a reason to divulge any information.

I leaned against a plane tree, tugged out her dead son's wallet, and flicked through his cards, picking out a student identity card. The photo was a good match for the kid who was lying dead in Belleville. The name matched the name of the kid I'd been hired to find. My client had said this woman was Pierre-Louis' mother. She would neither confirm nor deny. Then again, she didn't seem willing to confirm that we were in Paris.

I put the card into the back pocket of my jeans so I could easily take it out—she didn't need to see that I had her son's wallet. And she didn't need to know that I had his keys and a notebook whose contents I could barely understand.

She did need to know that her son was dead, and since I had the only obvious ID, it was going to take the cops a while to figure who the kid was and decide who they should notify about his death.

I returned the wallet to my jacket and pulled out his phone.

Everyone has only one mother, so if you've saved a number on your phone under "maman," then that's your mother, right? I pushed the dial button.

One ring.

Two.

Several floors up—possibly her apartment—a light came on. Dull, like a bedside light. And then the phone answered:

"Pierre-Louis? Are you alright?"

"It's Leathan," I said, faltering. My heart suddenly pounding. "Leathan Wilkey. We...I came to your door earlier..."

"What do you want? Why are you calling from Pierre-Louis' phone?" There was anger in her voice, hostility.

"Can I come up?" There was no response. "We need to talk—I'm outside."

She didn't say anything, but the sound of her trying to control her breathing told me she was still holding the receiver close to her face.

"This is important," I said. "We need to talk. I'm across the street—look out the window, you'll see me."

There was a movement at the window with the dull light. I raised a hand to indicate my presence. "Okay," she said. "The gate code is three A seven eight, and the door at the bottom of the stairs never shuts properly." I ended the call and hit the power off button—no need for the location of the phone to continue to be broadcast.

The keypad was dull with a brushed steel backplate, and the keys were sticky. I closed the gate slowly, not wanting it to squeak or bang, and walked under the arch and into the small courtyard shared by the apartments.

A few lights pushed their way through the dulled glass to give some background light in the shared space. It did little more than illuminate a few washing lines and in the gloom give the occasional glint off the damp cobblestones. As with everywhere in Paris, the paintwork looked like it could do with freshening up.

I took the stairs to Émilie Dubois' apartment—a narrow wooden staircase winding around an old elevator shaft. She was waiting for me when I arrived—her door cracked with an eye to the slit.

She opened the door to the width of her face but still stood behind the wood, obscuring herself and clearly delineating her space and my space. She probably figured I could kick the door, but still, she wanted to be clear that I wasn't welcome. I wasn't invited. I wasn't a guest.

"What's happened?" she asked. She made no effort to hide the fear in her voice.

"Can I come in?"

"No. Is Pierre-Louis alright?" Her throat was constricting—she knew that people didn't arrive at 2 AM, or whatever time it was, just to ask for directions to the Champs-Élysées. She could connect the basic facts: I had seen her earlier, at this exact place, when I asked her about her son. She had refused to tell me anything of note, and now the same guy who several hours ago was asking about her son was standing outside her door again, having called from her son's phone.

She knew something was wrong. But she knew she didn't know what was wrong.

"Please." My voice was barely audible. I stepped forward as if I had been invited in.

"No." From the dull light of the stairwell, I could see tears on her cheeks. Even in the half-light her moist eyes, wide and inquisitive, had a vigorous energy. They were the sort of eyes that men would stare into and want to possess, to control. They were the sort of eyes that I wanted to be close to for a few hours and forget what I had seen tonight.

But I wasn't here for me. I was here for her. "Two minutes and I'm gone."

She sighed, stepping back and opening the door far enough for me to enter her apartment. "Two minutes." She pushed the door shut and stood, waiting, expecting. A powder-blue nightgown peeked from under her dark blue robe. Both could be silk, but I wasn't really an expert on fabric and how to tell the difference between finest Chinese silk and manmade polyester. I was more of a cotton and leather guy.

"Can we sit?" I asked, looking at her bottom lip as it unconsciously twitched.

She said nothing but moved past the first door, turning on a side light as she passed. The room accessed from the second door was like its owner. Small. Compact. Not an ounce of fat. No unnecessary ornamentation. Presented simply. And yet, incredibly elegant with a grace that—in a city of many graceful sights and many graceful women—was still rare.

Two two-seater sofas—old, maybe antique, but well maintained—faced each other. There was no television, just a modest bookcase toward the window. She sat on the right-hand sofa. Even with a floor-length robe and in her own home, she sat with a delicacy. Maybe a lifetime spent being watched conditioned her to hold a perfect posture as she sat. Maybe it was not in her nature just to flop down onto a sofa. And maybe she was always like this with guests.

She hadn't mentioned my appearance, and I felt it best not to explain the blood on my knees, which the rain had washed into general patches of dirt. Usually I would prefer not to sit with dirty jeans, but all I was going to do was put my wet ass on her clean sofa. Bad manners on my part, but this news had to be delivered face-to-face, not from someone standing over her, and the sofa would dry out quickly enough.

She sniffed and looked up at me as I sat. Those expectant, inquisitive eyes.

I calculated. I probably had one question before I had to tell her. One question, and it wasn't about the answer she gave as much as it was about her reaction. I tried to keep my tone casual as I kept my gaze fixed on those softly glistening orbs: "Who's Marianne?"

She blinked once. A shrug. "In France…? You ask who Marianne is."

She was right—asking about the French national symbol may not be the kind of question to elicit the answer I wanted. "Is she a friend of Pierre-Louis?"

The tears started to flow more freely and she gave a single shake of her head, her dark, wavy, almost shoulder-length hair taking a moment or two to settle. "What's happened?" Her voice was steadier, almost accepting.

"Is your son Pierre-Louis Dubois?" She didn't react. I struggled to pull his student ID out of the back pocket of my jeans. I held it so she could see. "Is this your son?"

She went to grab the plastic card and then stopped, composed herself, and softly tightened her mouth. A subtle affirmation.

"I'm sorry," I whispered. "He died tonight." For a moment she was motionless—the only indication that she hadn't turned into a waxwork was the flow of tears. Then she bent forward, putting her head in her hands. The sound was quiet—it would barely reach outside the room—but the raw pain was clear.

She looked up. The glistening eyes, now red. "You're wrong." She stared at me—there was little left to say. She broke the stare and put her head back in her hands, sobbing.

I went to find the kitchen—like the rest of the apartment, it was small, but perfect. When I returned with a glass of water, she was sitting, her legs pulled up into a fetal position, sobbing gently. She tried to speak. She might have been asking "how" or "who" or "when." Her words didn't make much sense.

"Is there anyone I can call?" I asked. She shook her head and continued sobbing.

eight

Perhaps it was 2 AM. Maybe 3. I didn't feel any need for certainty. I was certain it was nighttime. I was certain it was still raining and the wind was still blowing.

That was enough.

I was pleased to be out of the apartment, feeling the damp freshness. While Émilie Dubois' apartment was clean, I wanted to be washed clean of the experience of telling a mother that her son—who from the few photos in silver frames I was guessing was her only child—had just died. There was still a lot I wanted to tell her, but I didn't see any point in continuing to intrude into that most personal grief. I'd go back tomorrow and tell her what I knew, so she could listen and ask questions when she wasn't trying to deal with her shock.

Doing that much seemed necessary.

And until then, I needed to look after myself.

As I got closer to the heart of the city, there were more people on the streets. The number of cabs and cars increased, and a few patrols cleaning the streets passed—small bug-like road sweepers, stopping at every trash can to empty it; guys opening the water vents to flush the gutters clean; and others just spraying down the broad sidewalk.

I called when I was five minutes away. "Nico! Leathan."

"Leathan." Hearing an Italian trying to pronounce a name of Scottish origin always made me smile. "How are you—are you coming in?"

"Can you take a cigarette break in five?" I asked. "Meet me around the back from your place. Bring my bag, and could you also bring a large envelope?"

"Sure. Five minutes," said Nico. "Ciao."

"Oh yeah—bring a large trash bag, too." I hung up.

Nico worked at one of the increasing number of boutique hotels for those who weren't super-rich, but who had cash to spend. These weren't the sort of people who shipped their Ferrari and the Bentley and their Porsche and their Koenigsegg to Paris for the six weeks that they stayed every year. Those people went to the big hotels everyone had heard of: the George V or the Ritz.

Nico's employer's market was the bohemian luxury seekers, after the *authentic* experience. Not so authentic that they actually lived like a Parisian and tolerated what Parisians tolerate on a daily basis, but instead looking for their notion of the Parisian experience, available if they paid.

I reached the end of the service alley that led to the back entrance of the hotel and waited. At the far end, a wash of light spilled out as a door opened. A character—presumably my friend—exited, closing the door behind him and returning the alley to darkness.

There was a pause. A flame. Then an orange glow. I could feel Nico's sigh of pleasure with his first hit of nicotine. The orange glow began to move toward me, and slowly Nico came into sight, dropping my bag before he went to embrace. I stepped back. "I'm covered in shit. You don't want this stuff on your uniform."

He smiled broadly. "Do you want a shower? A bed?"

"What I really want is a beer and some painkillers," I said. Nico winced—I knew he was wishing I had asked for these when we spoke earlier. I pulled out a €100 bill and held it for him. He took the bill and turned.

He might be a friend. He might feel in my debt. But I needed to make sure he knew—in tangible ways—that I appreciated the help he offered. I also didn't want him watching while I unloaded my pockets.

Nico had dropped the envelope and the trash bag I had asked for on the top of my bag. I quickly unloaded into the envelope 3,000 euros; Pierre-Louis' phone, having first removed the battery; the wallet, into which I returned the student ID; and the notebook. I kept the keys. The numbers in the phone that seemed important had been transferred to my phone as I sat across from the entrance to the apartment block, watching the cops and the forensics people come and go.

I sealed the envelope and swapped it for the trash bag, which I opened, flicking it through the air to fill it like a large balloon. Then I stripped. I dropped my jacket on the path—the wind against my bare chest seemed to find an especially unpleasant way to nip at my skin. Then everything else I was wearing—sneakers, jeans, socks, underwear—went into the trash bag. Before I dropped my jeans into the bag, I made some effort to use the soaked fabric to wipe any traces of blood from my knees, but the same darkness in the private alley that ensured I was not arrested for public nudity also made it nearly impossible to see whether the wiping had any effect.

The only shirt in the bag that Nico had brought out for me was a T-shirt that I slipped on first. I hate wearing those things—they always cling around my neck—but I'd be able to take it off soon. The jeans and sneakers were near replicas of those sitting in the trash, and while they were dry, I was wet, and trying to put on socks with wet feet while standing on a loose surface meant that I was filling my socks with grit.

There was the sound of one of the small, bug-like street sweepers. I jogged to the end of the path to find a guy emptying a street trashcan. I indicated the trash bag concealing my bloodied clothes and gave him an inquisitive look. He nodded toward the vehicle, where a rear panel was open and into which he tossed the trash bag he had just removed from the trashcan.

My garbage followed, and he dropped the side panel. "Merci, monsieur," I said.

I arrived back at my bag as Nico returned with my beer—the bottle already opened—and a bottle of painkillers. I took a swig. "Don't take this the wrong way, Nico—I'm grateful for the beer and all that—but this really is terrible stuff."

He laughed. "It's what the customers want and..."

We mumbled together, "...the customer is always right."

He continued: "The customers think it's authentic." He gave a weak shrug. "In a country that is famous for its wine, we still have people who want the beer, even if it's...well, you can taste for yourself."

As he talked, I opened the childproof bottle of painkillers and emptied some onto my hand. "What's the dose?"

"Two," said Nico.

I felt six pills in my hand. I knocked them back with another slug of second-rate beer. "Could you put the envelope in your safe and take the bag back to wherever you keep it?"

"Sure," said Nico.

I hoped my smile conveyed my gratitude, but in case it didn't, I pulled out another €100. "You know I appreciate your help, Nico?" I asked.

"Anytime, Leathan. Anytime."

"I'll be back in a few days to get the stuff back," I said.

"Not a problem," said Nico. "As long as it's my shift."

I turned with the bottle of unpleasant beer still in my hand.

nine

There's only so much authentic-for-the-tourists French beer I can drink, and tonight my limit was half a bottle. The remainder, along with the bottle, was consigned to the next trashcan I passed before I again moved off the main boulevard, preferring instead to continue my route along the smaller back streets. The streets less patrolled by the police. It was unlikely they would be looking for me—especially at this distance from the apartment in Belleville, and especially since I had turned off Pierre-Louis' phone a while before leaving it with Nico—but it wasn't a risk worth taking. And I wasn't going to take that risk when all I wanted to do was go to bed.

I pulled out my phone—she picked up on the third ring. There was the voice of a French citizen, living in Paris, talking English. She knew there was something buried deep in the psyche of this native English speaker that made him go weak when he heard English spoken with a French accent. Groggily, Cécile said: "That had better be you, Leathan."

I heard my name, and something inside me felt warm.

"Are you alone?" I asked. "I had a bad day at school. The big boys beat me up, and the bully took my lunch money."

She laughed—at me. Not unkindly. More in the way of an indulgent teacher with her favorite pupil. "Of course I'm alone. Shall I run a bath?"

As I arrived Cécile opened her front door, and I stepped into a hallway with steam wafting from the bathroom. She was wearing a white toweling robe pulled tight at the waist, and her long brown hair, flecked with gray, had been messily clipped on the top of her head. She didn't say anything; she just put her arms around me and held me.

When she let go, she said: "Give me the SIM. I'll flush it."

Cécile knew my routine. Put a new SIM card into my phone every morning. Take it out at the end of the day and dispose of it. Next day, put in a new SIM card. New number, new details, and a greatly reduced chance of being traced and identified.

When I was in London, I had upset a gang of Bulgarian people traffickers. Rather than stay and wait to be murdered, I had left, spending a few months traveling before I settled in Paris.

Although settle is not the right word.

Paris is big and crowded. It's the perfect place if you want to get lost—it's the haystack if you want to hide a needle. But if you want to hide, you need to take precautions, so for me, there were no credit cards, and mobile phones were something to be used with extreme caution.

And while I was being cautious, I never slept in the same bed two nights running.

I followed Cécile to the bathroom where the full bath was gently steaming and flicked the SIM into the toilet. The light around the mirror was switched on, with a razor and shaving gel left ready. She knew my routine. "Drink?" she asked.

A shake of my head was enough. We didn't need pleases and thank yous.

She indicated to take my jacket, which I slipped off. "This is soaked, Leathan. Have you been out in the rain all day?" The tightening of the muscles in my face confirmed.

"I'll put it in the airing cupboard. Can I empty the pockets, or is there stuff you don't want me to see?"

She knew me. She knew how I worked and how I thought. I carried out a quick inventory of my pockets: some spare SIM cards, the keys I had picked up at Pierre-Louis' apartment, some cash—over 1,000 euros. Nothing that she would wish I hadn't shown her. Nothing that would be out of place for a normal person.

I nodded. "You're sure? I *can* empty the pockets?" She smiled. "Let's get the rest of your clothes off then too."

As I dropped my clothes in a pile on the floor, she picked up my jeans. "These aren't *that* wet. Do you want them dried with your jacket—you've got another pair here, I think—or shall I wash them?"

I twitched my noise.

"Okay, I'll dry them." She looked up: "Nothing in the pockets?" I half shook my head as I turned to fill the basin, flicking water over my face from the growing puddle.

I heard her come into and out of the bathroom several times— the change in the slap of her bare feet from the wood plank floor in the hall to the tiles in the bathroom telling me when she was close.

She came back as I was rinsing my face with cold water and washing down the sink, clearing it of the last few bristles, having gingerly shaved around my new wounds. "Let's get you into the bath," she said. I turned; her robe had gone, but there was no change in her behavior.

Her body was curved, rounded, smooth, soft, comforting. There were no angles, no sharpness. She tilted her head toward the bath. "Get in," she mouthed, holding my hand to steady me as I stepped into the large white tub. She knelt beside the bath—her breasts full, perfectly formed in proportion to the rest of her body, and placed directly in my eye line.

There was a soft splash as she put her hands into the water, pulling them up again and lathering the soap before she reached for my leg closest to her. She lifted it out of the water as she soaped it, examining each minute section with the attention that a jeweler devotes to a diamond. When she spoke, her voice was soft, but there was a hint of tension: "Is this what the big boys did to you at school today?" She waited until I made eye contact. "Well, I'm going to write a very stern letter to your headmaster, insisting that those bullies are disciplined."

Cécile started to soap my other leg. She let out a small, stifled gasp. "That's probably where I was climbing down the balconies," I said.

"Shh," she said, holding a finger over my mouth. Her hand was wet, soapy, but gentle. "You don't have to tell me."

"I've got to tell..." What had I got to tell? I went to Cécile Renard when I wanted to talk and when I didn't want to talk but I wanted to understand. I was never sure exactly how old she was—forty-something I guessed, perhaps more, she never said, and I didn't care. She was older and smarter than me. Her brain was faster than mine. She saw possibilities that never occurred to me. She was more hopeful about people, she could always see the good they were trying to do, but she was faster to know when someone's intentions conflicted with how they presented themselves to the world.

"Claude sent me to see this guy—a diplomat. The diplomat wanted me to find a kid...a teenager." She was listening as she moved to soap my arm. "He paid too much. The job was too easy... no, not easy...too simple. Go find the kid; come back and tell me where he is. Here's five thousand euros."

Her eyes registered shock at the sum.

"Five thousand for a day's work." She picked up my other arm as I continued. "I spent the whole day and found the kid just after midnight. He had a bullet hole is his chest and died with me kneeling beside him. That's why my jeans aren't wet—I put on a new pair when I threw out the old ones with his blood all over them."

She gently pulled my shoulders to encourage me to sit up so she could soap my back. As I moved she turned me toward her, her breasts pushing into my face as she leaned over me, soaping my back. Then she softly guided me back and began to soap my chest.

"Do you trust Claude?"

"He's fundamentally untrustworthy, and he doesn't trust me. That's what makes him so trustworthy," I said. "We rely on each other's selfishness, and every now and then we scratch the other's itch." I thought harder. "He's never been dishonest with my money."

"This diplomat?"

"An honest man sent abroad to lie for his country." I let the thought lie as she put down the soap. "I only met him—and his minder—briefly. Of course I didn't trust him, but I trusted his money."

She frowned slightly as she stood up.

"It was what the kid said to me—as he was dying." She cocked her head, asking without saying. "He said 'protect Marianne.' There's no trace that I can find in his notebook, his phone, or anywhere of anyone called Marianne."

She stepped into the bath at the other end from me. Her hands disappeared under the water.

ten

I was aware of being awake, but was now torn between being asleep and the sensory overload of the bed—a warm cotton cocoon smelling of fresh spring flowers, on a just firm enough mattress, with bright spring sunlight knocking at the window.

There was a low creak as the door moved and Cécile Renard came in sideways, turning toward the bed as she entered, holding a tray with two mugs. I shut my eyes and listened as she placed one beside me, then walked to her side of the bed and sat.

"It's not raining," she said, "so you can wake up."

I opened one eye.

"Hi. How did you sleep?" She was still speaking in English.

"Well," I said, feeling a satisfied smile cross my face.

"You've slept, and last night's physical examination confirmed all of your vital organs are still fully functioning, so what are you going to do now?"

Her white toweling robe gaped open as she leaned forward, letting her right breast see the daylight. I stared—full and curved, a perfectly formed teardrop shape with a thick, rich pink nipple. In truth, I wanted to spend all day in her bedroom. I didn't want to get up. I didn't want to go out. I didn't want to think about anything apart from Cécile Renard.

"Are you going to see Claude?" She broke the spell, sitting and pulling her gown straight.

"The mother first. She needs an explanation, and she'll be ready to listen now that she's had a few hours to process the initial shock of the news. After that, then I'll see Claude. Then I should see the client, the diplomat—he did pay me."

She was thinking as she held her coffee to her lips. "And Marianne?"

I breathed in heavily. "Unless the mother says something, I'm not sure what I can do."

She sipped. Waiting for me to elaborate.

"Look at the options. There's a dying teenager—he says the name Marianne. At a guess, she's his girlfriend. The mother doesn't know about her, so she probably was a girlfriend *and* the kid knew his mother wouldn't approve. And he's been painting cutesy animals on the wall of a small room. That tells me Marianne's pregnant, which suggests that the view the mother would have of her is probably fairly accurate, if somewhat unfair since her kid's equally to blame for the pregnancy. And if I'm right that this kid has got a girl pregnant, then she hardly needs protection and she's not a priority."

"Grandchild?" She tilted her head, asking.

"I'm not being paid to find a granny for a baby that hasn't been born—and I've got other questions that I want answered first." She stared. "Not today—today's not the day to say, 'Your son's dead, but don't worry, you're going to be a grandmother.' But...yeah."

She looked across the room, pointing with her eyes. My jacket hung on the back of a chair with a pile of my clothes on the seat and my sneakers on the floor. My phone, the keys, and my cash were easy to see on the table next to the chair. "So the bullies at school didn't take *all* of your lunch money. They left you with enough to buy a snack for every tourist who visits the Louvre today."

eleven

It was a bright, crisp spring morning. The low sun came over the rooftops, cutting through a near-cloudless blue sky. In the sun, it was warm. Walk into the shade, and the temperature seemed to drop below zero. And when the biting cold wind whipped off la Seine, I began to regret only having a jacket, not a heavy winter coat.

I didn't need to nonchalantly wait outside the green gate, trying to look as if I was waiting for something else until someone opened the substantial lump of wood: Émilie Dubois had given me the code last night, and as she said then, the door from the courtyard to the stairwell didn't close properly anyway.

I reached the fourth floor and knocked on her door. A friendly tap, but loud enough to be heard. The door opened nearly immediately. Émilie stood in a white uniform. I might have thought she was a nurse had it not been for the embroidered logo over her left breast for one of the beauty companies. Her eyes—those soft pools into which I fell yesterday—were an angry red.

I expected grief. You lose your son—your only son, as far as I could tell—and you should be sad. Isn't that the first stage of grief? At the very least you take a few days off work. You cry a lot. You lose weight because you've stopped eating—or you put on weight because you comfort eat. Something happened—you react.

But this wasn't grief. This was anger. And confusingly, this was someone going to work.

She disappeared behind the door and then returned, putting on a heavy coat—the sort of coat I should have been wearing. "You. You got my son killed. Or did you kill him?"

She stepped into the hallway, locking the door behind her before starting to walk down the stairs.

I listened. The steps remained consistent through four flights, and then there was the squeak of the door that never locked and the tapping of her heels on the cobbles in the enclosed courtyard.

twelve

I've been inside Claude's apartment.

Once.

It was the middle of the night. He was asleep when I called. I had a problem.

The apartment didn't show the worst excesses one expects in the apartment of a middle-aged man living on his own. Claude has a cleaner who comes in once a week—she tidies the place, does his washing, and generally fusses. Not that Claude notices.

What struck me with Claude's apartment is that he doesn't actually live in it. Sure, he sleeps there. He keeps his clothes there. He washes in the morning and he washes in the evening. But the rest of the apartment is untouched by Claude. He restricts himself to the bedroom and bathroom. The cleaner uses the kitchen. And the only use the main room gets is the cleaner cleaning it every week, not that it actually needs cleaning.

And so for Claude, there is no necessity to change anything. The fact that his furniture feels about three centuries old when you sit on it doesn't worry Claude—he never sits on it, except during those once-in-ten-years events when someone like me visits unexpectedly. He's not going to benefit from getting new furniture—he's never home. He's always out: usually in a café or maybe a restaurant, or perhaps shuffling from place to place. I guess he has vices—he always seems to notice what might be called more matronly women—but those vices are for outside the home, not inside.

The café where I sat, like most cafés in Paris, spilled onto the sidewalk. Parisians like to watch. The rest of the world has television sets; Parisians have their cafés and their Haussmannian-fronted apartments to sit and watch the world pass. The café had an awning spreading over the sidewalk with two large heaters mounted above head height. I sat under one, feeling the warmth of its glow.

Around the outside of the overspill, reaching from the awning roof to the ground, was a thick plastic sheet keeping the wind out. If Claude looked out of his window, then the canopy would shield me. And if he proceeded with his regular routine—leaving the curtains untroubled, as they had been for every other day in the twenty-something years that he had lived in his apartment—then I would be ideally placed to see Claude as he left his block.

"Merci, madam." Coffee and a croissant were placed on my table. Like a driver focusing on the road ahead, my eyes remained fixed on the apartment block front door, but I was safe to flick my eyes away just long enough to acknowledge the arrival of breakfast.

I lifted my phone from the table and called the number I call every morning. It answered on the third ring. I gave my identity and the password details. "Good morning, Mister Leathan." The voice was young and female, and the English heavily accented.

When I left London—which I had to do in a hurry, having upset the Bulgarians—I gave a lawyer I knew, Daniel, power of attorney over my affairs. That was the last official act I performed. Since then, I've left no footprint that can be traced back to me. I don't own property. I'm not on any rental agreement. I don't have a credit card. Social media is largely—but not completely—an unknown world to me. And my phone has a new SIM card every day. I don't buy the SIM cards—instead, I rely on friends and acquaintances, like Nico in the hotel, to *find* SIM cards that I can use for a day and then discard.

My one consistent line back to civilization is what Daniel calls my *virtual personal assistant*. It took him a few months to persuade me, but now he pays a company to provide a personal assistant to take phone calls for me. A company located I'm not sure where. For a while I thought it was India. Then I thought it was the Philippines. Now I'm not sure. All I know is that every morning I call in and speak to someone very polite who gives me my messages.

"Hello, Mister Leathan," said today's assistant. I had long since given up trying to explain that Leathan was my forename and I was, in fact, Mister Wilkey. "Yes, I have one message for you." There was a slight gasp. There's always a slight gasp, and the gasp is the reason why I use the virtual personal assistant service. The slight gasp is the reason why I show up on no records and am largely untraceable. "I'm not sure if this is right..."

"It's correct," I said, knowing what was coming. "Just read it as it is."

There was a hesitation at the other end of the phone. English may not have been her first language, but she was polite enough not to wish to give offense. "It says..." she paused, steeling herself. "We know where you are, you worthless piece of shit, and today's the day we're going to fucking kill you."

Some might be worried. Me, less so. That was the same message that I had received every day for the last two months, since they found I used this service. It didn't get them any closer to me, but clearly someone felt good making threats that an assistant in Delhi, Manila, or wherever would convey to me.

The door to Claude's apartments opened. I ducked down as if tying my shoe, trying to get a better angle to look through the plastic. A couple, twenty-something, stepped out. Young, fresh, energetic—everything Claude wasn't. They looked as if they were catalog models, but in reality, everyone of their age seems to have a certain style, irrespective of their physical looks or their size. Everyone seems to *know* how to be stylish.

The door closed, and they moved off. I made another call, looking up the number I added to my phone yesterday. It was the second time I had called the number and the second time it had been answered swiftly. "It's Leathan."

Kasym Aitmatov grunted.

"It's important," I said.

I could hear the air resonating in Kasym Aitmatov's throat as he breathed. "Parc Monceau," he said. "Eleven AM." He hung up without waiting for acknowledgement.

I'm not keen on meeting people at specific places at specific times—it makes me too vulnerable. Maybe I'm over-cautious, or maybe today's message my foreign assistant had just conveyed was a useful reminder. But a meeting at short notice, in a public place with wide-open spaces, is probably less risky. In truth, the greater risk was probably from my client than from the Bulgarians—after all, it was him who sent me to the kid. Maybe he expected the kid to be dead when I arrived and hoped I'd literally get blood on my hands?

The door to Claude's apartments opened again. A middle-aged man—shabbily dressed and overweight—shambled out. Claude. I watched as the figure, still not fully engaged with the morning, tried to shut the door behind him, seemingly finding that it was fighting back. There was a narrowing of his eyes as he tugged several times at the door before he started uneasily up the street.

It wasn't simply that Claude was overweight. He was a big guy; he liked his food. It was that weight multiplied by gravity compounded by time had taken its effect. The heavy jowls tugged on the rest of his fat face, making him look like a cartoon character. The well-filled and regularly filled gut spilled over his belt—it seemed to me that when he needed to piss he would have to lift up several pounds of gut fat just to get to his cock.

And when you're carrying all that extra bulk, you walk differently. You walk more slowly, which was good: It meant there was no need for me to hurry. I finished my coffee and my croissant and left a €10 bill under my cup, waving my thanks at the owner as I left.

The brown leather jacket—old, with two buttons at the front, long lapels, and a belt that he had fixed behind his back—flapped in the morning breeze as Claude made his leisurely progress, occasionally running a hand through his unkempt and possibly unwashed hair. Claude seemed oblivious to the fact that the morning wind was cutting through every other resident of Paris.

If you're chased by a lion in the jungle, how fast do you need to run? Simple: faster than the guy next to you—he can be dinner. Claude is never going to run faster than anyone, but he'd sit down and have a chat with the lion, bullshit for a while, and persuade the big cat it would be in his interest to go and search for a gazelle.

The lion would happily pad off, but five minutes later, he'd think: what?

And so Claude continued walking without checking his environment, and I followed at a distance. I've never known him not being on his way to meet someone, then arriving and saying he had to leave to meet someone else. Claude was going somewhere and was taking the shortest route there. At every corner he turned. If there was an alley, a cut-through, a shorter way, he took it. And this was good. No one was following Claude on this crazy path.

I pulled closer. He wasn't looking around. He wasn't using the reflection in street windows to see who was behind. If the lion pounced, Claude would negotiate.

I saw the cut-through he was taking. He turned left. I turned right and sprinted. A short effort by me and I could get ahead of Claude and look back at his approach.

I stood panting as he came into sight. He was alone. He wasn't being followed. And he hadn't done anything in the least suspicious.

I called his number and put my phone to my ear. Claude slowed. Looked around. He stopped and started patting his pockets. My phone was still ringing. Claude felt something and pulled out a phone. He answered: "Bonjour." And as he answered, he started moving slowly.

"Claude, Leathan."

"Leathan!" There was a forced bonhomie in his voice. His face didn't show any joy.

"We need to meet. Now." I watched as Claude came closer, unaware that he could hang up his phone and shout to me.

"Can't do today. Tomorrow?"

"It needs to be now," I said. "You're not doing anything now are you?"

"I'm in a meeting, Leathan." He started to whisper. "These are important people I'm talking with, Leathan. I'll tell you tomorrow."

He drew level with me, not looking around. I kicked his foot, tripping him. He fell and hit the ground, rolling. He didn't seem hurt. Didn't seem shocked. Just slightly surprised to be on the ground.

"How about we meet now, Claude," I said, squatting beside him.

thirteen

I didn't need another coffee, but having one in front of me demonstrated to Claude that there was a period of time—the time it took to drink my coffee—during which I required his full attention.

"For once in your life, Claude, just tell the truth. Don't try to lay out the facts in a way that benefits you and that makes sure you can still take your skim. Just tell the truth." I wasn't sure whether the man on the other side of the table who was lighting a small cigar was going to be condescending or feign offense.

"Monsieur, non!" The café owner indicated the cigar to Claude. The two proceeded to argue as only two Frenchmen can. There was shrugging. There were questions with bottom lips pushed out. Voices were raised, but neither shouted. The founding principles of the Republic were recited and the treachery of the European Union agreed.

A compromise was reached. I wasn't sure what, but Claude seemed sanguine about the situation, even if he was unhappy with a law banning smoking. A law banning smoking where the national identity seemed to require that you smoke.

A law that Claude believed applied to other people. Not him.

"You know, Englishman…" I let the attempt to bait me and my Scottish ancestry pass. I've never felt pain at being called English—it always seemed there were worse things than being born south of the border. "You know, Englishman, how you tell a good restaurant in Paris?"

"Tell me, then answer my question."

"Cigarette stubs on the sidewalk outside the door." He seemed pleased with himself and slightly disappointed that I didn't respond. "The cigarette stubs tell you it's a restaurant that Parisians visit—you know they have been there because they are all forced out onto the street to smoke."

I forced a half-smile. "It's a shitty job you got me, Claude."

Now he was ready to feign and exaggerate offense. He took a different approach. "My ankle hurts, Leathan. You kicked me hard."

"It wasn't hard, and you deserved it. I'll kick you harder next time you lie to me, and I'll kick you harder still if you don't tell me what you sent me into."

Now the offense came. Now the incredulity. The Gallic shrug and a deep draw on his cigar bringing an angry scowl from the patron. "It was an easy job. Meet the diplomat..."

I cut him off. "The diplomat—that I have no evidence is a diplomat. It's not as if I met him in a diplomatic mission or anything as tedious as that." Claude winced, as if wanting to correct me. "The diplomat from the middle of outer I-don't-know-where-istan..."

"Kyrgyzstan."

"I can barely pronounce that, Claude, let alone point to it on a map."

Claude raised his hand, his index finger extended, pointing. "It's..." He paused, looking up as he thought. "It's..." He opened his hand, spreading his finger. Precision was now replaced by generality. "It's..." His face broke into a smile. "It's a long way away."

"'He's very westernized,' you said."

Claude went to agree as I continued. "Which is shorthand for saying he screws Western women, drinks the finest spirits from my father's land, and wears a suit instead of animal skins."

Claude frowned.

"Except when he's at home, when of course he wears animal skins to show he's in touch with the common man." I sighed. "You don't mean that he's westernized and believes in representative democracy, freedom of speech, and the rule of law...and that's before we talk about equal rights for women and homosexuals."

Claude sipped his coffee. He seemed to be happy to let me vent.

"'Why me?' I asked you yesterday. He must have people who can do this sort of thing for him, like that big lump Kasym Aitmatov." Claude showed no sign of caring—there wasn't a percentage to be made from caring, so he didn't. "'It's a personal matter, Leathan,' you said. 'It would be inappropriate for his government to fund an investigation into a non-national.'"

Claude returned his cup to its saucer on the small, round wooden table and spoke. Softly. Without apology. "You need as many friends as you can find with as much influence as possible, Leathan. I thought he'd be good for you. I thought he might help you."

"But is he honest?" I asked.

A slow grin spread across Claude's face. "Do you have many honest clients, Englishman?"

"Some," I said weakly.

"Excluding the women who cry on your shoulder and then never pay you a cent. How many honest clients do you have?" He let the question hang. "There's a reason why people come to you, Leathan. If a situation can be fixed by calling the cops, then people will call the cops. If it needs more than the cops can offer, if it needs an urgency the cops can't supply, if it has an aspect that someone wants shielded from the cops, then people come to you. And this...this was just a simple finding job."

"So you did know what the job was?" I asked rhetorically. Claude shrugged. "When you said, 'I don't know what he wants,' that was another..." I couldn't even be bothered to argue with Claude about the truth.

"All you had to do was find some kid," said Claude.

"And I found him," I said. "Then I watched him die. That's what upsets me."

"Die?" Somewhere under the layers of excess, somewhere in between the folds of loose skin, there were muscles in Claude's face. Muscles that tightened. "Die, Leathan? Who's dead?"

My voice was calm. "The kid. The kid I was sent to find—Pierre-Louis Dubois."

Claude leaned heavily on the small table, unsettling its balance and spilling my coffee as he lowered his head to his hand. He massaged the loose skin, looking up at me. "The kid...Pierre-Louis is dead?"

"Yup."

"Shit, Leathan. What have you done?"

"What have I done?"

"That kid's his son." I froze, fixed on Claude, willing him to repeat what he just said. "That kid is Tolomush Okeyev's son."

"What sort of fucked up...I mean—if he's so westernized—why doesn't he just do like normal parents and, you know, talk to his kid? Call him. Okay...why doesn't he do like normal people and text his kid, since teenagers only seem capable of communicating through grunts and text messages? What's wrong with direct communication?"

Claude spoke quickly and distractedly. "The kid was illegitimate—it was a strained relationship, if you can even call it a relationship. Okeyev wouldn't acknowledge the kid..."

"Because he's a shit," I said.

Claude didn't disagree. "And because it would cause him problems back home. If a diplomat is seen to be having too much fun, then questions are asked about taxpayer dollars or taxpayer goat shit or whatever they use as currency. And if there's a kid, then it's seen as a huge insult to the Kyrgyz womanhood. It would be bad for him and for the ruling family." Claude took another sip of coffee. "He's really dead, Leathan?"

"Really."

"How?"

"Shot."

"By?"

"Dunno. A guy with a girl to carry the gun. If I'd known what they were up to, I would have paid attention."

"Shit." He drew on his cigar, exhaling slowly. "Have you told Okeyev?"

I shook my head.

"Then don't. I'll tell him." It was the first thing Claude had said that I actually believed without considering whether he had an angle.

"If it's his son, then he deserves to hear what's happened from me. I was there...at the end," I said, standing to leave for my appointment and ignoring my coffee. I looked down at Claude: "And next time you offer my help, tell me everything. You'll still get your cut—I just want to know what I'm getting into."

fourteen

I didn't have enough time to walk to the meeting. I didn't have enough time to do anything other than take the Metro. Below the streets the Metro keeps moving, but on the surface, there's far too much traffic.

There was a direct route to the closest Metro and a longer route to the next stop. I headed for the farther station and followed a route that no rational person could explain. No rational person, apart from me. There had been times in the last few days when I had felt I was being followed. It was nothing more than a feeling, but there's something about getting a message every morning that today's the day that someone's going to kill me. Although, of course, the language of the threat was always marginally more flowery. Somehow that made me more cautious in the morning, and yet by the afternoon, I would start to lose my focus. I'd start to get confident. And confidence is where I'm most likely to trip.

My route started on the street and took what hopefully was a random pattern. I crossed over my path twice, there was a short distance I jogged, and for a few minutes I sat on a bench until I felt fairly confident that I was alone. But still, when I descended to the Metro, I let the first three trains go, each time confirming that the platform had fully emptied. I could have taken two trains with one change. I took six. It was enough to persuade me that there was no one on the Metro either.

Given that we were meeting in Parc Monceau, there was probably a smarter place to leave the Metro than Monceau station, but it was already three minutes after the scheduled meeting time as I stepped off the train and onto the platform. It then took another two minutes to reach street level.

By the time I was inside the park, I was unfashionably and impolitely late. The kind of lateness that gets people twitchy. If the diplomat—if he was a diplomat—had managed to pull together a group of people to watch me as I entered the park, then they were going to be getting frustrated by my late showing.

Frustration would lead to a mistake.

A mistake might give me a warning.

Might.

Before I came to Paris, I'd always lived in the UK—as a kid I was in Scotland; as an adult, I'd moved to London. In the UK, the approach to public parks is straightforward: They take some land, they enclose it within a fence or wall, they give the public access, and the people roam wherever they want to go.

Parisian parks are different.

Very different.

Like the Brits, the French take a piece of land and enclose it, and they give the public access. However, what they do on the inside is very different. Inside, everything is regimented. There are paths—clearly delineated paths—and there is grass. Between the path and the grass, there is a fence. In Parisian parks, one is expected to stay on the path—the stone-topped path that gets sodden in winter and is a near desert in the summer.

For a republic founded on the notion of liberty, there seems little liberty in public parks. Even the trees are regulated. They are planted in rows—perfectly straight lines. When the trees are cut, they are cut flat so that the row of trees forms a perfectly flat wall.

Allowing people to roam in clearly defined narrow lanes while keeping broad sweeps of green clear meant it was easy to look across the park and find Kasym Aitmatov. The large, physical presence of the diplomat's close protection man was hard to hide.

He was scanning the horizon, probably looking for me. I slowed my pace, keeping within a small group of people all wanting to roam freely, but feeling constrained by the ornamental fences directing us along the avenues. Unlike Kasym Aitmatov, I was a normal height—I didn't stand out in a small crowd.

As I walked, Kasym Aitmatov continued to scan. He didn't communicate with anyone. He didn't move his mouth, didn't pull out a phone, and didn't signal. His head just continued to move until he saw me when I was about fifty yards away. There was a flash of relief across his face, which was rapidly replaced by annoyance. His head turned away and tilted down. Doubtless his boss, Tolomush Okeyev, the man I was told was a Kyrgyz diplomat, was sitting on a bench next to him.

I winked at the obelisk of a close protection officer as I circled him, beginning to understand how the moon feels orbiting the earth.

The diplomat was a few inches shorter than me—five seven, maybe five eight—but he was stockier. My origins are in countries that industrialized nearly two hundred years ago. My origins are in countries that have had electricity and running water for everyone's lifetime and longer than that.

His origins were in a country that is industrializing, but that still has a strong heritage of people living on the open plains. A place where—irrespective of your age or your gender—you need to be physically strong, and you undertake hard physical labor on a daily basis. The labor crushes people as they get old and life expectancy is short, but for adults in their prime, there is no physical threat that concerns them.

While he was now a diplomat for his country and was wearing the clothes of people brought up with the luxury of central heating and clean water—a dark blue coat, wool, maybe cashmere, and a business suit to make a guess based on his trousers—he still had the presence of someone from the plains of Asia.

He was focused on his cigarette. He drew, then slowly exhaled before looking up. He raised his eyebrows—his rounded face, yellowed skin, and almond eyes under short cut thick black hair—seeking confirmation.

I nodded, he tossed the butt toward me, and I stamped it out.

He seemed far less concerned about my tardiness than his employee. "My apologies," I said. "I had something making me feel a bit queasy that I needed to attend to." I put a hand on my stomach. He made an assumption and responded with a small hand movement, as if he were lazily moving a fly away. I didn't correct him.

"You said it is important."

"You sent me to find your son." Statement. Not a question.

There was a twitch at the side of his face—more a contraction of a few tiny muscles. A twitch, but no denial. No attempt to explain.

"I'm sorry. Your son is dead. He was shot last night in his apartment."

He was the second of the parents that I had told in the last nine hours. I didn't see a future for myself as a bereavement counselor. It was a hateful thing to have to impart this news, but I'm sure it said something for my place in heaven that I felt bad doing it. Didn't it remind me that I still had some link to humanity? Surely if I found giving such news to be an easy task, that would be worse.

The diplomat remained motionless from the neck down.

Tears started to roll down his cheeks—one or two at first, but then enough that I couldn't distinguish one from another. Somewhere between the edges of his mouth and his jaw, something began to tremble. He controlled it at first, but then was overwhelmed. There was a sob, and he leaned forward: "My boy. They've killed my boy..."

Kasym Aitmatov looked at me. "He's got some grit in his eye that he needs to clean out. Go and buy yourself an ice cream and play on the swings."

I strolled away from the diplomat and watched the people in the park on the bright spring morning. Groups of mothers pushing strollers. Clumps of kids playing games on the stone-topped paths, oblivious to every other user of the park who now had to walk around their game. The occasional tourist, looking but not quite sure what they were seeing, and unaware of what they were meant to be enjoying. Local office workers who had slipped out for a cigarette and a mid-morning bite to eat.

All seemed calm. All seemed happy. Only one man in the park looked in pain.

A gust of wind blew. A few older people enjoying one of the first days of spring without rain pulled their coats tighter. The kids were not distracted from their games. Me? It was still too cold to get an ice cream.

I watched from a distance. Kasym Aitmatov stood tall and firm. The sentry guarding. The diplomat was leaning forward—clearly it was a considerable lump of grit in his eye, or maybe there was more than one lump, each of which needed to be removed individually.

After a while the diplomat sat up. My cue. As I returned, the diplomat placed a hand on the bench next to him. I sat without facing him and recounted the outline of what had happened since we last spoke, twenty-four hours ago.

I told him first about my research at a computer.

I told him what I did. But I didn't tell him where I did it—the Sorbonne—or why I went there—because they have guards. It had cost me €100 to get past the guard, which seemed a small price for several uninterrupted hours of work in an environment that's far more secure than an internet café.

I had sat in front of a computer for two hours, finding everything I could find online about Pierre-Louis Dubois. I had googled him, which produced few results. Then I had checked his social media profiles. That gave me something, but not much. Mostly what it gave me were links to his friends; his friends who had posted photos; photos that had GPS data embedded. His friends may have thought they were posting a hilarious selfie taken at college. I didn't even try to understand the joke—I just knew the picture had been taken and uploaded within the last day, and it told me exactly where it had been shot. With every picture taken within a fifty-yard radius, I had a fairly good idea about where his friends congregated. And I knew what his friends looked like.

Okeyev listened without interrupting. Occasionally he sniffed or wiped his nose, but mostly he sat motionless, waiting as I recounted.

It had taken a few more hours to find his friends IRL, as the kids say...in real life. They weren't just sitting and waiting for me to arrive—they had their own lives. Classes to attend, girls to chase, food to eat, whatever.

His friends had seemed surprised. Surprised Pierre-Louis wasn't around. Surprised someone was looking for him. Somewhat cautious about letting out any detail or even about talking to me, but they gave me enough that I could piece together.

I had spoken to the mother, and she was less helpful. She wanted nothing to do with me and told me nothing. But her protectiveness told me that she was indeed Pierre-Louis' mother and there was a strong bond there.

From there, I had pieced together a few of the details from what his friends had said. In among the comments about him being an engineering student—which I'd already found—they mentioned he was a happy, funny, engaging guy. The all liked him, but they all found him a bit standoffish, maybe secretive. Perhaps prone to have a focus or minor obsessions. Nothing they said suggested anything other than he was a teenager and was perhaps introverted. He hadn't found religion, he hadn't expressed disgust with his life, and he still loved his mother and thought she was cool and the most beautiful woman he had ever seen.

Maybe his doodles had changed. Instead of drawing cars and spaceships, he seemed to be drawing animals—mostly jungle animals—and drawing them over and over, as if practicing and perfecting.

Odd words had been slipped in—places, people. Belleville was mentioned a few times. An apartment was mentioned, but there was skepticism. His mother was mentioned frequently. A father, never. Siblings? There were only two of them who lived in that apartment, said the kid who had been to their apartment—mother and son. But then he mentioned Belleville again.

I went on to explain to Okeyev that by the evening I had been knocking on doors for property agents in Belleville. I showed a photo of the kid, and there was recognition. The fourth guy I spoke to had shown him around a few apartments in Belleville, but nothing had been right for what Pierre-Louis wanted. And did I want an apartment, by the way?

He couldn't find something that suited Pierre-Louis, so he referred him to another agent. It had taken two hours to find that other agent. He knew immediately who I was talking about. He hadn't been able to help either—Pierre-Louis wanted a second room, didn't care how small, but didn't have the cash to pay for more than a single room—so, again, he had passed him on to another agent. Maurice.

Could I have Maurice's number, please? Sure. But he's not there—he left a few days ago. He's on a cruise with his mistress and won't be back for three weeks. Maurice had fairly low-level security, which made it simple to review his records. I left 200 euros to cover the damage I caused breaking in.

At the block, I had followed two people through the door—a girl and a guy. I didn't pay much attention to how they looked—I was more worried about not being seen than about seeing. A shot. I went in. I knelt next to the Pierre-Louis as he bled, trying to talk with him. He died; I looked around the place and left via the balcony.

I didn't feel the need to tell him what I took.

I figured if Pierre-Louis' mother hadn't met Marianne, then Okeyev wouldn't have either, so I didn't mention her.

It felt that I had given him enough explanation to justify a day's labor and to satisfy him that his money had been well spent.

He was still staring into the distance when he began to talk. "Who have you told?" Four words without emotion.

"His mother. Émilie Dubois." I hesitated. "A mother has a right know that her son is dead."

I wasn't sure whether he was rocking or nodding. "Anyone else?"

"Claude."

He was still rocking gently. "Thank you for your kindness in being with my son in his dying moments."

I wasn't sure how to respond, so I sat mute.

"Do you know where they have taken his body?"

"There were ambulances and police and scientists. He'll be in a morgue somewhere."

The father was still rocking.

"Find who killed my son, Leathan."

I stood and turned to face the mourning father. "I'm sorry for your loss. Truly. But I'm not the guy for that job."

I stood and left him sitting on the bench.

fifteen

I left Parc Monceau by a gate on the east side—exchanging the fenced-in and regimented walkways for the sweeping boulevards of the Paris streets—and as soon as I could, turned south.

As far as I could tell, I hadn't been followed into the park. As far as I could tell, I wasn't overlooked while I was in the park. Now, having left the park, I decided to go somewhere—there was no pre-planning, no arrangement.

And so I found myself, after twenty minutes' walk, without my usual paranoid search for any tail, stepping into Galeries Lafayette, the somewhat snooty department store on Boulevard Haussmann in the 9th. My nostrils were immediately assaulted by all manner of different smells from the perfume counters. Intermingled and sometimes cross-pollinating were the makeup counters. Different brands that I had no conception of, all wedged together over the single floor, with narrow aisles giving prominence to the stalls and making passing difficult.

I've never felt the need to buy makeup.

I don't wear it myself, and it always seems like an atrocious gift: I think you should improve the way you look...here's some help.

Perfume works as a present—an invisible addition to perfection—but not makeup.

Makeup is about the magic—it's all in the preparation, and it's done behind the scenes. It's something highly personal, and when it's done you pretend it has no effect. You don't say, "Wow! You've done your eyeliner really well," or, "You've applied that foundation and powder combination well." It's possible to get away with "You're looking very sparkly," but a compliment to the paint is a damnation to the canvas. Tell the canvas she *is* beautiful, and if she asks—even though she will have spent a long time preparing—just say, "Oh, are you wearing makeup?"

The makeup floor was open to the huge, iron-domed glass roof many, many floors above. All of the floors above had been set around the outside of the building with balconies—decorated in gold—so that customers on the higher floors could look over the makeup floor as if they were going to the coliseum to watch the

Christians and the lions slug it out for a few hours. Watching pretty women apply makeup to other women was now a spectator sport, apparently.

I walked the grid of passages crisscrossing the floor. I was a stranger here—this was a land for women, run by women. They were not against my kind—there were one or two men allowed at the perfume counters—but this wasn't for us.

I spent about twenty minutes looking and trying not to be seen. I tried to remember the logo on Émilie Dubois' uniform. I tried to bring to mind the letters and shapes, but failed. I looked at the brand logos around me. Up close, minute differences were apparent. From farther than three feet, each logo looked the same and whispered, "I will make you beautiful in a way those other brands cannot."

I gave up.

She may have seen me. She may not work there. She may work there, but had on balance decided to go back home today, which would not have been unreasonable—it was less than twelve hours since she learned her son had died.

I pulled out my phone and called her number. It rang with no reply. Okay. She was probably not at home. The only practical option I had was to see if I could find her somewhere else.

I'm not Mister Fashion—clothing stores aren't meant for me. Sure, I wear clothes. Sure, I have to buy clothes somewhere. But I buy clothes with an eye on the practicality—I'm more concerned about whether there are enough pockets, not whether it's this season's shade of Egyptian Sand or whether the Sea Storm is stormy enough.

My clients don't expect me to present myself as one who has an understanding or respect of fashion, which is good when my entire wardrobe—which largely consists of jeans, oxford shirts, sneakers, and a few leather jackets—is spread across Paris, and my choice of clothes is usually determined by where I sleep. I wear what I was wearing last time I visited that bed, assuming my host has been kind enough to launder the clothes for me.

And as one who knows where to buy jeans and plain cotton shirts, I've never immersed myself in the world of the stores in Paris, so I've never really understood how the hierarchy works. This left me to try anywhere I could think of—each time guessing more wildly about the sorts of places that would have a makeup counter.

Having failed at Galeries Lafayette, I tried the Champs-Élysées mall, Beaugrenelle, and Carrousel du Louvre. I tried a few boutiques and a few beauty parlors. With one or two minor exceptions, I would have received a warmer welcome if I had told them I was looking for small children to roast on a spit. I even tried Forum des Halles, which left me dejected and fearing for the future of humanity.

After three hours, I started to understand why women throng to the makeup counter. When everywhere else you go tells you there is something wrong with you, that reinforces the need to change yourself, and how better than with makeup? Great insight, Leathan. Profound. The profundity that only a dickhead can muster. Now tell yourself, where is Émilie?

And the only answer I could come up with was Galeries Lafayette—the place I had started. Surely this was the best—or the least worst—place to work if your line was troweling samples of makeup onto dowdy women trying to compensate for the derision they had been shown when they tried to buy clothes.

I made my way back to where I started, under the domed roof with iron supporting glass.

This time, instead of throwing myself into the belly of the beast and walking between the altars to beauty where women could venerate, I went to the place for my people. The people who were allowed to look down and wonder, but who were never allowed to take part in this ritual. A tribal ritual passed down from the ancients to ward off obstreperous sales assistants. A tribal ritual to apply paint on the outside to make the canvas on the inside feel good about herself.

I went up a floor, stood by the gold embossed balcony with a glass shield to ensure no one jumped, and looked into the cavernous hole opening below like someone would peer over the edge of volcano about to spew molten lava.

Young pretty things, dressed in clinical white uniforms reminiscent of nurses at a high-end clinic, tended to old women.

Young pretty things—maybe the same age as Pierre-Louis Dubois with the same life experience as Pierre-Louis Dubois— telling women twice, three times their age how they should live their life. Young pretty things suggesting they themselves do something to look young and pretty when all that had happened was beneficial genes and a lack of years on the planet.

Young pretty things, weighed down by the amount of makeup on their faces as they explained to their eager customers that their new makeup product would cure whatever their problem was. Husband straying? We've got new lipstick. Feeling frumpy? Look at this blusher. Truly a medicine show for the twenty-first century.

Young pretty things, ubiquitous and indistinguishable. The beacons of white uniforms cut across a sea of mismatched fabrics on sagging bodies, but one beacon stood out.

She wasn't young. She wasn't pretty in the way that a teenage girl might be pretty. She wasn't buckling under the products applied to her visage.

When I had met her, I hadn't been able to tell her age. It's considered poor form to cut a woman in half and count her rings—added to which, I didn't care. And I still didn't care, but I was struck by the comparison—she was the oldest assistant, and not by a small margin. And she stood out because of a double negative—she was the one who didn't look immature. Put a supermodel next to a three-year-old, and the supermodel's skin is going to look older.

But she's still a supermodel, right?

Émilie Dubois stood out like a supermodel next to a crowd of three-year-olds. They were pretty; she wasn't. She was beautiful—beautiful inside and beautiful outside. Her movements were small, delicate, considered. The others moved to be noticed—every move a clumsy paint-by-number attempt to strike some pose. What they tried to do, she was. She had lived a life—she had given birth to and lost a child. She had lived what some of her customers might have experienced, but she was the oddity in a circus of freaks.

I spent another ten minutes watching her.

Watching! Who was I kidding? Captivated by her. It was the oldest cliché in the book—man looks at beautiful woman and thinks, "I can save her; I can take her away from all this." I wouldn't have been the first to think that, and I wouldn't be the last.

But I couldn't take her away. What was the deal? Come away with me—there's a bunch of angry Bulgarians trying to kill me. You'll sleep in a different bed each night, and most of your day will be wasted making sure no one's following you.

Oh yeah...and there's no money to support us.

I found some stairs to sink me into the cauldron. Disoriented in the foreign land of the makeup counter, it took a few minutes to find her concession stand: a white-and-mirrored block with shelves and counters pushing many products. The drug trade could learn...

She was leaning over a woman sitting in a chair and looking like a bad Halloween joke. Half her face was a nightmare created from the imagination of someone abused in childhood. The other half was the model of serenity. Émilie talked to the split-faced woman: "The secret," she began. I lost the conversation after that. There was talk of layers, blending, facial washes, and regimes. And those were just the words I understood. But I wasn't really listening to the words; I was hearing her voice. The customer didn't notice, but I could hear the catch in her voice—the tinge of pain as she spoke.

I picked up a tub of...I wasn't sure what it was. There were words. I understood the words, but I didn't know what the combination of words meant. And I suspected that neither would the woman sitting in the chair—she would just understand the basic transaction: Spend money, feel better.

"What tone do you recommend for an olive complexion?" I asked.

"I'll be with you in a moment, monsieur." Émilie Dubois didn't look up.

"Is this best for greasy skin? And skin with some sun damage."

"A moment, monsieur." Still without looking.

"What about skin with acne scarring?"

There was a small sigh, probably an eye-to-eye communication between her and the woman in the chair, and then she turned to me. She was about to speak when she recognized me. Her face remained still, the inner confusion given away only by her darting eyes. I waited for the eyes—those eyes—to meet mine. I didn't say anything. I couldn't.

She broke the gaze and stepped forward, whispering quickly. "I'm on a break in twenty minutes—we can talk then."

She pulled away. I waited for her to offer more.

"See that counter, over there, by the wall." Her voice was clear, audible to the customer. She leaned forward, whispering again. "There's a door behind which leads to the staff break room. Just walk through—no one will stop you—and wait for me there."

She turned back to the customer.

I made a note to take a trip out of Paris on Halloween.

sixteen

She had been right: No one did stop me as I walked through the door, crossing the threshold from public to non-public. What she didn't tell me was the size of the back-of-store area. I'd never really thought about it, but as I started moving through the passageways at the back—wide enough for the carts carrying fresh stock to pass—I began to see that the store was like the painted ladies being attended to at the makeup counters. On the surface, with young pretty things troweling on the latest in cosmetic science, they were gleaming. The surface was perfect and ready to be displayed to the public. Behind the façade lay years of neglect. Stretch marks from where the needs of the public areas pushed and pulled. Loose skin from a diet. The results of a bit of botched plastic surgery, too many late nights, and too much stress.

All were here.

I headed for our rendezvous: the staff break room. A tedious box of a room with an easy-wipe table standing on an easy-wipe floor and surrounded by easy-wipe plastic chairs that offered no comfort and little support.

Sitting at the far end was a man, maybe twenty-five, probably of North African descent—the obvious guess was Algerian parentage—wearing a dark shirt with a logo that meant nothing to me. He looked down into his lap, distracted by something that was beeping and whirring.

I sat on the other side of the easy-wipe surface, looking toward the door. The Algerian descendant looked up: "Hi." Then he looked back to the game he was playing on his phone without seeking any further human interaction. Five minutes later he left: "Bye."

Through the glass panels set into the door, I could see people passing. They all seemed to be the kind of people who used the word "because" frequently. "I'm doing *this* because..." There was a higher power that controlled their lives—they were slaves just trying to avoid a beating.

Twenty minutes became thirty.

"Not here" were the only words she said as she stood in the doorway. I followed.

The drop suggested we were going lower. She could have been leading me along the back passage to the land of make believe—I really couldn't tell. It all looked the same to me. Then again, I was focused on the slim figure in front of me. She walked with a correctness...a controlled posture. I hadn't noticed her ass before. Now I couldn't drag my eyes away from its gentle oscillation as she walked.

The background noise became louder, and the temperature dropped further. The door we reached was different—rougher, heavier, and painted black instead of white. I followed her through. She frowned, wiping something from her hand—a stickiness she had picked up from the door.

We had entered into another cavern.

The first big cavern I had seen was open to the public. It had a domed roof with an iron frame supporting glass covering the makeup counters. This was a smaller cavern without a glass roof.

We stood at the top of a rough concrete ramp edged with a safety rail constructed from iron pipe and painted in shiny blue paint.

Now on the outside, leaning against the rail, I could see that our exit was actually an access. But looking down over the rail I could see cigarette butts—a small heap, dropped without being stubbed out, suggesting this location was frequently visited by the staff.

Across the cavern's floor sat three delivery trucks—each painted with a different company's logo, each with its back open and men unloading. To the right a broad road swept down into the cavern—the gullet leading from the mouth feeding the beast.

There was a rattling sound as one of the porters began to push his stacked cart across the loading bay. He stared at Émilie and made no attempt to hide his attention. He briefly looked away as the cart hit the curb, but returned his gaze as he clumsily turned the corner beginning his ascent of the short ramp. I opened the door for him. He didn't seem to notice or offer any thanks or acknowledgement—his gaze was fixed—until I dropped the door after he had passed.

"Why are you here?" she asked.

The logical answer was: I wondered if you wanted to talk. Or perhaps: Why are you here and not at home grieving? Maybe: Why do you think this is my fault?

There were many questions I could ask, but I wasn't going to. I wanted to know what she was thinking. I wanted to know what she wanted to talk about. Sure, I'd been a pain in the ass—I'd embarrassed her at work, in front of a customer—but she'd agreed to see me. One word—"Security!"—and I would have been gone. But she didn't call them—instead she agreed to see me.

That had to mean something.

So I waited with the uncomfortable unspeaking silence hanging between us.

When she spoke her voice was annoyed. Not angry, just annoyed—a lighter shade of gray. "Why did you send those men?" she asked.

"What men?"

She exhaled rapidly. Disapproval. A small twist of her head. Disappointment.

"What men? When?" I enunciated each word. "I didn't send any men. I don't have men to send."

She had a look that said she was getting annoyed. She was used to men playing games with her—I was just another man playing games.

I tried again. "Did the men say I sent them? Or did you ask whether I sent them—and they just agreed?"

She went to speak—more to react angrily—then stopped. She looked up as if playing through a scene in her head, and then her face flushed red.

"It's alright," I said. "It doesn't matter."

"I haven't got long," she said. Still annoyed, but probably more frustrated with herself.

I shrugged and started walking down the concrete slope, away from the door, away from her, and turned toward the ramp the trucks drove down. I stopped, looking up at her. "I'll be around when you want to talk."

I headed toward the ramp before she could respond.

seventeen

It was midafternoon—or at least, as I worked my way up from the cavern under the large store, it seemed like it should be midafternoon.

Rationally, I knew that I had spent maybe three hours of the day effectively chasing my tail. The rest had been spent, on the whole, just chatting with people. But it still felt as if I had spent weeks running around a hamster wheel without a break.

For half of the time on my hamster wheel, I'd felt that I was being followed. This is a good feeling—if I think I'm being followed, then I can look for the person who is tailing me. And whether I can find them or not, I can do something to change the situation and make it harder to be followed.

For the other half of the time I spent running around Paris looking at every makeup counter in the miles between La Défense and Disneyland, I felt that I wasn't being followed. This is a bad feeling: If I'm wrong, then I lose, and if I'm right, it doesn't stop someone from finding me a moment later.

But for the last hour I had spent in Galeries Lafayette—in the public and non-public areas—I had felt that I was alone. I felt that no one was following me.

The broad ramp twisted upward, like the ramp on a multistory parking lot. The ramp became straighter, the angle of ascent flattened, and the outside became visible through a tiny square mouth. A single horizontal bar, striped in red and white, showed the dividing line between "inside" and "we don't care."

To the right of the gate was a tiny office—a building within the building, peeling wood-framed windows caging a man wearing a white shirt. He stepped out from the office and onto the track as I drew close. "Hey!" he said, gripping a clipboard in one hand and pointing to a plastic sign screwed to the wall: A figure, probably intended to be walking, inside a red circle crossed through with a diagonal red line.

I kept walking. I couldn't even be bothered to shrug. I had bigger issues to think about like whether to turn left or turn right.

I went right, soon finding myself in front of the windows of the store. Displays crafted to say, "Step in...we're friendly here...we *know* what you want even if you don't."

Some way up ahead there was a figure, trying and failing to look casual. He wasn't drawn to the expansive window displays, he wasn't carrying shopping or just passing, and he certainly didn't seem concerned by the wind, which was still whipping off la Seine.

Instead, there was a figure that most people would see as being a few inches taller than average, stockier than most, and having a darker skin tone. Given his physical presence, some might assume a driver or maybe security for one of the customers. Maybe a customer who didn't want this lump of a man to keep staring at her in the intimate moments as she allowed herself to be vulnerable at the temple to makeup.

They might have seen that.

I saw Kasym Aitmatov. The bigger and yet the more junior of the two men from Kyrgyzstan.

I turned and walked in the opposite direction.

eighteen

I checked the time. It was too late to get over to the college and talk to Pierre-Louis' friends. By the time I got there, the kids would have been gone for the day—or if not gone, they wouldn't be congregating.

I thought about going to Belleville to have a look around the apartment. Take a look without the police or SAMU banging on the door and without a dead body lying there. The scientists were probably still there lifting fingerprints and taking samples, and there would almost certainly be an officer posted outside.

I wanted to think.

Needed to think.

Different people think in different ways. Pierre-Louis Dubois thought by translating the ideas swirling in his head into marks in his notebook; words and images put onto paper in an attempt to codify and structure his feelings into something he could recognize. A plan that he could come back to, a fleeting new piece of knowledge made permanent by the intersection of paper and ink.

For me, I think with my first beer. The second is for pleasure, and the third ruins any bright ideas I had while drinking the first.

And it was too long since I had eaten. Despite Kasym Aitmatov's suggestion of an ice cream, I hadn't eaten since I had the croissant while watching Claude's door.

Albert's café was close—not the closest, but close enough. I had been there a number of times and was on nodding terms with the proprietor. He could recognize my face, knew I had been living in London, but couldn't remember my name. But most people struggled with my name, so I wasn't going to get too bent out of shape about that.

Café owners can be useful people to know. People talk in cafés—they spill out their life story to a complete stranger who must give them his full attention because he's got nowhere else to go. That's what makes café owners useful for me—someone has a problem, the owner knows a solution: me.

But the guy needs to know me and trust me before he's going to recommend me. And I need to know he is someone I can trust before I open up—even a little bit. And how is trust built? By spending time together.

So going for a beer was little more than a salesman making a call to a prospective customer.

As I walked into the café, Albert was surrounded by a group of Japanese tourists. They seemed unsure as to who had eaten and drunk what and who was liable to meet what share of the bill. All Albert seemed to know was it was going to take a long time before he got paid.

He caught my eye as I closed the door behind me. A grin—half in welcome, half acknowledging his present plight. He pointed to the beer tap, indicating the beer I had drunk last time I was in. He might not know my name, but he knew me where it mattered.

I sat at the end of the bar, away from the white noise of the Japanese. The debate continued as Albert poured my drink and put the glass in front of me. "Evening, Leathan," he said, proving me wrong. "Food?" He put a menu next to the beer and returned to the tourists.

I flicked the menu open as I reached for the beer, then lazily let my eye wander down the list of dishes. By the third sip, the tourists hadn't resolved their internal conflict, but I had decided what I wanted to eat. I turned the menu upside down and caught the patron's eye. He took two steps toward me while facing the Japanese. I laid my fingers to point to my order. "Coming up," said Albert, returning his full attention to the Japanese, who were swapping currency between them as if involved in a bizarre international version of pass the parcel.

Albert wrote something on a small pad, ripped off a sheet, and posted the page through the window to the kitchen. There was a good-natured shout from the kitchen, and Albert returned to the tourists who were counting out bills on the bar.

I returned to my beer. It helped me think.

I was dealing with two parents.

Both had lied to me.

Not necessarily in what they said, but they had both lied in what they held back.

He told me lies, and I walked away. I refused to help and refused the implicit offer of cash associated with giving help. She told me lies, it drew me to her, and I had sought her out.

He was my client—she wasn't. I guessed that made a difference, or did it? He had asked me what happened. I had told him, and when I had told him everything I sensibly could, I walked. But she didn't ask the question. Doesn't every parent—at some level—want to know how his or her child died? However painful the hearing might be, wouldn't you want to know? Almost certainly not immediately, but at some point, you have to hear it. Don't you?

I was halfway down my beer, but my decision was made.

I couldn't explain to Albert—no rational human being would understand what I was doing—so I made a big show of suddenly *remembering* I was meant to be somewhere else as I pulled out a €20, which I trapped under my glass before I headed for the door.

One day I'll market my own diet and exercise regime: Stay slim by following people around Paris. Like all the best diets, it's very simple: Don't eat; walk around a lot.

nineteen

The bright spring day had given over to a clear night.

The lack of sunlight changed everything, and as I stood, I was getting colder. The guys in the car parked on the other side of the road could run the engine and get the heater working. Every now and then, the lights flicked, suggesting the engine had gone on.

The gray Peugeot sedan had been there when I arrived. A gray car on a gray night parked just down from a large, dark green gate, which looked gray in the gloom. Armies spend millions buying camouflage—they could save a fortune by hiring the same guy who designed such a forgettable car. It really was that unremarkable.

And the two guys who sat in the car seemed completely unremarkable, conforming to the whole monochrome vibe without adding any personality. I was tempted to ignore them, but I suspected their presence here wasn't coincidental. More significantly, the last two people I had encountered who I thought I could ignore were very much the opposite. And while I had been occupied with making sure those two didn't remember me, they had been occupied with making sure Pierre-Louis became dead.

The lights on the car flicked—the occupants were feeling the cold too. It wasn't below zero, but it was close. The temperature wasn't the problem; it was the wind. The wind, although not strong, was biting, and I was standing still. I was leaning against a plane tree, which I was now on first-name terms with, but it didn't offer any protection. Not that my clothes offered enough protection for standing, watching, waiting. Jeans and a leather jacket are great when I'm on the move...building up a sweat. Less so when my heart rate drops to near-hibernation levels.

Partly for my own sanity and partly to try to force my body to generate some warmth for itself, I would walk. I'd only go as far as I could go while keeping the green gate in sight—or at least, even if I couldn't actually see the large chunk of wood that opened onto the courtyard behind, I made sure I could continue to see the sidewalk in front of the gate so I was aware of anyone arriving and anyone leaving.

At a distance I felt less likely to draw attention to myself I jumped up and down, shook myself, and jogged on the spot, sometimes throwing in a few sprints—all to force the blood to flow. Warmed, I walked back—staying across the boulevard from the green gate that looked gray and the gray car that looked invisible—and continued past the target as far as I could go in the other direction while still keeping the patch of sidewalk in front of the gate in sight. After warming myself again, I would return.

And so it had been for the last two-and-a-half hours.

One hundred and fifty minutes of wishing I were a lizard. Or a polar bear. Or anything but a bored human being who'd had a stupid idea while sitting and drinking a beer.

But the gray Peugeot told me it wasn't such a stupid idea.

Somewhere at the far end of the boulevard, at the lower end of the slight incline, masked behind pedestrians and plane trees, there was a new figure.

Small. Nondescript. In the half-light provided by municipal electricity, the figure looked gray.

A gray figure among other gray figures. Some taller, a few shorter. Most broader, most bulkier. I couldn't make out a face. I couldn't see any physical characteristics with any certainty. But it was her.

The guys in the Peugeot hadn't noticed.

But it was her.

The posture. The walk. She had a shopping bag in each hand, but still she held herself in an upright position. Where everyone around her seemed doubled over, holding themselves as if their stance would protect them from the cold, she was walking as she would walk wearing a tight dress—the movements of her thighs were restricted with a slightly exaggerated sweep of her calves. Each step was short, precise. There was a military-like precision, but with a grace as if she were floating—her legs gently propelling her on a cloud.

The guys in the Peugeot started to wonder but weren't sure. Maybe it was her, maybe it wasn't. One seemed to think yes, the other no.

She settled the argument. Her pace changed. The rhythm of her step, wafting her on a cloud that invisibly supported her, broke. She was like everyone else—now heavy paces expressed her anger. The subtle flicks of her knees gave way to deliberate movements from her hips. Delicate steps were now heavy stomps. Her head—previously floating on top of her neck—was now angrily pulled into the top of her shoulder and pointing at the gray Peugeot.

What can you divine from a change in how someone walks? Anger? Fear? Joy? All that seemed clear was there was a recognition of the men in the car.

As she reached the passenger window, she transferred both shopping bags to one arm. With the other arm she pointed— aggressively gesticulating, her hand reaching from outside to inside the car. Her voice was raised. Across the boulevard what she said was unclear, but the raised voice was audible, even with the noise of traffic.

The two men remained impassive.

She returned to her upright posture and turned away. A few steps to her green gate, and she was gone.

But the Peugeot remained.

twenty

The gray Peugeot sedan remained, and the two guys inside behaved as if nothing had happened.

I waited. Counting time in my head and visualizing the route. Maybe the stairs? With shopping, she'd probably take the elevator. I played it through: Go through the green gate, under the arch, and across the corner of the cobbled courtyard. Open the door that didn't lock properly, then two steps up to the elevator. Hit the button, wait. Step into the elevator, punch the button, wait, and then get off at the fourth floor. Three steps to the front door, unlock the door, step in, drop the shopping on the table, turn around and lock the door.

The question was: Would she then go to the kitchen or would she turn on the light in her living room?

The light went on at the fourth floor. One question answered and confirmation that she was home.

I waited. I timed it: five minutes. Five minutes, and the guys in the sedan seemed to have done nothing. No calls. No checking in. No requests for help. They didn't even turn over the engine to fire up the heater. They just sat.

But she had recognized them. Their presence had been enough to break her reserved demeanor. Two guys sitting in a car had been enough to pierce the veil. Which told me that they were the guys that had said I sent them...when she asked.

I didn't send them, leaving the obvious question: Who did? Who knew she lived here to send the two guys here?

While that was an interesting thought, the bigger question for me was: What was my opening gambit? How was I going to start the conversation? I stood away from my plane tree leaning post, shook myself loose, and hoped to push some blood around my body and fight against the cold that seemed to have found every joint in and was attacking each and every one with a hammer.

I decided I'd figure what to say by the time I got there. Necessity and invention, and all that stuff.

Reflexively, I looked left. How long before I learned? I was in Paris now—look right when crossing the road...unless it's a one-way street.

I looked right and felt a hand on my shoulder. A big hand. A firm grip. Not necessarily aggressive—it was a hand on my shoulder rather than a fist to my gut—but definitely intended to get my attention.

I spun.

Shit.

I had been cautious in the morning. I had been smug in the afternoon when I dodged my pursuer, leaving him outside Galeries Lafayette. But in the evening, I had been over-confident and got sloppy.

Kasym Aitmatov, the diplomat's close protection officer, had his hand on my shoulder. The side of his mouth was lifting, and a look of quiet self-satisfaction had crept across his face. "Mister Wilkey," he said releasing my shoulder.

He was dressed for the sub-arctic—a heavy coat, scarf, fur hat—yet still had the smartness that would be expected of a diplomat's aide, apart from his boots, which didn't seem to match with the legs of his business suit visible under his coat.

"I was just passing," I said.

He looked at his watch. "Just passing?"

"Mmm."

"It takes you nearly three hours to *just pass*?"

Shit. The best magic is always explained by misdirection. Was this all the guys in the Peugeot were? Misdirection? I had been looking at them while Kasym Aitmatov had been looking at me. A simple trick, perfectly executed, and I fell for it.

"Aren't you going to tell your boys to go home now?" I said, nodding to the gray Peugeot.

"Not ours."

"Not yours? So what are they doing here?"

He shrugged, a huge movement of a big man covered with ample padding. "They were here when I got here."

"Which was when?"

"When I lost you."

I looked up at him, questioning. "I saw you on the balcony looking at her in the store. I saw you talk to her. I saw you both disappear through the door at the back—you first, her later. I figured it was only a matter of time before you came here."

Shit. Predictable and caught.

"Well, now you've found me." He stared mirthlessly as I continued. "You've won your prize, and now I'm going to get warm."

I turned. The hand was returned to my shoulder. I let him see that he had my attention, and he released.

"Maybe you're not understanding, Mister Wilkey." The voice was measured—there was no anger, no menace to his tone. "This wasn't a training mission. Tolomush Okeyev didn't send me running around Paris just to amuse me for a few hours. He feels the two of you need to have a chat."

"Great," I said. "I'll swing by tomorrow."

A gentle shake of the head. Almost a shared joke.

"Day after?" I tried.

"Now."

"I need to get warm."

"The heater in my car and the heated seats will warm you faster than any bar," he said. His voice lightened: "And I don't need to point out that most citizens in the European Union don't carry guns, but diplomatic immunity affords me certain privileges."

The car was parked two streets away.

twenty-one

Kasym Aitmatov, the man whose home was on the plains of Asia, let the Mercedes move off gently. The engine's deep rumble hinted at power, but there was no feeling of being forced back into my seat or of having G-forces pull my face tight like a nightmare facelift. He respected speed limits and traffic signs. I know we went around corners, but I never felt the centripetal forces moving me from my seat.

All I felt was the warmth from the seat that Kasym Aitmatov had promised me and the warm air pumping into the cabin.

After about ten minutes, the big man pulled up outside a restaurant. I knew of the restaurant but had never been there. *They* say the food is very good. *They* say the food is unpretentious and if the owner smartened up the place and added some *je ne sais quoi*, he could put the prices up. But *they* also say that he doesn't want to, because he likes the kind of clientele who are attracted by a place that chooses food over flourish.

Aitmatov led into the small entrance foyer and, instead of walking into the restaurant, turned to the right and followed a winding wooden staircase enclosed on each side by dark wood paneling. At the top there was a broad corridor with untreated floorboards; the walls had dark wood paneling up to the midpoint with white plaster above. Breaking the line of the wall were three doors, all shut. At the far end of the passage, someone I presumed was a waiter—a man with a white shirt and black trousers, a white towel over his arm—rested against the wall.

Outside the middle door stood a man in a suit. Ten years younger than Kasym Aitmatov. A few inches shorter and many kilos lighter. He genuflected as the man who had driven me across Paris approached, implying a hierarchy. The senior aide tapped once at the door, paused, then entered, looking back at me to indicate I should follow.

In the room there was a round table that would comfortably sit four—two chairs were at the table, the other two had been moved to the side. On one chair sat Tolomush Okeyev, his attention drawn to his companion on the other chair.

She was maybe nineteen, perhaps twenty, and was wearing a clingy purple dress revealing excessive cleavage, not that she had that much cleavage to display. If you wanted to be cruel, you could describe her looks as pretty but slutty. If you wanted to be charitable, then with her hair tied back in a ponytail and a white uniform, she would fit perfectly as a girl working at a makeup counter in one of Paris' leading department stores.

"I'm sorry, this is important," he whispered to her, reaching into his pocket and taking out several €100 bills.

She tried to pull a pouty sad face. She tried to suggest she was disappointed that their evening was cut short. Her eyes told a different story: She had been paid for a night's work after an hour's labor.

She took the bills as she stood, slipping the cash into her grab-bag, then bent forward—pure affectation to make the best use of limited assets—and kissed the diplomat on each cheek. As she leaned forward, the hem of her dress barely covered her ass, and two sturdy legs came into view.

Returning again to the vertical, she pushed out her bottom lip, gave a tiny wave to her sugar daddy, and tottered out of the room. "Take her wherever she wants to go," the diplomat said to Kasym Aitmatov, his eyes fixed on his guest as she left.

With his eyes still staring at where he had last seen his guest, although the door was now closed and there was no ass wrapped in tight purple fabric—nor sturdy thighs—to be seen, the diplomat spoke: "Sit."

He indicated the just vacated seat next to him, pushing it a comfortable distance from him while his eyes were still drawn to the door.

The table was covered with a white cloth that didn't lay quite flat due to the creases acquired in storage. There was no cutlery, no napkins, no plates, no condiments, no flowers, candles, or other table decoration. Just an expanse of starched white cotton that had enough frequent flyer miles from its trips to the laundry to buy a ticket to Pluto.

There was a knock at the door, and the waiter who had been at the end of the corridor stepped in. "Drinks, monsieur?" he asked.

The diplomat looked at me: "Have you eaten, Leathan?" I gave a small shake of my head, and he turned back to the waiter. "Two steaks and a bottle of red." He turned back to me: "Red alright for you? Or would you prefer a beer or something else to drink?"

"I'm good with wine," I said.

The diplomat looked back to the waiter. "That's it."

"Merci, monsieurs," said the waiter, leaving the room.

The diplomat saw the slightly puzzled look on my face and smiled indulgently. "In what they call my line of business, you will understand that I meet a lot of people, and we often do our business over dinner."

"I suppose."

"Again, you will understand that much of my business is about appearance. We must perform a ceremony so that people understand the grandeur of what we do. I represent a country of fewer than six million people. We can shout and scream all we like, but at the end of the day, we have to acknowledge that if our nearest neighbors, Russia, China, and India, want to dominate us—as indeed the Russians have—then we would be powerless. We could launch a guerilla war, but we could never repel the forces of a country with a population ten times, twenty times, or more, larger than ours. We could never repel a country with access to weaponry that we cannot afford and do not have the scientists to develop."

"I suppose." To be honest, I didn't really suppose—I didn't care. I wanted a beer, but a glass of wine would make an acceptable short-term alternative.

He continued. "We will never be at the top table, and I am happy to accept that. But some of my confrères—if I can call them that; the people who hold a similar position to me—they behave as if their tiny country means something, and by extension, that they have some level of importance because they have been *chosen* to represent their great nation. And how is this great power manifest?"

He looked to me. Maybe the question wasn't rhetorical. "Tell me," I said.

"Through the choice of food." He laughed at his own anecdote. "They believe the choice of food is how you communicate your power, your breeding, and your understanding to your brother diplomat."

The door opened, and the waiter returned, a wine bottle in one hand and three glasses in the other. He placed the glasses on the table, then stood next to the diplomat, opening the bottle. "This is what I like," said the waiter to the diplomat. "Try it. If you don't like it, we'll get you something else."

The waiter, who I was beginning to suspect might be the proprietor, poured a small measure, picked up the glass, swirled the dark red liquid, sniffed it, and took a sip, leaving only the dregs in the glass. "Mmmm. It's good." He filled each of our glasses and then left, taking his glass with him.

The diplomat smiled. He knew that normal restaurant protocol had not been followed. He knew I knew that. He took a sip of his wine. "He's right—it is good. Try it, Leathan. You'll like it."

I tried the wine. I'm not a big wine drinker. I usually get disappointed—the experience never meets the promise—but this was a good. The kind of wine I could happily drink all night and would then wake with a rampaging headache tomorrow.

"I have lived most of my adult life outside of the country I represent, the country of my birth. Indeed, since the age of twenty, I have cumulatively—cumulatively—spent less than six months in my own country." The diplomat was talking again. I took another sip. "One thing I've learned: There's no point in asking an expert something and then, when they give you their opinion, thinking you know better."

He had my attention—it seemed he might be getting to the point.

"What's the best wine here?" He paused a beat. "I don't know. But the man who has tried all the wines will know. Is the wine corked? Is there something else wrong with the wine? How am I meant to know? But the proprietor will. What's the best food to eat here? How should it be cooked? This place is renowned for its steaks, so that's not a hard choice, but after that? I just say steak. They choose the cut, the chef then cooks it how he believes the steak should be best cooked and presents it in a way he thinks gives the best meal."

"So your buddies all flap around like peacocks, but you get the best meal?"

"You understand me, Leathan. You understand me." He put his wine down and continued. "And you're the expert I need to help me with my current problem."

I grimaced. We'd had this conversation this morning.

"We got off on the wrong foot, Leathan."

Wrong foot? He lied. Or at least, he held back a key piece of information: The kid he paid me to find was his son. And I was betting there were plenty more details that he had held back. It wasn't enough to suspect—or even to know—that he was lying. I needed to understand what lies he told, what lies he thought were untruths, and what lies he regarded as a matter of interpretation, and that took time. And it would take more than a meal together to understand how this man thought, and how he thought when he was under pressure.

"I hope you'll reconsider," he said. "Or do I need to call my Bulgarian friends to help persuade you?"

"Don't fuck with me!" I surprised myself by how quickly I moved. My anger had propelled me from my seat to the door. I was now scouring my mind for an insult to throw, and then I'd be gone.

"Or?" It was a simple question. I'd never tried negotiating with a diplomat before, but I guessed he was much better at it than I was. He patted my seat—indicating with his eyes that I should come back to the table. "Or?"

"Or nothing," I said, returning. "Just don't fuck with me. It's not big and it's not clever. You just make yourself look like a petty little asshole."

That seemed to amuse him. "Not quite the language that we use in diplomatic circles, but I take your point, Leathan. And I apologize. I'm sorry. That was unnecessary."

It might have been unnecessary, but it let me know that Claude had told him more of my background than I would have hoped. Sure, Claude can recount his version of my CV—anyone who wants my help wants to know why I'm the right guy—but telling them my weaknesses just puts me in danger.

"I need your help—and Claude tells me you are a man who can help."

"Kasym Aitmatov seems like a guy with some talent," I offered.

"He is exceptionally talented, but he's also on the diplomatic payroll. He has his—shall we say, a *day job*—and I need some distance. You are deniable. I can deny you at home. I can deny you in France. Leathan who? Doing what?"

He reached into his pocket and pulled out a small stack of Euro bills, putting them on the table in front of me. At a guess, as before, there was 5,000 euros: ten bills of €500. I looked at it without touching.

"Tomorrow's fee. You didn't do any work for me today, so here's tomorrow's fee."

I stared at the stack, still not touching the bills on the crisp white cloth, but I did speak. "You need to be honest with me." He looked unconvinced. "Honest. Open. Frank." He seemed to relax, as if accepting that he wasn't going to argue against my basic proposition. "Who's Marianne?"

The sudden movement of his eyes told me that my shift from employee to inquisitor had been noticed. His reply was swift. "Someone trying to get money." He relaxed back into his chair, picking up his wine glass. "Are you telling me you didn't do stupid things in the past?" He looked up, a broad grin across his face.

I nodded back, acknowledging that it was the choices I had made that led me to where I was: living in Paris, sleeping in a different bed each night, minimizing any trace of my existence, and taking scraps of work that other people would walk away from.

"We all have a past, Leathan. I have a past and I have a position—both of which make me vulnerable. My position also means I am able to do favors that others cannot—I literally can get some people out of jail for free. I can help you get away with murder. That makes me even more vulnerable to my past." His tone was wistful, and he was focusing in the far distance. "And no, I don't *need* to be honest. But I understand your concern and apologize if you think I misled you."

The contemplation was broken as the door swung open. The waiter followed by a younger woman dressed similarly and carrying a large tray. "Has Kasym Aitmatov returned?" asked the diplomat.

"He has and he's already got his food, monsieur," said the waiter, starting to lay cutlery for each of us. "He's having the same as you." He turned to his colleague with the tray and took a plate in each hand, holding the white porcelain with a towel. "The plates are hot," he said as he placed a steak in front of each of us, before turning back to the tray and reaching down for a large bowl of fries and a plate of vegetables.

"Thank you," said the diplomat.

"Bon appétit," said the waiter, closing the door behind him.

I looked at my steak for a few moments before continuing to talk. "If you don't need to be honest, then confess your sins. And if you don't want to confess your sins, then at least tell me what I'm dealing with."

twenty-two

I believe the word is convivial—as in, apart from one small spat when he clumsily threatened me, it was a convivial evening that I spent with the diplomat from Kyrgyzstan.

Which surprised me.

I had thought he was somewhat of a dickhead when I first met him, but as he relaxed, I seemed to get the full diplomatic charm deployed. He seemed astute—he could read people. He was smart—he listened to experts. And he showed consideration—maybe it was a small point, but he made sure Kasym Aitmatov was fed, and it was clear that the restaurant knew his requirement that Kasym Aitmatov be fed from the same menu as him and before him.

So his choice in women might be questionable. Ah well...let he who is without cast the first, and whatever... We can all be smart when it comes to women that hold no allure for us.

But do we make the right choices when there's something we can't walk away from?

"Kasym Aitmatov can drop you anywhere," said the diplomat as I went to leave after dinner.

I thanked him but chose to walk. I didn't want him to know where I was going, and if I was honest with myself, I was hoping that the walk and the chill of the early February night would dissuade me from my course.

I knew it wouldn't, but still I hoped.

The diplomat's money was in my pocket, and now I was getting paid to do what I was going to do anyway. I was getting paid disproportionately more than I would expect to be paid—as in, get out of town for three months' money for two days' work. Two days' work, ignoring expenses and assuming I didn't get jumped.

On the plus side, I'd got money. On the minus side, I'd found a patron. There was no plus without the minus, and while his explanations had been reasonable—and I liked the guy and I had enjoyed a good steak—I still didn't trust him. He had said a lot, but he hadn't told me much. After I first met him, I had spent a few hours on the internet looking through the social media trail left by Pierre-Louis Dubois, the kid I now knew to be his son. I'd

also briefly googled Tolomush Okeyev, still uncertain as to who he
was. Google had told me as little about his history as he had told
me tonight.

Nothing he had said had given me anything useful for the task
he wanted me to perform.

I arrived at the location of my new best friend forever—the
plane tree—and waited for ten minutes, feeling the warmth from
my walk beginning to fade and being replaced by the chill of a
February night.

The gray Peugeot remained where it had been when Kasym
Aitmatov had placed his hand on my shoulder about four hours
ago. The same two unremarkable guys remained, just sitting, doing
nothing, communicating with no one.

The light at the fourth floor window looked unchanged.

Now there was no Kasym Aitmatov to stop me. I could have
that chat with the unremarkable gentlemen. But one thing that had
twigged in the last four hours was that they weren't looking for me.
They probably didn't know who I was, even if they might know my
name.

That would quickly change if I banged on the window. They
would know that I was here, paying attention.

I pulled out my phone. "It's Leathan." Émilie Dubois answered
on the first ring, as if she were sitting next to the phone waiting for
a call. "I wanted to check you're alright."

"Oh."

"...to see if you needed anything...make sure no one..."

"I'm fine," she said. Two words. Two words from which I could
try to diagnose a diversity of feelings, each at a different intensity
and with a different scale. It wasn't that there was something wrong
in what she said—but something wasn't right. She was upset—of
course she was upset, dummy, her son had just died—but there was
more: She was anxious. The call didn't seem to upset her—she wasn't
worried about me or my intrusion, but there was a nervousness that
didn't sit well with the upset.

"No unwanted visitors?"

She was hesitant. "N-n-no."

"I was waiting outside when you got back. I saw those guys in
the car."

"Oh."

"You do know they're still there? Watching. Waiting."

"Where are you?" The tone said surprise, not shock.

"Across the road...by my tree. I'm looking at the gray Peugeot now."

"Oh." I'm not sure if I just wanted to believe or whether I was letting my hopes run away, but that "oh" sounded different to me. Positive. Expectant. Pleased, perhaps.

"Do you want me to come up?" I asked.

twenty-three

"Why are you here?"

It was a simple question—I just expected the front door to be closed before it was asked. Maybe I thought it might be prefaced by some pleasantry, like "Hi."

"I don't mean why are you here, I mean *why* are you here?" The emphasis was subtle—she didn't mean why, she meant, what is your actual purpose, Leathan?

The entrance hall was plain with little adornment. It was like the entrance hall you would step into as you entered many apartments in Paris, but somehow this felt intended. This was arranged to her will and was more than the space between the front door and the rooms in the apartment. "I'm here because something's not right," I said.

"My son has died. My only child has died. The world will never be right again."

I couldn't argue with her basic premise—I was there in part because I knew her world had changed. But I was trying to point to something outside of her situation. I could never know how she was feeling, but I could see what she had done—how she had behaved—in the last day, and compare that to how others had behaved.

"The world never will be right. But there's more, isn't there?" I wasn't sure whether the confusion spreading across her face was genuine. "There are people outside your apartment—they've been there for at least six hours. Your son dies and within a few hours of finding out, you go to work. But when you leave here, you look terrified and blame me. Everyone grieves in their own way—and I'm not one to tell you how you should grieve—but something feels odd to me."

She had changed out of her uniform since she got home and was now wearing tight black leggings and a loose sweater. The dark blue sweater was baggy, but the excess fabric was by choice, not accident, and it didn't swamp her, leaving an untucked white cotton blouse to poke out around her neck, wrists, and ass. Her hair—dark, thick waves that didn't quite form curls—had been loosely clipped back.

"It's gone eleven, and you're not asleep...you don't even seem ready for sleep."

"I don't think I'll ever sleep again." Her voice was flat. Resigned. Matter-of-fact. She could have been telling me she had no cheese in the fridge.

"I thought you might have questions," I said, trying to give a more honest answer to the question she had posed when I arrived.

She seemed to accept that explanation without acknowledging the veracity of the statement, and turned, leading through to her lounge. The same two sofas facing each other. The same bookcase. The same radio. The same lack of television.

We sat, facing diagonally. "I don't know what I can tell you," I began, "but I was there." She didn't respond. "Some law of the universe says if you were there, you have to find those who the person loved and tell them what you can."

She let out a small sob, curling forward and beginning to weep. Her head turned so she could half look at me. "I want to know. But not yet."

She returned to her sobbing. I returned to sitting and watching her.

"I'm not ready to hear." Her voice was apologetic. Her cheeks were moist as she looked up. "If I hear what happened then it's real. Once the police turn up...then it's real."

"The police will take a while," I offered. "They probably haven't identified... There were no details in the apartment, and the rental agent is on a cruise."

She looked up, annoyed. These were the details she didn't want. Facts, proof, evidence. Cold, hard, empirical. She had just told me she wanted to keep the warmth of the unknown—while she didn't have proof, she could lie to herself that her son was not dead.

"But it still doesn't tell me why you're here. Here, now," she said. "You're not the first man to call me late at night on a pretense."

I felt the slap of her rebuke for my crass insensitivity.

"You look disappointed," she said, continuing with her thought. "You're not French, are you?"

Was it my accent? Was it my attitude? "I believe in liberté, égalité, fraternité. I believe in the ideals of the republic. Isn't that enough?"

There was a wry smile under the tears, but no response.

"No. I'm not French. But I'm not *not* French. My mother was French."

She noticed the past tense. Her lips moved involuntarily: "I'm sorry."

"My mother was French, and my father was Scottish. They met in France, but I was born and bought up in Scotland, in a town called Grangemouth."

"I thought I heard English—that worried me," she said, wiping her cheeks, "but if your mother was French, you will know that we French are less concerned with some affairs that seem to vex you English."

"I'm not English," I repeated softly. "Scottish."

"Oh dear." She seemed ready to smile. "The Presbyterians are worse than the English. At least the English have the aristocracy— and the aristocracy know how to have fun. The Presbyterians..." She let the thought hang—waiting, expecting, encouraging me to explain.

"I'm here, because..."

Because? Because, I thought she might have questions. But she could ask those over the phone...or in daylight, or...

"Those guys outside. Are they the ones who...?" And I was back. Back asking questions about a subject she didn't want to discuss. "They seemed to upset you...to worry you. Do you want me to stay?"

There. I had blurted it.

"As I said, Mister I'm Scottish Not English, you're not the first man to call me late at night on a pretense."

I felt my cheeks burn and my throat go dry. When I started to speak, I could hear the tremble in my voice. "That's not what I meant—I'll sleep on the floor, here." I indicated the broad area of uncluttered floor. "You must have some blankets."

She seemed amused—she had played this game before. I didn't realize I was in a game—I thought I was here to impart knowledge. But somehow I had found myself sucked in, and now I was in a game squaring up to an opponent who was far more skilled than I.

I cleared my throat and continued—my voice steadier. "We both know that if I spend the night on the floor—then when dawn breaks tomorrow morning, I'll wake up and find that I'm the guy who sleeps on the floor." A whisper of a smile under her moist cheeks agreed. "And there's no way that the guy who sleeps on the floor become the guy who sleeps in the bed."

The whisper of a smile became a broad grin, and she stood. Effortlessly moving from the seated position to the vertical before leaving the room. I heard her walking along the hall; then there was the sound of a squeak of a door opening, followed by some soft thudding.

Her footsteps got closer, and she returned, her arms wrapped around blankets, sheets, and pillows, which she dropped on the floor. "I'd like you to stay, please. I'd feel better having someone here."

twenty-four

She didn't sleep.

I didn't sleep.

I didn't sleep because I was lying on the hard floor with only a few blankets as padding, although I was probably experiencing no more discomfort than her son had experienced for the weeks he had been living in the apartment in Belleville. And I didn't sleep because I was listening to her.

She didn't sleep, because… Who knows—I guess she didn't sleep for any number of reasons and some combination or permutation of those reasons. All I knew for certain was she was in the next room, separated from me by masonry and plaster, and yet I still knew she was awake.

Which was no reason for me to be awake—at the end of the day, I was the guy who slept on the floor in the next room, not the guy who slept in her bed. And I wasn't going to be the guy who slept in the other bed in the apartment—her son's bed—because.

Just because.

But I would have liked to have a look in his room.

Whoever they were that came here after my visit last night, they came for a reason. They knew the kid was dead, and yet they came here. Twenty-four hours later, and they were still waiting outside. They didn't come to notify. They didn't come to offer condolences. They didn't come to apologize.

But they didn't come for no reason. The simple guess: They came for *something*. They didn't find *something* at the apartment, so the next logical place to look for *something* would be the kid's mother's apartment.

Something. What? I fluffed the pillow and got myself as comfortable as I could, then closed my eyes. Concentrating. Something. What would, what could, what might a teenager have? What would be enough to get the kid killed? Was it enough that he *had* to end up dead, or was there a disagreement and he was shot? I kept my eyes closed, letting my mind wander, hoping to find possibilities, options…

The thing about sleep is you're never aware of actually falling asleep. You only know you fell asleep when you wake and the logic kicks in: To wake means I must have fallen asleep. And often the logic then follows: So what woke me? I was becoming aware of what woke me.

She was sitting on the edge of the blanket, watching me. In the half-light seeping in from a single side light in the hallway, I could see that she had changed and was now dressed in a similar style to how she had been last night: a night dress with a silk robe that she was pulling tightly around her.

I looked up. Even in the low light I could see her eyes were dry, but they seemed raw. "Come and talk to me," she said, holding out a hand as she stood.

She led me by the hand from the lounge through the hall—the side light like a mini sun—and to her bedroom. The room was lit by the light that pushed in from the hall—the light in the hall that had just killed my night vision, leaving me able to make out shapes but not to see detail. With my newfound blindness I became more aware of the scent. Not the sort of scent that comes out of a bottle, not a perfume that is developed in a laboratory and pushed into the world with gas propellant, but more a fragrance. The sweetness of the clean smell of flowers on a spring morning in a meadow still damp with dew.

A hand on each shoulder—gentle, but intended—and she moved me more fully into the room, releasing and then pushing the door, leaving a gap wide enough that she could slip out sideways if she wanted.

Her hands moved to her waist and untied her robe, letting it fall from her shoulders. In the half light, there was outline but no detail. The outline was enough for me: slender shoulders giving way to a figure wrapped in what I was guessing was silk, which covered the small breasts, narrowing waist, and gently sculpted hips. She hung the robe on the back of the door—with each movement, the fabric of her nightdress pulled itself tight against her skin—and then turned back to face me. When she spoke, her voice was a whisper: "You can sit there."

She looked around me, using her head to point at an armchair in the corner of the room toward the foot of the bed. "There's blanket you can wrap around you." I followed her gaze.

When I turned back, she was sitting in her bed, pulling the sheets tightly around her neck. The perfect symmetry of her face was broken—one side was lit by the light that had found its way from the hall; the other was in shadow. A shadow to hide the dark thoughts she must be feeling.

The chair was soft and yet somehow held me tight. It was the kind of chair you would sit in when you wanted to read: Four hours later you'd remember that lunch was under the grill, the kids needed collecting from school, and there was a world outside of the world you were reading about. I pulled my legs up into the fetal position and wrapped the blanket around me. It felt far softer than the ones I had been dozing on in the other room.

"Everyone I spoke with said Pierre-Louis was a sweet, gentle kid. Kind. He cared about things... He loved his mother." I couldn't see the detail of her face, but I heard the soft sob. "Tell me about him."

She was silent apart from her sniffing. I waited. Slowly, she began to talk.

"He was sweet. He was kind. He was gentle. He was all that and more. But there's a bond between a parent and child—it's something programmed deep, deep, inside from when we were apes swinging in the trees. And there's a bond...a special sort of relationship that forms between mothers and sons. As a parent on your own with only one child, you form a different kind of unit. I've got a sister—as kids we could fight each other and we could fight against each other. But when there's only one person in your life—when there are only two of you—you don't have any choices. You have to make it through together, and that makes you stronger. So much stronger."

Her voice was steady. Calm. Controlled. But every word seemed measured. Every word seemed to come from a memory she was picturing in her mind's eye.

"He was changing—he was growing up. There was college. His own apartment. He had secrets." She paused as if searching for the right word. "Not secret secrets. There was just more that he didn't tell me—he wanted to think things through on his own, he didn't want to bother me, he didn't want to worry or upset me."

"The apartment?" I asked, wondering if I was pushing too hard... getting too close to how he died. She didn't react, so I continued. "Have you seen the apartment?"

"No." There was no upset—she hadn't made the connection between the apartment and the place her son died. "Pierre-Louis didn't even want me to know where it was until it was finished. Belleville was all he told me, but that's a big district...lots of hills, lots of Chinese restaurants. 'I'll show you when it's done, maman. Wait until then.'"

A slight movement of the sheets, twitching the whole bed, told me that she had shrugged.

"You can't hold them too tight or you'll smother them. You've got to trust them—if you've done your job right as a mother, then they'll make the right decisions. But I've felt alone without him here—without him sleeping down the corridor."

She sniffed and reached for something to wipe her nose, returning to her position with her sheets wrapped round her and the light illuminating half of her face. There was a change in her tone—a hesitancy and yet a certainty. "I used to feel that he came back when I wasn't here."

I tilted my head, waiting.

"The place smelled different—nothing you could say for certain, but teenage boys smell different. Or something moved. Just a millimeter or two. Enough that I noticed." She sighed. "Or did I just hope and want to notice?"

She went quiet.

"You haven't asked about his father." Her voice took on a harder tone—accusatory, as if responding to something she thought I was thinking. "The question usually comes up."

"Why would I ask?" It was her turn to wait for me to elaborate. "If there's anything I want to know, then I'll ask him directly. He'll probably lie to me, but at least I can ask him."

"He...?" She sounded as if she didn't know how to phrase the question. And if she asked the question, then that would take us back to the subject she didn't want to talk about.

"He hired me," I said and swiftly moved the conversation forward. "But tell me about you. What's your story...? It's obvious that you're not the same as the girls on the makeup counter."

"You mean I'm older?"

"No—that's not what I meant." I laughed softly. "Yes, of course you're older...but there's more of a difference. They're pretty—but you're beautiful. They seem to smear themselves in powders and creams all to achieve something that you have achieved...just by being you."

"I've already told you," she said, a hint of playfulness in her voice, "you're not the first man to..."

I cut across her. "I'm sure I'm not the first man to tell you you're beautiful. I'm sure you hear it often enough that it's like saying there will be weather tomorrow. But that doesn't mean it's not true... And I'm making an observation. I'm pointing out a difference. I'm wondering how you got to here."

The room went quiet apart from the sound of cotton ruffling as she shifted, sitting up straighter and pulling the bedding tighter.

She seemed to be weighing up my comment. She knew she was different from the makeup counter girls. She knew most of them were the same age as her son. She knew it looked strange from the outside—she probably knew that customers noticed, and she almost certainly knew that she wasn't part of the circle of the young and pretty things with too much makeup.

And then she started to talk. Tentatively. Haltingly. Stories not in chronological order. She talked for maybe two hours, getting slowly more tired before she finally fell asleep halfway through a sentence.

I slept fitfully—it's never comfortable to sleep in a chair— waking at 6:30. I left the apartment without waking her.

The gray Peugeot was still parked outside.

twenty-five

"You look rough." It sounded like a comment that I should take as a mark of respect. Clearly in Albert's world, to look rough was a good thing. "Husband get home earlier than expected?"

"No."

As I had walked to Albert's café, the sky had a thin layer of high gray cloud—about the same color as the Peugeot stationed outside Émilie Dubois' apartment. The cloud simultaneously kept out any rays of warm spring sun while trapping in the cold, damp night air whose chill was compounded by the wind coming off la Seine which was now pushing through the door to the café that the delivery guy had propped open.

"But it was a woman." A statement from Albert, not phrased as if it might be a question. In his mind, there was only one explanation for my appearance.

I hoped he didn't have any views on religion.

"Yeah. It was a woman, Albert. A woman who wanted to talk..."

"And you left without shaving?"

My lack of shaving seemed to signify something to Albert in the same way that teenage boys—hell, boys of every age—talk about *how far* they got. Clearly for Albert, leaving early and leaving without shaving were two markers. I just wasn't sure why they seemed to be such a good thing in Albert's mind.

"If you want a shower and shave," he said. "It's up the stairs on the right. It's going to be a while—the chef's running late and there's this delivery..."

I stood. "Have you got a phone charger?"

"Sure," said Albert, holding out his hand for my phone. My phone, which didn't have a SIM card in it yet. Yesterday's had been flushed shortly after I arrived at Émilie's apartment. The new card could be added once I had refreshed myself.

By the time I returned—my hair still damp, and wearing yesterday's clothes—calm had broken out, and from the sound of clattering in the kitchen, the chef had arrived. I sat at the bar as Albert walked over, giving an angry look in the direction of the kitchen. "We have a chef. You can eat." And then quietly. "It's good food—it won't make you run out on us—*he*," his eyes went back to the kitchen, "is just an asshole."

It had been more than twenty-four hours since I'd got in a scrape or hurt myself. I had examined the graze on my face while I shaved—it hadn't gone away, but it was much less raw than yesterday. My joints ached, but that was probably more to do with the amount of walking I did yesterday, and my cuts from climbing and falling down the side of the white apartment block in Belleville at least seemed to have formed a scab.

Which all seemed like quite a positive outcome to me—and small victories should be celebrated, so I ordered croque-monsieur and coffee. It may not be what a Roman Emperor would have ordered for a feast to celebrate a famous victory, but sometimes the only option is ham and melted cheese.

Albert passed the order to the kitchen, his tone sour, and then went to take an order from a customer at a table by the window. When he returned, he poured my coffee in front of me. "So? She wanted to talk?" He smirked. "Where exactly did she want your tongue to be wagging?"

I sighed. Albert clocked that his humor may have missed its target. "This wasn't *the talk*, was it, Leathan?"

I snorted. My tone was dejected. "No...no. I would have preferred it if it was."

This was clearly outside of Albert's experience. He obviously had an expectation of the roles men and women fulfill in relation to one another. Clearly you either fuck, fight, or have deep discussions where she talks about emotions. Those were the choices, seemingly.

So...he was a Neanderthal. He was emotionally illiterate. But that didn't make him a bad person. That didn't mean he couldn't become someone I could rely on. That didn't mean he wouldn't be someone to help me—he had already offered me a shower without any indication of expecting reciprocation. I tried to do the mental calculation of plusses and minuses to balance where the risk was. I figured I ought to keep the details generic; only mention a few elements; make it about me, not about her; and see how he reacted.

"Sometimes I get asked to help. To find people." His eyebrows raised. "I got asked to find a teenager two days ago."

"Did you find him?" asked Albert.

"Of course," I said, mock offended. "But not before someone else had shot him. I was there as he died."

For the first occasion in the short time I had known Albert, he seemed to be silenced. There was no witty quip, no sexual allusion in his armory with which to react.

"It was the kid's mother I was with last night. She wanted to talk."

"And there's nothing like a dead kid to kill the chance of a good fuck," said Albert, feeling he was feeling my pain—feeling he could again relate to my experience last night.

"I think she said a lot because..." Why did she? Because she wanted to blot out the pain and didn't know how else to. "Because... you don't know how to react when your kid dies. There are all these emotions, fragments of memories, joys, regrets, paths not taken, dreams, hopes. And there are conversations she doesn't want to have..."

Albert was listening intently—there was a calculation going on in his head: Was this a new way to persuade women into bed?

"She doesn't want to hear how he died, so what started as me telling her about the kid became her telling me about herself."

"And?" said Albert.

"Interesting woman. We all make decisions... We do things once, twice, or just for the summer...or until this happens...and five years later, what was short-term is what you do, and what you do is who you are."

He sensed I'd said all I was going to say about her and was only talking for my own benefit. A shout from the kitchen took his attention away.

As Albert talked to the chef—a relationship that seemed to involve both men shouting rhetorical questions past each other—I pondered. It was time for a trust exercise, and how much could I lose? I had 5,000 euros the diplomat had given me last night. Split the difference: 2,500 euros. Albert returned with my croque-monsieur.

"Thanks, Albert," I said as he laid the plate in front of me. I leaned forward, keeping my voice low. "Can I ask a favor?"

Albert seemed offended that I needed to ask.

"Obviously my private banker would usually handle these things..."

"Obviously," said Albert, laughing. "My private banker handles everything for me. Everything apart from the duties performed by

my private driver, my private dresser, and my private cock sucker."
He leaned forward, sotto voce. "Although, to be honest with you, I
think my private cock sucker might be sucking other cocks."

"You understand the situation," I said. "I'm not comfortable
carrying around cash, and my private banker isn't around to take it
off me. Could I leave some money...?"

"Of course," said Albert, not waiting for me to finish the request.
"Of course, Leathan."

I paused, assessing. He was a man who seemed obsessed with
sex—if he thought with his penis, then he mightn't have the
foresight to rip me off, but would he have the intelligence to keep
my money safe? Only one way to find out: I reached into my pocket
and pulled out five €500 bills and discreetly passed him 2,500
reasons to screw me over.

Furtively, he counted the cash and put it in his back pocket.

"And you couldn't break this down, could you?" I asked holding
another €500. He winced but took the note and went to the till.

He dropped a stack of notes in front of my breakfast. "So why's
the kid dead? Why did he get shot?"

"I don't know," I said, taking a mouthful of my breakfast. "That's
what I'm going to find out next."

"And then," said Albert, a lascivious grin spreading across his
face.

"Nah. I was there when the kid died. I want to know why he
died—that means I've got to find who killed him. If it helps her,
great. But this is for me."

Unconvinced, Albert raised the side of his lip as a new customer
came through the door.

"How much for breakfast?" I asked.

"On the house," said Albert. "Storytellers eat for free." He
turned to his new customer. "Bonjour, monsieur."

twenty-six

The reinforced cement levy forming the bank of the canal was laid as three steps up to the edge.

Three steps to clearly delineate water and land, while leaving a convenient seat on which to sit and watch the barges cut across the city. Barges where there should be cars. Barges because there was a canal that had originally been built to supply water to the city.

I say convenient seat. In the summer, I'm sure it would be a great place for the students to congregate. What's better than sitting by a canal, letting the soft breeze calm the summer's fierceness? In February, all I had was a cold, cold, cold lump of cement holding back the cold water and freezing my ass off.

But as I sat on the bank, I was just some guy. If I stood, if I moved toward them, then something primeval would make me noticeable. Peripheral vision notices movement, not stillness. If I stayed here, they wouldn't see me.

And the students didn't seem to be seeing me. They were involved with each other—small clusters, laughing and joking, some holding earnest discussions, others seemingly angry and outraged. At one community college in Paris, all life was here to see. Young but standing on the cusp of adulthood, experiencing everything for the first time with a freshness and vitality that people like me could barely recall, even though I was probably only a few years older than some of them.

I saw him walking on his own—a row of broad white teeth on a bobbing head. When I had spoken with him two days ago, I guessed where his family originated from: perhaps India, maybe Pakistan.

I stood and waited as he scanned the horizon; Bilal Dareshak's gaze finally fell on me. There was a brief confusion before the recognition, and then he jogged over to me.

When we had spoken before, he had seemed over-eager and keen to please—all positive traits as far as I was concerned. "I am very worried. Pierre-Louis has not been back since I spoke to you."

His speech was fast, his voice heavily accented. "I tried calling him—it goes straight to voicemail. Look..." He pulled out his phone and called Pierre-Louis, holding up the phone's screen so I could see. "See. Voicemail."

The voicemail wasn't surprising. The phone was in a hotel safe with its battery removed.

"No one else has been looking for him? No police or anything?" I asked.

"Police?" The mention of police seemed to suggest to Bilal that this was even more serious than he may have considered. "I have seen no police—should I call them?" His phone was still in his hand.

"I don't think so," I said. If the police hadn't been here, then likely they still hadn't figured out the identity of the dead body. And if you start talking about police, then some kid is bound to have a parent who is or works with.

"Does the name Marianne mean anything?" I asked.

Bilal was noncommittal—as if he were guessing at an exam question and looking for assurance that he was on the right track. "I...I thought she was his sister."

"Sister?" Even I could hear the surprise in my voice. "Sister, not girlfriend?"

The possibility of her being a girlfriend seemed not have previously crossed Bilal's mind. He looked behind, and when he continued, it was in a whisper: "I always thought he was...gay."

He misinterpreted my lack of expectation at his remark.

"I'm not...you know...well...hmmm...you know...anti-...." He was stammering. "It's just...you know...my family...they're..."

I was guessing he was shooting for "prejudiced" or "narrow-minded" or "homophobic" or "just plain ignorant."

"I've never met a gay person before—my community doesn't acknowledge homosexuality. I just assumed that was what they're like." He continued, a small child muttering to himself. "He's *really* close to his mother. I like having a gay friend—he's less aggressive than the other guys, and he never calls women bad names."

I triangulated between what he said and what Émilie Dubois had said: Pierre-Louis was bought up as an only child to a single mother—they were close, and he was respectful to women. He probably wasn't gay; he was just more responsible than his years might have suggested.

Bilal Dareshak was still trying to explain. "Look at my skin," he said. "It's dark. People know my heritage is not French, but they have problems talking about my ethnicity because they're scared of everyone who looks like me."

I understood. I still wasn't sure about where his ethnic origins were located—but that didn't matter. Whether he was from India, Pakistan, Bangladesh, Afghanistan, Sri Lanka, or anywhere else didn't make any difference to the information I wanted from him.

"And like people who don't know how to talk to me about my ethnicity, I don't know how to have a conversation about Pierre-Louis being gay. Not that I needed to, because..." He tailed off, seemingly having reached the end of his explanation and found that I wasn't telling him he was a bad person.

"What about his father?"

Bilal Dareshak went quiet, thinking. When he started to talk again, he seemed to have lost confidence in what he was saying. It was as if he sensed from me that he had got the whole gay thing wrong and that meant everything he thought or said was wrong. "I don't know...I'm not really sure." Then he brightened. "You need to speak to Thea. She would know."

"Can you find her?" I asked. "Now?"

Bilal nodded, then disappeared.

twenty-seven

I pulled out my phone and felt around in my jacket's pockets for a SIM card—there were usually two or three to be found in there if I looked. It took ninety seconds for my phone to reboot and find the signal, and as I waited, I sat on the canal bank looking at a passing barge.

A sister would make sense. With a sister all the pieces fit into place: Marianne is pregnant, and her brother has found an apartment for her, which he's decorating. That explains how a teenager can afford an apartment—or how he isn't affording an apartment.

Instead, she and maybe the infant's father are paying. That explained why Pierre-Louis hadn't really left home. And the sister was probably a half-sister—Émilie would have mentioned another kid, wouldn't she? There would be more silver-framed pictures with a daughter. So that might go some way to explaining why Pierre-Louis didn't want to tell his mother.

I checked my phone: It had a signal, so I called the number I call every morning. It answered on the third ring. I gave my identity and the password details. "Good morning, Mister Leathan." The voice was young, female, and the English heavily accented. The same as yesterday, but a different person.

"Yes, I have one message for you." There was no gasp—I had probably spoken to this person several times, but still she was readying herself to impart the hate. "It says..." She paused. Even if it wasn't her first time, for anyone with a shred of decency, it wasn't an agreeable thing to say. "We know where you are, you worthless piece of shit, and today's the day we're going to fucking kill you."

I didn't even notice—my mind was already miles away. I stared over the canal, my eyes falling on an empty passenger cruiser slowly moving against the current. But I wasn't really seeing the boat. I was seeing a darkened room with Émilie, half lit by the light pushing through a cracked door, telling me her story.

I thought she might want to talk about her kid. She did. But she didn't. To talk in the present tense was to acknowledge he was gone. To talk in the past tense allowed her to remember how he was and to hold on to the notion that he was still alive.

So she talked about the past—and talked about herself. Maybe she felt guilt for decisions taken. Maybe she was confessing—as she sat isolated from the man she was talking with and barely able to see him, and yet he was close and the only person who was hearing what she had to say.

And maybe she wanted me to give her absolution.

She told of a smart girl, an intelligent girl, a good-looking girl, from a family that didn't have much. Around the time she had turned eighteen, she had some friends and the group of them were often invited to bars and clubs and sometimes TV shows, just to pretty things up.

That led to invitations to more exclusive parties, often with rich businessmen and sometimes politicians or civil servants. There was always a group of girls, and they were always there to pretty things up. They got some expenses: travel to and from, a few Francs to put in the bank, but nothing more than a good time and an evening with free alcohol.

She didn't have a serious job, so when she was offered work as a companion for visiting guests—businessmen, minor diplomats, and the like—she took the work. It paid, and all she had to do was be seen on the arm of whoever was paying. She got money, they got to look normal—or at least what passed for normal. And they got company—they paid for her time and nothing else.

But she liked the men, some of the men at least, and they seemed like her. They said she was smart, intelligent—certainly she had read a bit. They said she was witty, which was another way of saying youthfully cheeky, and she could hold a conversation. Some men were telling the truth. Some were just saying what they thought they needed to say to get what they wanted to get.

Applying a label to what she did was tricky. She wasn't a good-time girl, and she wasn't a prostitute. She wasn't in a stable relationship, but there were relationships of sorts. She got paid for her time, and increasingly there were other less obvious forms of payment—travel, clothes, jewelry, and expensive gifts. One man set her up in her apartment, others paid for her furniture. It wasn't that she was doing things for money—it was more that she found fun where the money happened to live. Some of the men she liked. Really liked. And this was France, so things happened. She had a good life and she grabbed it with both hands.

She didn't say so, but if she ended up with a child, then there were bound to be other women in the same situation. She wasn't the only beautiful single woman in Paris, and having seen Tolomush Okeyev up close, it was clear that he liked women—as a species. And indeed he seemed to be keen to keep exploring the species.

If he had one child, then there was likely another, if not many others.

And these men and women didn't just happen upon each other—the meetings were arranged. There was an organizer, a procurer, a fixer. Call it what you will, there was someone who knew what was going on and who probably knew what happened.

twenty-eight

Something drew my gaze from the canal.

There was a fuss. Two people arguing. Arguing as friends, not as enemies. Disagreeing on something where they both had a stake. Bilal Dareshak was arguing with a ginger-haired girl.

Many redheads self-define as auburn.

This girl could never. This was ginger, and at the orange end of the ginger spectrum. Long, lank, ginger hair. One day she would embrace the ginger and learn to love it. That day had yet to come. For now, she wore her hair like a ginger stain.

I hadn't seen ginger the other day when I came looking for Pierre-Louis. This was good—a new perspective. But she was locked in an argument with Bilal Dareshak—that was bad. Somewhere between the two, they might agree on the story they were going to tell. Somewhere between the two they might negotiate and agree on what facts they knew. I didn't want that—I wanted to know what she knew and what she thought she knew, not what Bilal Dareshak told her she should know.

Realizing they were at their destination, ginger went quiet. In front of me, a stranger to her, she was shy. She was holding back. Reticence and an agreed version of history. I wondered whether it was too early for a beer.

Bilal Dareshak began. "This is Thea. She's studying mechanical engineering, like Pierre-Louis, and she's in the same tutor group as him." She looked down, seemingly unaware that she was being talked about, and pulled her shapeless jacket tight over a black-and-white gingham blouse.

"So you know Pierre-Louis quite well?" I tried.

Her head lifted. A weak smile. A noncommittal shrug. She looked to Bilal Dareshak: "He's not gay, and she's not his sister."

The thin youth who had interpreted gentleness and Pierre-Louis' strong bond with his mother as homosexuality went to talk.

She cut across. "No. You're wrong; he would have told me if he was gay. He would have told me if he had a sister." She turned to me, her eyes pleading: "What's happened to Pierre-Louis? Why are you looking for him?"

"His mother is upset," I offered. "I'm just trying to help."

This didn't seem to help Thea: The flood defenses holding back her tears weren't going to survive for long.

"Does he have enemies?" I asked. "People who might want to hurt him? People he upset?" The banks burst—the tears flowed. There was little more she was going to tell me, so I might as well try and make her feel better, even if it was a lie: "I've been looking for him for two days—no one's told me there's a problem."

She wailed and left. Bilal Dareshak seemed pulled between the two of us. "Go on," I mouthed, pointing toward Thea. He caught up with her, slipping an arm around her shoulder. She wriggled free, growled something at him, and walked away.

twenty-nine

I watched the ginger girl.

She was walking away from me and from the college. It took a few moments to realize that she was probably heading toward the café. Small, unnoticeable, but it seemed to have its customer base—students—well catered for.

I waited until she disappeared from view before I moved.

As I got inside, the café felt smaller than it looked from the outside, and I felt older than I looked from the outside. I was probably ten years older than every customer, but those ten years spanned so much change that I might have been a time traveler in this land.

Thea was nearing the counter. By the time I had pushed my way through the youthful vigor, she was ordering. I held out a €10 to the cashier. Thea turned, shocked, her eyes still moist. She weighed up whether she was offended, angry, or pleased by a simple act of kindness. Her contemplation was broken by the cashier offering me the change on a small chrome tray. Thea smiled a thank you and picked up her coffee, which was placed on the counter in front of her.

She seemed to know the ways of navigating between teenagers, and we were quickly outside. I had lied once, why not twice?

"I can see you like him." That was true. That was blazingly obvious. "His mother says there's a girl he likes, but he's shy. His mother thinks her son doesn't know how to tell the girl how he feels. Is that girl you?"

She shrugged, trying to keep the excitement from showing. Then her face fell. "I saw her once...with him."

I waited.

"She wasn't much to look at." There was a certain irony in a less-than-spectacular girl calling out another. "She had that sort of...triangular look." She made the shape of a triangle with her hands around her coffee, the point at the top. "You know, that sort of Dutch look?"

To my mind, the Dutch are more than one sort of body type, but I waited for her to elaborate.

"You know—they're thin on top, but they sort of go out at the ass. It's like they're two halves of a person stuck together. That was her."

"Hair?" I asked.

"That sort of blond, Dutch hair," she said.

"Did you talk to them?"

She shook her head, the ends of her lank ginger mane flicking. "No, I just saw them on the Metro. I saw them...and..."

It made me almost nostalgic. The pang of first love and first rejection. The youthful jump to conclusions not based on any facts—only a simple assumption.

"I think he might have been helping that girl," I said.

Her eyes widened. Suddenly, there was hope for her.

"Do you know where the girl lives?"

The head shook again, less vigorously. "He once said someone's mother lived in Seine-Saint-Denis." Which was a bit like saying: I know there's a needle in one of these three haystacks.

She pulled out a phone and checked the time before shrugging again. "I've got a class," she said.

I watched her walk away. She had walked about thirty yards when it hit me. The sound of my running alerted her, and she turned. I almost felt out of breath as I began to speak. "Is there anywhere at college that people store things? Lockers or something?"

thirty

In the months I had been in the city, I hadn't paid attention to the universities and colleges of Paris.

And why would I? It wasn't as if I had a child who was going to go to college, and there were no cousins or extended family in the city for whom further education was issue. To me, the institutions were all the same and their essential function was to work as a landmark in the same way that Metro stations and the many squares did.

I had found my way into la Sorbonne—getting access to the prestigious university's campus in the Latin Quarter when a lecturer had needed my help. The guard on the door at first seemed like an impediment. Later I saw their utility—I only had to slip one a bill and I could get unrestricted access to the student areas while having some reassurance that I wasn't going to be followed...there being guards outside and all that. And while I was on the inside, I could use the computers and the other facilities without interruption.

That was my experience with education establishments in Paris, and I had assumed and extrapolated from there when I asked Thea, the ginger girl, to help me get into the college that both her and Pierre-Louis Dubois attended.

She hadn't been keen—there were lots of "but what if...?" questions. Each displaying an increasingly creative mind, but lacking in any practical possibility. Usually at this point I'd pull out a bill or two—it's amazing how a few euros can help someone wrestling with a dilemma.

But Thea was different. She wouldn't want money—it wouldn't influence her. In fact, it was likely to offend her. I had to call on her sense of hope. I had already lied to her and suggested that Pierre-Louis was interested in her but was shy. That lie would hit her hard when she found he was dead: She would find her friend had been murdered, and she would be left with a whole bunch of what ifs that would spin through her head, probably for the next fifty years.

"We've got to help Pierre-Louis," I said to her. "Clearly something is wrong and no one seems to be taking this seriously. If we don't do something, then no one else will."

"Really?" she said. "You think this will help?"

"Mmm."

"But do we...you know... It's his locker; won't he...?"

"It's his locker, and he would want us to help him." I paused, locking eyes before I continued. "Have you got any better ideas—if there's anything to find, then it will be in his locker, won't it?" I really had no clue, but I wanted to see what was in the locker.

The ginger girl considered my argument. Every instinct she had screamed "no!" but still something said to her, "If you help, then you'll prove that you love him." Love won, and she started leading me toward the college.

There was no security. No one stopped us; no one questioned us. There were other students, none of whom seemed to notice that a stranger was passing through. For all the effort in persuading her to help, I could have walked in on my own. However, where she did help was in taking me to the lockers and pointing. "There. That's Pierre-Louis' locker." For that piece of knowledge alone, I was grateful for my guide.

The lockers were set as two rows of gray metal doors with little identification and no ornamentation. The metal cabinets were a few years old, showing some signs of scuffing and wear, and a few on the lower level had been on the receiving end of a foot moving at speed—but none had been forced open. The feature that set most lockers apart from their neighbor was the padlock: the choice of each individual to protect his or her possessions.

"How are we going to get in?" she asked.

In truth, I hoped that getting past the lock was going to be simple. However, I didn't want Thea to know how I had Pierre-Louis' keys. "We pick it," I said.

"Really?" I could have told her that gravity didn't exist—she would have been less amazed. Her voice was a low whisper as the last few groups of students filed away. "Can you pick locks?"

"Yeah." I was casual, but my suggestion hadn't had the desired effect, so I tried again. "That's a fairly simple lock—it shouldn't take more than about forty-five minutes."

"But I've got a class." The whine was back. "I'll be late. I'll..." Her instinct to conform through a lifetime of conditioning was back.

"You go—I'll stay."

There was a slight frown. She felt a duty to go, but she wanted to stay.

"It's going to take forty-five minutes—maybe an hour. There's no need for you to be here. There's nothing you can do apart from wait." She was struggling with a dilemma. "Give me your number. I'll call you if I find anything."

There was hope in her eyes. For someone whose default response is no, there may be a way to say yes. But she still wanted to say no.

I pulled out my phone and handed it to her. "Put your number in." She was sure there was an angle she was missing. "Then call your phone—that way you'll have my number, and you can call me." And there was an angle she was missing: I'd throw out this SIM card in a few hours so the number she was getting was useful only today. More than that, if my phone rang, then I'd know who was calling since she was the only person with my number.

But she didn't know that.

She punched in the number and called her phone. An annoying chirping sound emitted from the backpack hanging from her right shoulder. She smiled and handed my phone back. "I'm late..."

I cut across whatever she wanted to say. "Go. I'll handle it and I'll call you if I need anything."

As her footsteps slapping on the linoleum floor faded, I pulled out the keys I had been carrying since I found Pierre-Louis in his apartment. Everything else had gone into the safe at Nico's hotel, but I was sure I'd find a use for the keys, so I'd carried them around for the last thirty-six hours.

I looked at the lock and looked at the keys, then back to the lock, trying to guess which key would fit. The lock was a few months old. I looked at the keys—some of them were old, scratched, bent. I ruled those out immediately. I ruled out what looked like house keys and I ruled out the kind of key that fits in a deadbolt: It might be a padlock, but this was a pin tumbler lock.

That left three keys. Three shiny silver-colored keys.

The second slid in and twisted smoothly, opening the padlock with a click. The door opened fully, knocking into the next locker's padlock as I tugged it with rather too much enthusiasm, and then I stared.

If there were people who thought Pierre-Louis might have hidden something in his mother's apartment, then it was only a matter of time before they started looking elsewhere. And that elsewhere would likely include this locker.

There was a logic.

And if I was right—I thought as I stared into the empty locker— they were going to be disappointed, like me.

thirty-one

I clicked the padlock shut, then was out of the college and moving quickly within a minute of my disappointment.

I knew where I was going—at least, I knew the quarter I wanted to reach—but I didn't want to go directly. I had been caught out yesterday, and that always made me twitchy. Also, I wanted to think.

A bus passed me, heading to a stop about fifty yards ahead. I jogged to catch it and jumped on, following an old lady with a shopping basket. No one got on after me, so if I was being followed, they were going to have to follow the bus, wherever it was going—and I didn't know where it was heading.

When I started out this morning, I had a feeling that there was something missing and that all I needed to do was to find one of Pierre-Louis' friends, who would give me that piece of the jigsaw—the piece where the sky and the roof of the building meet and you can finally see where all the other pieces fit.

But Bilal Dareshak and Thea had just contradicted each other, and my sudden inspiration to check the locker had turned up nothing. The best I could hope was that there had been something, and someone had already been past. Someone who knew how to pick locks and could get a padlock like that open in a few seconds, which is all it would take if you had a clue as to what you were doing.

My phone buzzed. An infrequent occurrence. I pulled it out and checked—a text from Thea. Typical teenager, why call and interact with a real person when you can send them a message of 140 characters or fewer?

Or in Thea's case, eight characters, including a space I wasn't sure was necessary: "Well ???"

There was only one suitable response: :-(I hit send and contemplated deleting her from my contacts but decided against it: I might want to ask for her help.

The phone buzzed again. Thea: ?

"Completely empty," I texted back and returned to looking out the window as the bus left the main boulevard and headed into...

into I wasn't quite sure where, but I could at least keep thinking. And thinking told me I had questions and needed answers. I wasn't going to get a straight answer—but hopefully I could get enough of an answer to lead me somewhere else. No one was going to tell me who Marianne was, but clearly my assumption that she was just his girlfriend was wrong. Sister or girlfriend, she was significant in Pierre-Louis' life.

We passed a Metro station, and I got off, quickly descending to the underground rail network. I took three trains—at the second interchange I waited for the fourth train, allowing the platform to clear after each train so I could be sure I hadn't picked up a tail.

Sometime after 11:30, I made my way above ground. The Left Bank; the south side of la Seine. Location of Claude's apartment and Claude's habitual home with its proximity to the French National Assembly. A magnet drawing politicians, civil servants, and various flunkies, not to mention Claude. A rich source of people who need help, but who need to keep some distance from their problem—all there for Claude to consume, like a whale swallowing plankton.

In many ways Claude's day-to-day existence is much like my own. We both spend our waking hours out on the street talking with people. The difference is that he has an apartment, where I have to ask for a place to sleep each night. But his apartment is of little value to him: It really is just a hotel that he happens to own.

At the fourth café I tried—on the corner of a small square overlooking a church—I saw Claude sitting, talking with a woman in a well-tailored business suit. She didn't look Parisian. She didn't look French. It was more English tailoring applied to the female form rather than the understated Parisian.

Claude noticed me as I entered. His eyes said: "Don't." I ordered a coffee and sat at the bar.

As I waited, I checked my phone. "So what now?" Another text from Thea.

"Any ideas?" I texted back and immediately regretted sending the message. She wasn't going to let this slip—I was now her friend, helping her find the love of her life.

I checked my call log—it had been nearly two hours since I last tried Émilie, and as had been the case two hours previous, there was still no reply when I tried.

The phone buzzed again. Thea again. I returned the phone to my pocket and waited for Claude.

thirty-two

"You're not going to kick me over today, Englishman?"

"You're dealing with all the English today," I said, letting Claude's intended insult pass as I pointed to the woman in the well-tailored suit who was hailing a cab outside the café.

"She's not..." Claude began as I sat in the chair vacated by the woman, the noise of the busy café masking the bumping of the round-backed chair on the wooden floor.

"She's English, Claude. No Frenchwoman would dress like that." Claude slumped back in his chair, silently acknowledging that she was indeed a British citizen.

"Tolomush Okeyev," I said. Something on Claude's saggy face twitched. "How many children does he have?"

I could have asked Claude to detail his favorite sexual positions—it would have seemed a more reasonable question to him. I could have asked Claude to explain quantum computing—he might have felt he had a better grasp on the subject. He seemed incapable of forming a coherent response, instead settling for vague sounds, half-shrugs with hand movements, and a wobbling bottom lip.

"You knew he had a son," I said.

Claude was still struggling. "Of course."

"So why don't you know about other kids?"

"It's not a question I've asked," said Claude, pulling some coherence into his speech, the loose skin on his slightly sweaty face flapping. "People tell me what they want to tell me. He never told me about any kids—I didn't know he had a son until he told me he wanted the kid found."

"Because you're the soul of discretion?"

"Because it's bad for business, Leathan. People come to me because I can help. They come to me because they know I'll listen and then I'll sort their problem. They tell me their faucet is leaking, I find them a plumber—I don't rip out the whole kitchen or tell them they need a new hot water system. I don't try to fix some other problem for them because it will make me feel better or because I thought the universe wanted it sorted." The table shook as Claude gripped the edge, leaning forward so I could hear him clearly as he spat out his whisper.

"Yeah, but you know stuff," I said calmly.

Claude snorted. "Everybody knows *stuff*. It's how you apply what you know that makes you useful—and keeping your mouth shut keeps you alive."

"You know about Tolomush Okeyev—you know how Pierre-Louis Dubois came about."

Claude relaxed back into his chair, dropping his right hand toward the jacket pocket over his right hip. He patted the pocket—feeling for one of his small cigars—something he did when he was getting agitated.

"I'm presuming the kid came about in the regular way: man on top, woman underneath, or maybe woman on top, man underneath." He gave half a smile, then continued. "But you know how it works, Leathan—surely one of these women you're always chasing after must have taken you in hand and shown you how it works. This is Paris, not London. We do have sex here."

"I know how sex works, thank you, Claude. But I need a name."

"Claude," said Claude. "If you're telling me you've got some girl pregnant, then I would be honored if you would call your baby Claude. Thank you, Leathan. I'm touched."

"Let me elaborate." I ignored Claude's barb and continued. "About twenty years ago, there was a young man in Paris from Kyrgyzstan. He was attached to the country's diplomatic mission. He loved Paris. And who wouldn't, Claude? Only an idiot or a Philistine wouldn't love Paris. But he really loved Paris—and he loved what Paris had to offer."

Claude seemed to be thinking three steps ahead—he had twigged where I was pushing the conversation. He seemed determined to push me off course. "You don't know this, Leathan. These are only stories."

"Stories told to me by Tolomush Okeyev and Émilie."

"But you..."

"Shhh." Claude paused as I told him what I knew. "One thing that Tolomush Okeyev loved in Paris was the company. He had the opportunity to meet so many interesting people. Some people he would meet through his work, but some would be introduced by a...let's call him a fixer."

"Leathan." Claude threw the disappointed parent face at me: soft voice, head tilted, slight twist to the mouth. Not a direct scold, but a call to my better nature.

"This fixer would find women. Now, these weren't prostitutes— these were women who were elegant...sophisticated...witty... good-looking... You have a drinks soirée, and there's a list of things to do: sort a venue, get the alcohol, get the nibbles, hire the waiting staff—oh yeah, and don't forget the girls to pretty things up."

Claude had shifted from disappointed parent to teenager being scolded. He sighed, his gaze scanning the room, but looking over their heads so he wouldn't make eye contact.

"Whenever the need arose, this man—this fixer—would find, procure, organize, use whatever verb you want, a bunch of women. And the women would happily turn up because they got paid and they got to mingle with a bunch of rich guys. There was the chance that one of these men might be interesting or husband material. And if there wasn't suitable husband material, then there was suitable *having fun with* material."

"You're reaching, Leathan. This never happened."

"It did. This is exactly what Pierre-Louis' mother told me happened. She met a bunch of guys this way, over a period of several years. Some were a-holes, but she liked others. Liked a lot. Liked enough to lie down for King and country, or whatever it is you lie down for here."

"In this country we lie down for sex because we like sex. We're not repressed like you English. We don't have your rules and regula- tions—as long as two adults consent..." He saw the grin on my face and realized that the implied slur on the French national character had been enough to trip him.

"So we're agreed. There was someone who worked as a go-between. Someone who had a useful contacts book who could bring a group of girls of a suitable caliber." Claude didn't disagree. "I just want a name. Twenty years ago, or thereabouts, who would have organized these events? Who would have known Tolomush Okeyev and been able to find girls? Who would have known when the girls got pregnant, because I'm sure there will be other women and other children out there?"

"You're asking dangerous questions, Leathan."

"I'm asking for a name, Claude. Nothing more."

"But you're asking questions about the past. You're asking about people who did small jobs way back when. Anyone could get girls."

"But not the right girls and have contacts," I said. "This isn't a pimp with a stable of whores. This is a guy servicing his high-level contacts."

"Think about it, Englishman. We all grow up—where would a fixer, as you call him, be twenty years later? Don't you think he might be fixing bigger or different things?"

"Just a name. I just want a name."

Claude's face was becoming pained, pleading. "This guy was a kid back then—he's a man now."

"A name. It's my risk, not yours—and I'll be careful."

"It's my risk if they find I've given you his name." I stared at Claude, waiting for elaboration. "Tolomush Okeyev is his cash cow. A good farmer tends his livestock and will protect his livestock."

"Enough of the farming, Claude. A name. A place I can find him."

"Gaston Blanc," said Claude, sighing. "He owns a bar called the Shillelagh on Boulevard Montmartre. He owns a lot of pubs, clubs, and bars, but that's where you'll find him."

I half stood, leaning forward on the table to whisper into Claude's ear. "Thanks for that, Claude, and I'll be sure not to mention your name as long as you do me a favor and stop mentioning that the Bulgarians in London would like a chat with me."

I could feel his blush as I exited.

thirty-three

I stood on the corner of the square outside the café where Claude's English client had stood to hail her cab, and I hit redial. Again the call went unanswered.

It was lunchtime—too early to go crawling around clubs looking for some guy who twenty-something years ago arranged girls for diplomats and businessmen and who now, apparently, milked these former clients before selling them off to the slaughterhouse. At least that was the story I heard from Claude. The part of the story I didn't quite understand was what this man, Gaston Blanc, also did that was enough to make Claude twitch.

I took a few back streets and passageways moving between medieval Paris and Haussmann-reengineered Paris and back. Small, narrow, and individual to broad with consistent architecture, finally working my way to la Seine, crossing at Passerelle Léopold-Sédar-Senghor.

The pedestrian footbridge ensured that anyone following me in a vehicle would be putting plan B into action—someone would have to get out and follow me on foot. I stopped on the single-span crossing to look at the river, allowing my gaze to fall back toward the direction from which I had come. There were cars everywhere—it was Paris on a cold February morning; there were going to be cars. Trying to identify one that had stopped was impossible.

I'm not sure who first had the idea to put padlocks on bridges. Whoever he was, he was a dick. Originally there was only one bridge over la Seine with locks. The tourist couples would come to Paris, they would attach the padlock to the bridge apparently as a sign of their love or something—the notion of being chained together having no negative consequences—and then would throw the key into la Seine.

Stupid idea.

But never underestimate the stupidity of people. And soon the one bridge was filled with locks and tourists didn't know where that bridge was, so the locks spread like a deadly virus engulfing Paris. Now, every bridge—apart from those with the stone balustrades—has padlocks spreading like a thin covering of mold.

They might be a stupid idea, but they gave me the chance to squat down and look at the locks. Perhaps do the tourist thing and photograph them—at least point my phone toward them as if I were taking a photo of them while I looked around to see if there was anyone on his own who was waiting in an overly casual manner...waiting for me to move again.

Big locks, small locks, brass locks, old locks, chrome-plated locks, and more. My eyes came to rest on a combination lock. However much I sneer at the locks, at least I can believe they come from a true place: I can believe in couples throwing the key into la Seine to signify the permanence of their relationship.

So what does a combination lock with a thousand permutations tell you?

It didn't tell me much, except that I was cold and I couldn't see anyone following me.

Reaching the Right Bank, I crossed and entered Jardin des Tuileries—yet another miserable Parisian garden where pedestrians are marshaled along set paths, the grass is only available for birds, and trees are meant to be square.

By the time I reached the other side of the gardens, I was sure that I wasn't being followed, so I took the shortest route, heading to Galeries Lafayette. Thirty minutes of quick walking, plus some pauses to look behind.

Something told me to be cautious, so I went two levels up from the floor flooded with beauticians, perfume, makeup, and unhappy women looking for a way to change their lives by spending money. This time I knew where I was looking—but now my face was recognizable. You don't spend several hours telling a guy your life story and forget what he looks like by the next morning.

I stood at 90 degrees, looking across the floor. Looking across her booth.

She was there. At work. A woman sitting in the chair in front of her—probably with half of her face looking shocking and the other half a subtle understated elegance, reassured by quiet, comforting words.

We all handle grief in different ways and we don't know how we will handle grief—especially the grief of losing an only child—unless and until we have to handle the grief. Maybe she was still telling herself I was mistaken and Pierre-Louis would walk back through the door at any moment. She hadn't seen the pictures of his dead body—she didn't need those images seared into her memory—so she could tell herself that he was alive.

Maybe work was therapy for her. The gentle repetition of a mindless task, the offering up of words of comfort more a habit than heartfelt reassurance, all a subtle displacement activity to allow her brain to slowly process what had happened.

Or maybe it was about money. She had no man to provide her with an income. She had no savings—she might be nearly fifty years old, but everything she had earned had been spent on her son.

I didn't understand. Or maybe I did—I just realized how much I didn't know and how much she hadn't told me.

But I did know two things. First, she was at work, which meant her apartment was empty. Second, I didn't want her to see me. I ducked back and took the escalator to the ground level, leaving through the closest door and heading north again.

thirty-four

The gray Peugeot was still there. Still parked in the same place it had been yesterday evening. In the same place it had been this morning when I left.

There was one change.

Instead of there being two unremarkable guys sitting in the car down from the green gate that led to Émilie's apartment, there was now one unremarkable guy. A human need—the need to pee, the need to find food—had overtaken, and one unremarkable man had chosen to go and do an unremarkable thing.

One man in the car, instead of two, halved the chances of my being seen. Halved the chances of him noticing me and remembering: Hey, that's the guy who left here early this morning. Halved the chances of him saying: Hey, didn't that guy turn up here last night?

The Peugeot shuddered, and a small puff of smoke coughed from the tailpipe. So the guy who was left was unremarkable, but he did feel the cold. The same cold that the rest of us felt in this broad boulevard as the six-floor buildings blocked the low spring sun.

I spent another ten minutes trying to find something remarkable in the unremarkable guy behind the steering wheel, but I failed. I hoped that the other unremarkable guy would return. My hope was in vain—I was going to have to go through that large green gate and into the cobbled courtyard, knowing that there was an unremarkable man out of the car...moving freely. It's easy to hide from a big, bad ogre—you know what he looks like; when you see him, you can run. But when a guy's so unremarkable, you don't know what you're hiding from.

I walked down the boulevard—away from the Peugeot—for about two minutes before I crossed. The street was as busy as it was going to get—in other words, not very busy—and I wanted to be out of easy eyesight before I crossed. As I walked back up the slope of the boulevard, I fought my natural inclination to walk swiftly, dropping my pace to keep step with my fellow travelers on the broad sidewalk.

Fellow travelers who provided cover as we passed the unremarkable gray car. Fellow travelers who provided cover as I slipped through the green gate, shutting it quickly behind me before I stepped through the arch and into the cobbled courtyard.

There was blue sky above the courtyard, but, as with the street, the sun was too low to throw any beams into the deep funnel formed by the six floors of apartments looking out onto the small cobbled square. I opened the door with the broken lock and took the elevator to the fourth floor. The slow ascent gave me a few moments to flick through Pierre-Louis' keys in the hunt for one that looked like it might fit an apartment.

This apartment.

This apartment I was about to enter, breaking every sort of implied bond of trust between me and Émilie.

Probably breaking quite a few laws, too. But then, I hadn't been in Paris long enough to acquaint myself with French laws. Maybe their penal code said ignorance of the law was acceptable? Maybe Code Napoléon—Napoleonic civil law—which differed in ways I could not really understand from the common law that apparently governs England, where I had spent most of my adulthood, would give me an out. Or at least a good argument.

The elevator door opened. I selected the key that looked like it should be a door key and that was oldest and most battered. With some effort, it slipped into the lock but wouldn't twist. I pulled it. Shit. Jammed. I pushed it; pulled it; twisted; leaned against the door, hearing it creak under my weight; and finally it shifted.

I felt the withdrawn length of toothed metal—newly warmed under the stress—then chose the next possible door key. It didn't fit—either way.

The third key slid in, giving a reassuring zipping sound as the teeth passed through the lock. I turned the key—it didn't want to move. I leaned on the door and tried—it still didn't want to move. I pulled the door—the wood moaned softly—and I heard the machinery move, making the security bolts attached to the lock rattle, but the door didn't unlock. I turned the key the other way. There was a reassuring clunk, thunk, and the lock turned with the bolts releasing themselves.

I let the door swing open and stepped into the wood-floored entrance hall; the side light on the table was now extinguished.

Softly I closed the door behind me, listening to the gentle metallic sound as the latch clicked home.

There was the squeak of a foot on the wooden floor.

When I turned from the door, the first punch hit me squarely in the gut.

I tried to look at my assailant—all I could think was that he looked unremarkable.

The second hit to the gut was anything but unremarkable, and I felt myself doubling over, assisted by his hands, which were thrusting me down.

There was pain. I knew my head hurt. I knew my head had made contact with something solid. And that was the last thing I knew.

thirty-five

There was something about the wooden floor.

It might be practical as a floor covering. It might look good with its herringbone pattern.

But it wasn't a good substitute for a bed, and a man who has been knocked out—so comprehensively, so quickly—needs a bed. Or at least, he needs something soft to lie on.

I stayed where I was. It was uncomfortable, but while I remained lying I couldn't fall.

At some point I decided I was, if not alert, at least awake. Conscious. Past the point where I should be dramatically sprawled over Émilie's entrance hall, leaving myself like some tribal peace offering.

Slowly, I pushed myself up and rolled over into a sitting position, finding some comfort in leaning my back against the door. My eyes caught the side table; it had some new additions keeping the side light company: my phone, the keys I found in Pierre-Louis' apartment, and my money. A small collection of objects telling me the unremarkable man had been through my pockets.

A small collection telling me that this guy wasn't a thief—he was looking for something else in my pockets. My identity, perhaps?

It hurt to stand up. I leaned forward to pick up the contents of my pockets and felt the pounding as the blood rushed in my head. I sat down on the floor again, waiting for the dizziness to pass and looking at my cash.

It was enough cash to be annoying if I lost it, and with a throbbing head I couldn't defend myself. I took off my sneakers and spread 2,000 euros between each shoe—two €500 bills under each insole. They could have my remaining cash if they jumped me—they could get very drunk for nearly €500.

I found my way to the kitchen and let the faucet flow—cold water for my face, cold water for my throat, and solid cabinets to support me—while I stared out of the window and over the open space above the cobbled courtyard to the apartments across the way.

He was an unremarkable man, but with a remarkable punch—a blow like that was one I wouldn't forget anytime soon.

Unremarkable people don't do unremarkable things—that's why they're unremarkable. But as his fist had just demonstrated, I had been wrong: He was a remarkable person—he just looked unremarkable.

I closed off the faucet and made another attempt to stand up straight, unaided. As long as I moved slowly—and held myself as if I had spent years in deportment classes—I could move without pain and dizziness.

I paused in the kitchen doorway before turning to the bathroom. It was as it had been yesterday and as I had seen it this morning. Some of the towels had been moved, maybe the soap was in a slightly different position, but there was no dead body in the tub.

The front room looked much as it looked yesterday. My makeshift bed of blankets had been removed, and order had been restored.

I slipped through the half-closed door into her bedroom. The bed had been made. The blanket on the chair where I had sat had been refolded and placed just so. And the gentle fragrance wafted through the air, reminding me that the weather outside was anything but spring-like.

I didn't know what Pierre-Louis' room looked like normally. I had wanted to take a look yesterday, but it had seemed at best impolite. At worst an intrusion. And if I sneaked a look while she was sleeping, that was a breach of some implied trust.

Not that letting her remain ignorant that I had her son's keys wasn't a breach of trust, albeit a minor breach when compared to me letting myself in and then looking around her apartment while she was at work.

However Pierre-Louis' room had looked, I guessed it hadn't looked like it did now.

I went back to the bathroom to find some painkillers. I threw back a small handful and took a few more for my pocket—this was going to hurt later—and then returned to Pierre-Louis' bedroom.

The room smelled. It was an unpleasant smell. A smell of a human. A human who had been there recently. A human who had been there working fast and sweating. Working hard to find something he was looking for.

In my experience, most teenage boys are messy. In my experience, most mothers of teenage boys accept the messiness but try to impose some level of order. There are basic minimum requirements that come with living under the same roof: Clothes will go in the wash, beds will be changed, no food to be kept in the bedroom going moldy or attracting flies, there will be semi-regular cleaning of said room, and so on.

While the apartment in Belleville had few items, those items had implied a certain level of order. Or at least a minimum level of teenage boy-like behavior.

Which all told me that a room where the occupant couldn't even reach the bed for detritus on the floor was unusual, different, out of place. Just plain wrong. Émilie would not have left this mess when she thought her son had moved out. She would have asserted at least some order—if only over that pungent human smell.

That pungent human smell that was fresh.

The unremarkable man had been here. He had opened the closets and pulled out every piece of clothing—dropping each item on the floor after checking. Shirts, trousers, jackets, shoes, all scattered across the floor. Books—school textbooks, fiction from kids' stuff through to Proust, prizes from school, engineering textbooks—all lay opened and scattered atop the clothes. From the marks on the walls, there had been posters—these too had been included in the monolith that had become the room's floor area.

There was nothing that said: "This is how I was before that smelly man came." I couldn't be certain, but my guess was that the unremarkable man had looked everywhere for whatever he was looking for, and if my pockets were any indication, he was a thorough man. And if he was that thorough, there would be nothing here for me.

I shut the front door behind me and turned the key. The deadbolt slid home, locking the chaos and the smell for Émilie to find later.

thirty-six

Walking was difficult.

No. Walking was easy. Staying vertical and at the same time moving forward, *that* was hard.

The Metro seat felt unusually comfortable. That was my first warning: If you find the seat on a Metro is comfortable, then something is wrong, very wrong. The walk up from Belleville Metro was tedious—as I followed hill after hill, it dawned on me that maybe I wasn't in Belleville any more. Somewhere this became le Quartier du Combat, but that was a border that never really stuck in my mind.

The ascent made me breathe more heavily and made my heart beat faster, seeming to pump blood with extra vigor, each pump reminding me that my head hurt. A lot.

When I got to the white concrete wall topped with a steel fence, I waited, casually mooching around outside the gate until someone came out, giving me the opportunity to slip in. It took a bit longer until someone came out from the door that I had propped open with my jacket two nights ago. When he came, he noticed me hanging around outside the door.

"Thanks," I said. "She's going to kill me—what is the number?" I waved the keys as if that and some vague assertion of trouble with an unspecified female were reason enough.

He nodded sympathetically, as if he too suffered. "Two, two, three, three," he said, turning away.

The elevator pinged as it reached the fourth floor and I stepped out, loosely swinging the key ring around my index finger. By a process of elimination, I was down to a choice between two keys.

The front door had police tape sealing it closed. There was the sound of the door opening behind me, and a voice, an older voice. He might have been speaking to me; I wasn't paying attention.

"Wrong floor," I said, turning. I recognized him from Monday night—I had seen him through the spyhole as he went to consult with his fellow neighbor, although now he was wearing more than pajamas and an old dressing gown. I suspected he might have seen the two people I had seen. I suspected he might be the person they had told to return to his apartment while they ran, knocking me down in the stairwell.

"You're the second person in ten minutes!" He was clearly delighted. When he continued he was more conspiratorial. "Everyone's making the same mistake—it's alright, I'd probably come here and have a look... We don't get excitement like this every day."

I held my hand up, surrendering. "You got me," I said. The old man's face told me he was delighted with his detective work—he could show those young police officers who had been around how to read a person. I took advantage of his need to talk. "So this is where that kid was shot?"

The old guy nodded—one movement that both conveyed the answer to my question and signaled the gravity of the situation.

"Who was he?"

This question delighted the old guy. "*That* is what the lady detective keeps saying! 'Bastien,' she says, 'we've got his fingerprints, but we haven't got him on record.' There were no papers in the apartment and no wallet. The agent who rented the place is on a cruise. And now they're going to try that...you know...take some blood like the American TV shows."

"DNA," I suggested.

"Exactly. The lady detective says they're going to use that to find out who he is."

"And no one around here knows him?"

Bastien, as I now knew the old guy, shook his head. "Nice young man. Very quiet. Very respectful." He brightened, but offered nothing more.

"Why was he shot?"

The headshake continued—a look of hangdog sadness in his eyes. "We've all told the lady detective everything we could, but she doesn't know. She said sometimes crimes just don't get solved."

He didn't seem to know anything more and he didn't seem to understand that the conversation had reached its natural conclusion. My head hurt, but I figured five minutes spent walking around the compound wouldn't make it much worse. I could come back—quietly—and slip into the apartment.

The elevator dumped me at the ground floor, and I walked out the door, turning away from the gate and into the heart of the huge complex.

My initial reaction when I walked around the outside—that this was a vertical city—had been right. This was a city with a few shops so you could pick up a newspaper or some food. There were community areas; there was a nursery and preschool for the kids. There was everything you could need.

My initial reaction—that a vertical city was a bad thing—had been wrong. Sure, *I* didn't like it. But I wasn't a mother with a young kid. This seemed a great place if you were trying to bring up a kid: There were lots of other mothers to meet and lots of kids to play with, all within the bounds of the high walls keeping danger out. There was no need to ever leave the place, but if you wanted to take a night off, then finding a babysitter would be simple.

But still there was a question niggling me: How did Pierre-Louis Dubois afford this apartment?

He had no obvious sign of money. He might have had a part-time job, but that wouldn't be enough to pay the rent here. His mother was working a low-income job, and her apartment would already be sucking up any spare income, not to mention she needed to save for her own retirement.

The only obvious answer was that he was milking the cash cow, too.

So did the cash cow turn against his new farmer? Did daddy pay for his inconvenient little bastard to be killed? And did he send me along to get in the way?

Shit, Leathan, what have you stumbled into?

thirty-seven

I was still turning over options as I got into the elevator—I did not want to believe that Tolomush Okeyev had paid for his own son to be murdered. Maybe the kid had savings and could pay a month's rent or two months' rent. But after that?

Pierre-Louis was bright enough—he would have figured that if he stopped paying his rent, then he'd be out. Or his girlfriend/sister/whatever she was along with his son/daughter/niece/nephew/whatever would be back on the streets.

And if he was intending to drop out of college, why had he been attending so regularly? He missed one day and everyone noticed. It wasn't a simple three-day weekend or "yeah...sometimes he..." His friends expected that he would always be there. Always.

I got out of the elevator at the fifth floor and walked down to the fourth, slipping silently through the door onto the landing, making sure I didn't alert my new friend, Bastien, that I had returned.

I tried the key that wouldn't fit in his mother's lock. I was right on my first attempt and ducked under the tape across the door and into the apartment before Bastien, the neighbor, would have got to his spyhole.

The apartment had changed since Monday night. There was no dying/dead kid—but the now-dried pool of blood remained. The pool had been smeared, perhaps as they finally moved the dead body. Or maybe they were reaching into a back pocket looking for his wallet or keys.

The clean, characterless walls—a blank canvas for a young family to imprint their personality—were now covered in finger-print powder. Anywhere someone might have touched had been brushed with black powder. Had I been cautious enough to wipe away all my prints or were my marks now being fed into some police computer?

There was powder on the balcony door—I peered through to the balustrade, which had not been dusted. Maybe I had been cautious enough. Maybe I had been lucky. Maybe I didn't want to try to find out. And maybe I could figure a good enough excuse for having been there—it's not as if fingerprints are date-stamped.

I stepped into the bedroom. It had been cleared—there was no table, no makeshift bed, and no pile of clothes. Just some fingerprint powder liberally spread. The nursery had been treated similarly—the paint cans had gone, and the covering on the floor had gone. All that remained were the animals on the wall, and they were now smeared with black powder.

But the scientists—at least I presumed it was the police forensic people who had done all of this—had done more. As I looked at the floor, I noticed that the beading that would usually hold the laminate floor where it met the walls had been removed. Someone had lifted the laminate floor. Someone had looked under. Someone with time and better tools than me.

I followed my path back to the bedroom and through the main room. The cracked blood confirmed that the flooring had been lifted. I wandered into the bathroom. The side of the bath had been removed and had been placed vertically in the bath, leaving the plumbing under the tub exposed.

Whatever they were looking for, they were thorough. Whatever I was hoping to find here had gone.

The faucet turned easily, even with my jacket pulled over my hand, and I took a mouthful of water before picking a few painkillers out of my pocket. I threw them back and closed off the water, then returned to the kitchen area.

There was nothing here, but it was a quiet apartment where I could spend the next hour calling some of Pierre-Louis' other friends to see if any of them knew where I could find Marianne. I hoped Thea would have made my introduction and told everybody that someone was helping Pierre-Louis' mother search for her son—and as part of that search, Marianne was a legitimate line of inquiry. And if I still didn't have any luck finding her, then I would go to this Irish bar and see what it was about Gaston Blanc that worried Claude.

Cautiously, I lowered myself to the floor, my back against one of the kitchen cabinets, and looked across the room and out the window.

I still wanted to know how Pierre-Louis was intending to afford the rent.

thirty–eight

Everyone knew there was someone looking for Pierre-Louis Dubois.

No one knew anything.

Many suspected.

Most had theories.

No one could actually come up with something tangible. A name. An address. A phone number. Some way—any way—to contact Marianne.

As I called through the list of people I had copied down from Pierre-Louis' phone while I sat across from the apartment block watching the police arrive, the conversations quickly became repetitive. Everyone wanted to help, but no one knew anything. They understood the urgency and would call me back today if they found anything out.

I didn't want to tell them that tomorrow was too late—today's SIM card would be gone at some time around midnight, and along with the card going, this number would die.

The people I spoke to were kind and concerned, but it was frustrating. As I left the elevator and walked out the door of the block, I played the conversations through in my head, looking for any nuance, any hint that something was wrong, that someone was withholding.

I couldn't see any. All I could see was that I had one option: Gaston Blanc.

I ignored the rustling behind me. When she spoke, I didn't realize it was me who was being threatened. "Do I need to show you the gun, or are you going to behave?" A hand was buried in her olive green jacket.

"I always behave," I said, recognizing the dirty red jeans from two nights back, "but sometimes I behave badly."

Her eyes were twitchy. Twitchy like they had been when I first saw them. The gun didn't scare me—the person carrying it did. She had been there, and for all I knew, she had pulled the trigger. I was her puppy dog, ready to be led wherever she wanted to take me.

She pointed toward the gate with her nose, her dry, frizzy hair rustling with the movement, and then followed ten yards behind me.

At the gate she pointed right with her eyes, still keeping her distance.

A brown Renault door swung open, and I was pulled into the car. My escort dropped herself into the front passenger seat and turned, showing me that, indeed, she was carrying a gun. Dark, black, menacing, and pointing at me.

To my left, I recognized the other guy from Monday. He had changed since then—a green olive jacket replacing his denim jacket—but apart from that he seemed to have the same jeans and tennis shoes. The driver sat silently—the hobo, I guessed, from Monday night. The unwashed hair and voluminous beard certainly fit the part, and his brown jacket was at least twenty years old.

Bastien, the neighbor, had told me I was the second person in ten minutes to check out the apartment. I wondered which of these three had preceded me.

"Give us the money," said the guy next to me in his green jacket that matched the woman's.

"What money?"

"It's our money, not yours," he said, falling silent as the gun holder caught his eye.

"What are you doing here?" she asked, the gun twitching on each syllable. Big gun, small hand—I was ready to argue, but not ready for a fight.

"Talking with the neighbors," I said.

The gun twitched.

"I talked with the neighbors," I repeated, enunciating each word clearly.

"Go ask him. His name's Bastien and he's like a jack in the box. The elevator pings, and he's out his door to see who's there."

The driver gave a grunt of affirmation from somewhere deep within the mass of his beard.

"He went in," said the guy next to me. He turned to me: "You went up—for the second time—and you disappeared. You were inside."

The gun holder frowned at him—that was one less lie they could catch me in. "What were you doing?" she asked.

"Looking for money." It wasn't true, but it seemed like an answer they would believe. She nodded, the gun barrel mirroring the nod. Her eyebrows raised, she was waiting for elaboration. "They've cleared the place out. The forensic guys have been over everything—they've even pulled up all the flooring. The place is stripped bare. There's no money there."

"You mean there's no money there *now*," said my fellow back-seat passenger, turning to face me. A flick of her eyes gave him permission—suddenly his hands were over me, patting me down, feeling for whatever I was carrying, and reaching into my pockets.

"How much are you expecting?" I asked, feeling powerless to stop the intrusion.

"Hundred," he said.

She hissed something to him, then turned to me. "What were you doing here on Monday?"

"I heard Pierre-Louis had come into money. I had an investment opportunity for him."

"And?"

"And the opportunity fell through when I couldn't raise the cash."

The hands going through my jacket had pulled out the contents of my pockets.

"So why are you back here now?"

"I think your friend adequately answered that," I said, looking to my left at the guy who was checking the contacts on my phone. "One hundred thousand euros."

He tossed the phone back to me.

"Why did you visit the kid's mother?"

"When?" It was a stupid question, giving away too much.

"We saw you going in." Their response was smarter than mine.

"Probably for the same reason you visited her," I said, noticing that I wasn't corrected. "Don't we all have one hundred thousand reasons to visit her?"

The keys were tossed back in my general direction. I picked them off the floor. He was counting through the cash he had found in my jacket. "It's not one hundred thousand, is it? It's not anywhere near one percent of that. As I said—I haven't found the money."

He grunted and passed me a €10 bill, his hand continuing to reach across me for the door handle. The door swung open, and he shifted his body, kicking me out of the car with both feet. I fell to the sidewalk, lying still and holding my head as I watched the battered old brown, wedge-shaped Renault pull away.

thirty-nine

"Sit. Wait. What do you want to drink?"

I'm not sure that a barstool has yet been designed that offers real comfort. They may be an acceptable place to perch for a moment or two, or even for the length of a drink, but not for any longer than that.

This barstool was unpadded, with no carving to shape some comfort into the unforgiving wooden seat. The dark-stain giving each stool at the bar a uniform color had then been worn back to the wood's natural blond color, confirming that these were cheap pieces of softwood and not expensive pieces of crafted mahogany.

Not that I was criticizing. If I owned an Irish pub, I would fill it with cheap furniture.

I'm sure that I, too, would apply liberal amounts of green paint. In this case, Gaston Blanc had chosen a shade of green that was too dark to be called emerald to frame the doors and the windows. The rest of the wood—the bar, the barstools, the benches, the barrels called into service as tables—was dark. Dark and rough, as if recovered from a sinking ship carrying famine victims fleeing their homeland.

Dark seemed to be a theme in the Shillelagh.

As I reached the pub on Boulevard Montmartre—the broad boulevard that comes off Place de la République and makes its way toward Arc de Triomphe—just before it flows into Boulevard Haussmann and somehow surprisingly close to Galeries Lafayette, the change from outside to inside was striking. Outside there was a wide-open avenue with several lanes of traffic flowing in each direction. Inside it was dark, oppressively dark. Technically, there were windows to bring light to the dark wood and to the dark, untreated timber floor, but if you removed the glass panes and replaced them with thick steel, just as much light would seep through.

The barman looked at the whisky that I'd been nursing for the thirty minutes I'd been waiting. I'm no great connoisseur, but it was an enjoyable drink and it was a free drink. I was welcome to have more, but I didn't want more. The effects of alcohol would put me at too much of a disadvantage.

The barman's eyes questioned. "No thanks," I said. "Just the one." Starting on the spirits at 5 PM sounded like the prelude for a great evening. Or might have been the prelude for a great evening if my head wasn't still hurting and I hadn't been kicked, literally, out of a car, falling awkwardly into the gutter. I rummaged in my pocket and found two more painkillers, which I washed down with some whisky.

"Fuck it," I whispered to myself and looked up to the barman. "Yeah, I will have another."

I slipped the barman my only €10 bill as the second short arrived. "It's on the house," he muttered.

"And this is a small thank you, to you," I said, leaving the bill. I never know when I might need the comfort that a barman can offer. I figure it's always better to be in credit.

The bill disappeared into his back pocket. I drank to his health.

Somewhere in the darkness, between the very dark and the exceptionally dark, there was a movement of moderate darkness. "Take your drink," said the barman. He caught the flick of fear in my eyes. "They don't do anything here... Too much risk. This is home—they just talk here."

I nodded my thanks and deep appreciation, picked up the whisky, and headed toward the darkness. Through the dark wood door, it was like the back of most pubs, bars, and restaurants: plaster walls painted white—probably a long time ago—utilitarian flooring, in this case concrete, all lit by occasional strip lights. It wasn't much light, but my eyes struggled to reacclimatize after the seeming near-blackness of the bar.

I followed along the corridor and into a room on the side. It was small and windowless with a table against the wall being used as a desk. The dark figure who had led me into the room indicated to a small leather sofa pushed against the end wall and forming a right angle with the table.

A guy working at the table—fifty-something, neat, well-groomed—turned and looked toward my guide. "Is it?"

The other man nodded once and pulled out a phone to show the guy at the table something on the screen. He smiled weakly. "Leathan, right? You said you want to talk."

I nodded.

"How's your head?" The phone disappeared as the seated man continued, seemingly responding my confusion. "You took a bit of a tumble earlier, didn't you? You were out cold."

My guide, still standing, grinned. He was so unremarkable that as my eyes had struggled to adjust to the light, I hadn't put two and two together. Usually I'd remember a guy who hit me and avoid him. This time I found him and didn't recognize him.

"So where's the kid?" asked the man I was presuming to be Gaston Blanc.

"You mean..." I stammered.

My hesitation seemed to frustrate him. "You're banging his mother—you know who I'm talking about: Where is Pierre-Louis?"

"He's dead," I said, starting to feel my role in life was to notify of births, deaths, and marriages. "He was shot two nights ago."

Gaston Blanc lifted his hand, and his eyes widened. Slowly he let the weight of his skull rest on his hand as he took in the news.

"You're sure?" he asked, the certainty having left his voice.

"I was there when..." I wasn't sure how to describe my role when all that was asked of me was to verify that death had indeed occurred.

Gaston Blanc stood and ushered my attacker out the room, closing the door behind both of them. I took another sip of my whisky and surveyed the room. A dark room in a dark building. Despite the barman's reassurance that this wasn't the place for violence, I wasn't sure how Gaston Blanc would react if I started searching through his office while I was alone.

The door opened and Blanc returned, unaccompanied.

"Did you kill him?"

"No."

"So who did?"

I shrugged. How would I explain that I'd just seen the killers—or at least, the people I figured had shot Pierre-Louis—and yet I still didn't know who they were or why the shot was fired?

"So you're a family friend, banging Émilie? That's it? Nothing more?"

"I... No..."

He laughed. "So you haven't been given the keys to the magic kingdom, but you're hoping to get in?" He paused his onslaught, letting the silence admit my guilt. "Is that how you got her key?"

"I picked the lock," I said.

He laughed again, this time with less mirth. "Leathan, Leathan. Please don't lie. We're all friends here. When my friend ran into you," he indicated the man who had been in the room, "and he apologizes—you didn't announce yourself, hence..." He mimed a fist punching. "As you were lying...he checked you were alive, then checked your pockets. There were no lock picks—just a bunch of keys."

"I found them on the street," I said. "It was a lucky fluke that one fitted."

Something in my retort amused him. "Leathan. I don't care who Émilie sleeps with. She's her own woman—she can make her own choices. What's niggling me is that you know more than you're telling me. Do you understand?"

I understood.

"So...what were you doing at Émilie's apartment?"

"What was your man doing there?"

"I think you can guess, Leathan. He was looking for something."

"And so was I."

Gaston Blanc smiled indulgently, and gave a *what the heck* shrug. "We were looking for Pierre-Louis. We hadn't seen him in a few days. And now we know why." He seemed to be affected by the death—not hugely saddened, but at least understanding that at a human level, someone's son had died and her life had been permanently changed. He looked to me: "You?"

"I was trying to figure who was looking for Pierre-Louis and why he was killed."

Gaston Blanc's face remained impassive.

"You know he has a sister? A half-sister. Girl called Marianne." Blanc's face remained unchanging as I continued. "I figured she should be told." Still no reaction. "Have you got an address...a phone number...any way to contact her?"

A look of pained confusion crossed his face. The kind of look that a parent fakes with a child when they don't want to answer a question.

"Come on," I said. "We're just friends talking over a whisky." I took another sip. "We know you knew Tolomush Okeyev and Émilie. We know you were the one who introduced them. We're friends, and that's what friends do...."

The side of his mouth twisted in a smile.

"So it's not unreasonable to guess that you might know Marianne's mother."

"I knew them. I knew Tolomush and Émilie," he said. "They were my friends—and they still are my friends. But that doesn't mean that twenty years ago I knew everyone that they knew. Tolomush liked the ladies—he was quite capable of finding women without my assistance. I'm sorry, Leathan, but I've never heard of this Marianne and I can't tell you who her mother is."

forty

The sun had set before I went into the Shillelagh, Gaston Blanc's Irish pub, but still, walking into the pub—passing from streetlight to that weirdly un-Irish world—was like plunging myself into a vacuum that sucked out light.

Stepping back onto the street now felt like I was stepping into the midday sun in the middle of the desert. Without the heat.

The broad avenue of Boulevard Montmartre was packed with cars—two lanes going in each direction. Coming toward me, heading away from Galeries Lafayette, was a bus. I jumped on board and pulled out my phone.

Kasym Aitmatov answered on the second ring. "It's Leathan. I need some face-to-face."

He mumbled something about dinner and an ambassador from a country I didn't recognize, but I was sure the United Nations flew their very colorful flag.

"I can be in République in twenty minutes," I offered. He grunted and hung up. République—or if I'm going to be accurate, Place de la République—the eight-acre Hausmann-inspried public square crossing three arrondissements and bringing together eleven streets is harder to avoid than to give directions to.

I had two voicemails—a rarity, as I usually don't give out my number since it changes every day. This gave me some hope that one of Pierre-Louis' friends had come through. The first message was a hang-up—a long sigh as someone pondered what to say, before giving up and ending the call.

The second was much longer, but no more enlightening than the hang-up: A friend of a friend of an ex of a drug dealer of someone she once met who knew someone, their aunt...

I called the number of the hang-up first. "Hey, it's Leathan. You called."

She sighed again. "Look." Yet another sigh. "I don't know..."

"That's alright," I said. "I'm just looking for Pierre-Louis. I just want to find him so his mom can stop worrying."

Still no response.

"No one will know it was you. This won't trace back, and it might help."

Reluctantly she offered a name—a German-sounding name. She explained this was someone's mother and gave an address, or at least, directions to an address—a housing complex in Seine-Saint-Denis, a block name perhaps, a floor, give or take a few floors above or below, and instead of an apartment number, a location. The outer corner...the last apartment at the end of the corridor.

"I hope you find him," she said and hung up.

Then I called the guy who left the message. He had learned everything he knew about detective investigations from watching American TV shows.

Which pretty much made him as qualified as me.

My only claim was that I had been doing what I did for longer, had worked with other people, had been paid for what I did, and had seen some repeat business.

I focused on the call. After a long explanation as to whom he knew and how, eventually he offered a name—again German-sounding—and a possible address, again in Seine-Saint-Denis.

He then made his pitch as my wingman, suggesting he would be something between the world's coolest detective and its most insightful forensic scientist, and of course, this would all be enhanced with his own personal super powers.

I thanked him and hung up.

Seine-Saint-Denis was a thirty-minute drive when the roads were clear, so it would probably take an hour in traffic, and two if I got the bus. And then I wasn't sure where I was going, which all meant that I would be banging on doors late at night.

Banging on doors late at night. I couldn't see a way that would end well, or with me finding Marianne. I needed help.

"Nesrine, Leathan."

"Hi, Leathan, how are you?" she laughed. From the sounds in the background she was still at work.

"I'm good," I said. "How do you fancy skipping work?"

"Work?" she asked. "You mean that thing that helps me pay the rent?"

"This is France—no one ever gets fired, and you sound like you're getting very close to your statutory thirty-five hour limit. You would be doing your employer a favor by taking tomorrow off and coming with me on a road trip."

She laughed. "Where?"

I told her 8 AM and gave her the address of Albert's café. "Got it," she said. I hung up as the bus drew onto Place de la République.

forty-one

I spent ten minutes watching rush-hour stop/start traffic. Six lanes—three in each direction—going around three sides of the huge rectangle, the fourth side having been pedestrianized.

Each Mercedes caught my eye, giving me hope of shelter from the wind that funneled along the eleven streets converging on Place de la République, only to be dashed time and again. I was so busy scanning the distance that I didn't see the car pull up next to me with the passenger door open.

Kasym Aitmatov's sharp whistle drew my attention, inviting me into the passenger seat.

I felt the warmth coming from the leather that had offered comfort less than twenty-four hours previously and twisted to look at Tolomush Okeyev, who was sitting on the back seat—a white shirt, bow-tie, and dinner jacket reinforcing what Kasym Aitmatov had already told me: He had to go to dinner with another ambassador; his time was limited.

"I'm sorry that..." he began as Kasym Aitmatov pulled off, gently shifting the huge bulk of metal as if he were carrying a sleeping infant.

I held up a finger, stopping him. "Marianne." He nodded once. "When I asked you, you said she was someone who wants money." Three short bows of the head. "Why didn't you start by telling me she's your daughter?"

His round face with taut yellow skin remained still. There was no flick of emotion. No pang of regret. No surprise. No change—nothing. "You impress me, Leathan—your work is fast and thorough."

"I don't need flattery," I said. "You remember our conversation yesterday? The one where you agreed to be open and honest."

"To love, honor, and obey," he quipped. "I haven't forgotten my vows."

"So why didn't you mention a daughter?"

"Because she's not." Again, his face was blank, emotionless. "I have never played the role of father to her. I was not involved in her upbringing. I didn't know..." His face remained fixed, but he was now staring into the distance—the muscles around his eyes suggesting the brain was working overtime. "I have never had a DNA test. I believe the woman if her mother says I am the father, but I've never seen a need for confirmation."

He continued to stare into the distance; each breath seemed heavier as he controlled his exhalation, breathing out through his mouth, which he pulled into a small, tight circle.

"I described the relationship between the two of us in a way that I believe portrays its present state. She is a woman who has tried to extract money from me. She is not a daughter in any effective sense of the word beyond maybe carrying my genes."

His breathing seemed to normalize. "Have you found my son's killer?" His focus was locked on me as I gripped the side of my seat, keeping my body twisted toward him.

"Have I found the killer?" I asked. "Or have I found the reason he was killed?"

"Huh?" There was a narrowing of his eyes—a hint of confusion across his face.

I wasn't quite sure how to phrase the next question, and to be frank, I was more interested in his reaction than the answer. "It seems to me that there are many possible reasons for your son's death, and finding the right reason is the simple way to figuring who killed him." The confusion drained from his face as he contemplated the notion. "And it seems to me you could have had one hundred thousand reasons to want your own son dead."

The reaction was slow.

His head, which had been nodding as he politely listened, became still, cocked slightly to the side as if questioning. His eyes—wide as he took in new information—became narrow, inquisitive. His lips moved as if to speak—to ask for elaboration—but no sound came out.

And then he froze—only the pulse in his throat confirming there was still life.

I reminded myself: a diplomat, an honest man sent abroad to lie for his country. When he began to speak, his tone was calm. There would have been more emotional involvement if we had been discussing the weather or the traffic. "I don't know what you have found, Leathan. But keep searching, and you'll find I had nothing to do with my son's death."

There was an infinitesimal movement of his head, and Kasym Aitmatov drew the car to the curb. We had moved a mile and were just shy of Place de la Bastille. "Keep searching, Leathan. I need to know who killed my son."

He tapped lightly on Kasym Aitmatov's seat, and the big man pulled out a small stack of bills, handing them to me as his eyes made clear I was to get out of the car.

I placed the cash in my pocket and took out my phone as I stood, feeling the bite as the wind came off Bassin de l'Arsenal—the stretch of water linking Canal Saint-Martin and la Seine, which was originally a ditch to fill a moat around the Bastille fortress. The gusts were blowing with no buildings to break their intensity.

She answered before I had lost sight of the Mercedes. All I could hear were tears—she couldn't speak.

"I'll be there in half an hour," I said and hung up.

forty-two

I stood outside Émilie Dubois' front door and tapped with the pads of my fingers. Three fleshy impacts.

There was a change in the light behind the spyhole, and then the door opened. Before I was fully inside the hall she was clinging to me, weeping. I remained still and silent, but wrapped my arms around her as I waited for the storm to pass.

My eyes scanned the hallway. It looked very much as it had when I awoke from my slumber induced by Gaston Blanc's unremarkable man. There was one addition: a spray of white lilies. Enough flowers for three large vases, tied together with a piece of raffia—the bundle lay on the floor.

When we had spoken on the phone, she was crying. When I arrived, she was quiet, but the tears were still flowing. In my arms she began to sob, but now she was quieting—the sobs were becoming less frequent, and her breathing, punctuated by huge gasps, was becoming more regular.

Eventually she looked up and tried to speak. "Pierre-Louis' room." She began sobbing again—I didn't want to tell her I already knew what the problem was.

"They've been through his room," she blubbed into my chest. My shirt was now damp from her tears. I held her in my arms. I wasn't sure what else I could do—and at that moment all I wanted to do was to hold her in my arms forever.

She sniffed and looked up, trying to keep herself within my embrace.

This was the point where I was meant to speak. "Is anything missing?"

I felt her shoulders lift and watched as a new tear pushed itself from the side of her eye.

Her hands, which had been gripping my chest and shirt—clawing at me in a cat-like manner—moved to hold me around my waist, and she awkwardly tugged me along the hallway to her son's bedroom, wedging the single object that we formed into the doorway.

The room was exactly as it had been when I left. The closet had been emptied, the shelves had been cleared, and the contents had accumulated in a pile in the middle of the floor onto which everything else in the room had been dropped.

"Jeez," I offered. "Do you know what they were looking for?" I felt her head shake. "The rest of the apartment?"

She mumbled something; her face, with its cheek firm against my chest, was looking toward the room, surveying the damage.

"I can help."

Her head shook again. She hadn't been ready to go through her son's life yesterday—there was little that had likely changed since then.

"Those are lovely flowers," I said in an attempt to move the subject.

She responded with sobs and fresh waves of tears streaming into my shirt.

"I thought it was his father," she blubbed. "I thought the money came from his father."

She looked up at me, her eyes still streaming. "What money?" I asked.

"I thought his father was paying for that apartment and he wasn't telling me because he didn't want me to be upset." She saw my confusion. "I couldn't pay for an apartment for him—he wouldn't have wanted me to think..." She broke off and sniffed. "Now I know he didn't tell me because he knew how I would react when I found out where the money came from."

I waited for an explanation or elaboration. Neither came.

She sniffed again and released herself. "I need..." she pointed to her nose as she moved away. I surveyed the mess of the bedroom and closed the door on it. Out of sight, and all that.

I turned back into the hallway, feeling my head still throbbing and something hurting in my shoulder where I had landed as I was pushed out of the Renault. With the wind, my muscles all seemed to be tightening and throbbing.

There was the sound of padding footsteps and Émilie returned, tears mopped and a few tissues in her hand. "You look like hell, Leathan."

I felt the involuntary spasm of a smile crossing my face before I asked the question to which I already knew the answer: "Have you got any painkillers?"

She pointed to the bathroom. "In the medicine cabinet."

I threw back a few pills and stepped back into the hallway. She was closer, looking me up and down. "You look like hell—have a bath." The hint of amusement crossed her face. "You can scrub your own back—you're a big boy."

She pushed past me into the bathroom and started running the bath. "Soap. Towels." She pointed. "Hang your jacket up there." She pushed me out of the bathroom and indicated a row of coat hooks just inside the front door. I turned back from hanging my jacket. "Shoes." She pointed to the floor under my jacket.

I pondered whether to remove the bills under my insoles, but figured it would be too suspicious—not to mention sweaty and unpleasant.

"I'm washing those clothes," she said as I stepped closer. "Off. Now." It was as if she were ordering a child who had been playing in the mud.

She watched as I undressed, dropping each item of clothing in front of me until I stood naked. Her eyes surveyed, but didn't make contact with mine.

The running water distracted her, and she looked away. When she looked back there was a slight flush of red in her cheeks. "There's a robe behind the door." She stepped out of the bathroom doorway, pointing the way with her eyes, which then dropped to continue their survey.

forty-three

If you were eight or ten inches shorter than me and much more slightly built—for instance, if you were Émilie Dubois—then the toweling robe that had been offered to me would probably be a good fit. It would probably close with a good overlap and it would likely go a moderate distance down your thighs.

A smirk crossed her face as she saw me trying to adjust the robe— each move creating another gap. She tilted her head, beckoning to me to follow. With each step, I felt either my cock swinging free or my ass getting exposed as she led me into the front room.

A table I hadn't paid attention to before—square, old, dark wood; I guessed another piece of vintage furniture—had been moved into the space where I lay last night with a chair placed on either side. In the middle of the table was a roast chicken, its skin a crisp golden brown.

"I hope you like chicken," she said. "And before you ask—no, I didn't...I went round the corner while you were in the bath."

Which was her way of saying that this was a chicken that had been cooked in a rotisserie by one of the local butchers. It's something that only seems to happen in Paris and that I love about the city: There are many butchers, and every butcher has one or more vertical rotisserie ovens roasting chickens. The constantly turning racks allow for the chickens at the top to drip their fat onto the lower-down chickens, which are also turning and roasting, and at the bottom, potatoes are roast. The smell as you walk down a street is glorious, and it also means that it's faster to get a roast chicken than a hamburger.

I sat. The robe offered no help, and my ass made direct contact with the slightly chilled wood of the chair, but the table hid the fact that I was flopping out the front. "Are you hungry?" she asked, a carving knife in one hand plunging into the chicken.

"Yeah," I mumbled as she started moving hunks of flesh onto a plate. She added some scoops of the small roast potatoes, then placed the plate in front of me.

"Begin," she said, returning to the chicken and removing a few smaller pieces of meat. "You look like hell and you can't go anywhere because your clothes are in the wash, so you might as well enjoy your food."

I wasn't going to argue with a woman who I wanted to spend time with, when she was insisting that I spend time with her.

She sat and took a delicate mouthful. "There's something about rotisserie chicken—you get the flavor and the moisture." She was right. It was hard to think of a simpler means of cooking, and yet the results were so effective. I let my enthusiasm for the meal express my thanks and my agreement.

She poured us each a glass of wine—both glasses filled equally. "Whatever you're meant to have with chicken," she said. "I like red, and I like this red." She paused, a small smirk forming. "You probably want a beer...but you're having wine."

I sat back to savor the first sip of wine. "You seem less..."

"It'll work itself out—he's just messing with me to get at Tolomush...and to protect whatever he sees as his interest."

"He?"

"The guy who gave, lent, whatever the money to Pierre-Louis. I don't know what he's planning, but I do know he will have seen it as an investment, and every investment must provide a return." She was drinking her wine faster than me. I had more body mass to soak up the alcohol and I was eating more food. "If he thinks I'm going to repay the money, well..." She took another gulp. "I just wish Pierre-Louis hadn't got involved with him."

"So who is he?" I asked, cutting off another lump of moist chicken.

"I met him way back when. When life was a series of parties, expensive gifts, travel to new places that were exotic at the time. He was young, ambitious, wanted money, and wanted to do things. He wanted to be a music promoter. He thought he would arrange these huge gigs and then spend his days chatting with rock stars and groupies."

She pecked at her food before refilling her wine glass.

"He was quite an entrepreneur, so the notion of becoming a music promoter wasn't crazy stupid out of reach. He had the brains and had the drive. He started running nightclubs—he knew putting on events was a step to putting on bigger events. But as he started running nightclubs, he started meeting girls and guys with money who wanted female company, and he got good at using girls to get guys into his club. He would get some exclusive bait to pull in the high spenders. And very soon the clubs were less relevant, and he was getting paid simply to find female company for guys with a lot of money."

She took another large sip, then subtly wiped the red wine mustache.

"And that was where I met him. He looked after me for a few years, and then Pierre-Louis came along and we lost that symbiotic thing—neither was useful for the other." She took a smaller sip. "He never did become a big music promoter." Her tone took on a note of regret. "He found better income by running drugs through his clubs—or at least by taxing the dealers operating in his clubs—and the girls he runs have changed. In my day, the men bought your time and what you did was up to you, but now he makes much more money from the whores trafficked in from Eastern Europe and Africa."

She went quiet—her gaze stuck in the middle distance. She had told me what, but not who.

"I still see him occasionally," she said, an amused smile on her lips. "He's taken over this pub—it's an Irish pub, the Shillelagh—about ten minutes from the shop. Sometimes I walk in that direction."

It was like another punch to the gut. I felt the breathlessness, the pain, the beat of my heart, and the ache of my stupidity.

"The Shillelagh?" I asked weakly.

"It's a good front for him—he likes the location," she raised her eyes. "He took it in exchange for a debt and made it home. It's not too flashy, so it doesn't upset the police, and the druggy stuff can go on elsewhere."

"We're talking about Gaston Blanc, are we?" I struggled to keep my voice calm, remembering who had told Blanc that Pierre-Louis was dead. The kid whose debt—if I understood what she was implying—had now been passed to my host. My stumbling inquiry—her debt.

She nodded slowly. "Do you know him?"

"I'm more acquainted with the reputation." I took a sip of wine before continuing. "So does he still provide...?"

"Girls?" she asked.

"Girls, yeah...for...Tolomush Okeyev?"

Something amused her—I wasn't sure whether it was the question or the way I delivered it. "His best client? Does he still provide girls for his best client? Hmmm. I wonder." She snorted. "Of course! Who wouldn't want to have a pet diplomat?"

"Pet?"

She snorted again before refilling her wine glass. "I don't know what he's got on him... No, rephrase that—I don't know how much he's got on him, but Gaston will be in deep with him. I told you: For him it's all about the symbiosis. He will offer a whole world to Tolomush that no one else can provide, but Gaston will want something—lots—in exchange."

"What sort of exchange?"

"The sort of exchange that only a diplomat can offer," she said, letting the thought hang.

"Can't he...?"

She was amused again. "Refuse? Walk away? Call the cops? Hire a hit squad?"

"Yeah," I said. "Do something."

Her look of indulgent amusement wasn't fading. "Tolomush has a problem. His big problem is that he doesn't want to go home. He hates Kyrgyzstan. It might be beautiful, but it's remote, it's tribal, and the TV's awful. Most importantly, he doesn't have the stomach for Kyrgyz politics. It's a game he doesn't play well—the corruption and murder doesn't sit well with him. No, he wants to be in Paris... London...Madrid...Vienna."

I finished my last potato.

"That means he can't just go home, and so his past indiscretions become a lever. What he did—drugs, partying, fornicating, fathering children, and so on—are irrelevant by French, and indeed most western, standards. Diplomat has consensual sex with woman is hardly news. However, these deeds would be regarded badly at home."

She saw my slight surprise.

"He would be seen as having misused public funds, and the choice of *foreign* women would be a grave insult to Kyrgyz womanhood. So that gives him a choice—go home or play nice with Gaston Blanc. Gaston Blanc, who will incidentally continue to supply a stream of willing young women."

forty-four

"You're looking a lot happier this morning," said Albert by way of greeting. "You haven't shaved, but you've washed and your clothes are clean."

My clothes were clean, and I didn't want to tell Albert that they were still slightly damp too—as they were when I retrieved them this morning—but my body heat was finishing off the drying process quickly enough.

I eased myself onto a barstool. It somehow felt far more comforting than the one I had waited on nervously in the Shillelagh.

Albert continued without pause. "You went back to offer her understanding, didn't you? And she melted." There was a nervous beat as Albert calibrated my response—he had been wrong-footed when I told him that Émilie Dubois' son had died. "Congratulations, Leathan, you wily fox." He leaned across the bar and slapped me on the shoulder. "How is she? Dead son and all that."

"My guess would be that any mother who loses a child will never recover from that loss. Life may continue, but it will be permanently changed. There will always be that grief." I leaned on the bar. "And I'll have a coffee and a croque-monsieur."

Albert seemed happy that he had found a response—triangulating between his expectation and my lack of argument—and grabbed the coffee, pouring a cup as he greeted the new customer coming through the door.

I dug around my pocket—I was sure I still had several SIM cards, and yesterday's card had been flushed before midnight. "Have you got a payphone?" I asked Albert. He shook his head slowly, giving a pained expression.

He spoke, his voice faking a hint of wonder. "I think my grandpa told me about those." His arm came forward, a cordless phone in his hand. He held it, delicately gripping it between his thumb and index finger. "We use these things in my century...and sometimes," he was enjoying patronizing, "some people even have phones that they carry in their pockets. But if you've left your phone at your new lady friend's apartment, I quite understand. Use this." He stood the phone vertically on the counter.

"Thanks," I said. "In your century, you wouldn't happen to have a laptop or an iPad or something like that?"

Albert froze, his eyes questioning. His face cracked—a toothy smile spreading. "What is this? I've stepped back in time and ended up in Leathan's personal office. I thought this was my business, but clearly I was wrong. And clearly you were too busy having sex last night to think about these things." He turned and disappeared through the door that had led me to the bathroom yesterday and returned a few moments later with a battered laptop.

"It takes ages to boot, it's slower than getting a permit from the municipal offices, but it works." He opened the lid, hit the power button, and turned the laptop to me. "The password is: *I like big girls with big boobs*. One word, no spaces, all lower case." A small group of new customers had entered and were milling around, blocking the entrance. They had the look of tourists. They were enough to distract Albert. He looked back and shrugged. "I needed a password I could remember."

I had called enough that I could remember Kasym Aitmatov's number. He answered with his customary efficiency.

"I need to see him. Only for a few moments—but I need to see him soon." Kasym Aitmatov muttered something as I typed in the password. "Nine AM. On the monument." I hung up and waited as the laptop whirred and spluttered. Eventually it calmed down and let me open a browser.

I was focused, engrossed in looking at where I might be going. I knew it was Seine-Saint-Denis, and I flicked between the map, the satellite view, and the street-level view, trying to reconcile the details I had been given with what I was seeing. A hand on my shoulder— placed gently—broke my concentration. "Bonjour, Leathan."

It was Nesrine Walter. I stood and we embraced, kissing on both cheeks. "Just to warn you," I whispered quickly, "the patron is going to think we had sex last night." Nesrine stood back and laughed. "I'll explain," I mouthed.

"No need, Leathan." She looked me up and down. "Whoever she is, you're looking good for it."

Albert had noticed. "Coffee?" I asked. "Something to eat?"

"Bonjour, mademoiselle," said Albert—his eyes darting between us as he tried to play both angles. Either she was the woman he suspected was Émilie Dubois, not that he knew Émilie's name, or she was fair game. As he looked at Nesrine—slim, nearly as tall as me, mid-brown hair to her shoulders framing a soft face with a warm smile—there was a calculation going on in his head: Was this woman old enough to have a teenage son? And then the second question: Was this woman behaving like someone whose son had just died?

"Just a coffee," she said to both of us.

It would probably disappoint Albert to know that I had never had sex with Nesrine. I had met her when she needed help. Her younger brother had disappeared—she was concerned, and her parents were frantic. In the end it was little more than a lost weekend solved by me getting on a train to Marseilles and bringing the fool back to Paris.

Nesrine was broke—all her savings had been spent bailing out the idiot brother last time. She was grateful—disproportionately grateful—and felt in my debt. She had made an offer to settle the obligation. A very kind offer.

But not the kind of offer I would accept under those circumstances.

I'm sure Albert would have accepted. And it was not that she was unattractive or that I wouldn't have found pleasure between her sheets with her. But she would not have. She liked me. She respected me. She was grateful to me. But she wasn't attracted to me. She might have consented in a very legal sense of the word, but not emotionally.

Plus, there are many other ways that people can pay me, and she repaid me by driving me around occasionally. She was one of the few drivers that I really trusted. In a city of millions, I'm was pretty much at two drivers that I trusted, her and Kasym Aitmatov.

She knew I wouldn't tell her exactly what was going on—and she was cool with that—but she was also smart enough to tell me when she thought I was wrong or being stupid.

"Let me show you where we're going," I said, turning the laptop to face her as she sat down. "And you do have a phone charger in your car?"

forty-five

Tolomush Okeyev sat on the lower plinth under the huge monument in Place de la République. His usual pristine smartness lacking. Asian precision replaced by Western relaxation bordering on the kind of slobbery that the English do much better than the French.

He balanced his head in his hands, which were in turn supported by his elbows resting on his knees. "Good dinner?" I asked as the reddened whites of his eyes came into view.

He muttered something about the other ambassador and entertainment budgets, and seemed happy to sit—he was ready for sleep wherever his body was, and the chill of the clear spring morning seemed not to have penetrated. Or maybe it had penetrated and it was too late to save him.

Something was missing: I scanned the square, largely empty, but toward the eastern edge saw what was missing. Kasym Aitmatov was watching his charge at a distance—giving his boss privacy and standing far enough back to be able to assess what was happening. Or in this case, what wasn't happening.

"Here's an idea for you," I said. "You're clearly not ready for exercise or to expend energy, so if you want to do the minimum amount of work, then be straight with me. Don't go to the effort of lying—just let the truth flow." I paused. There seemed little reaction, so I continued. "What does Gaston Blanc want from you?"

"What do you mean when you say 'lying'?" he asked, dropping his hands, his head suddenly capable of self-support, his eyes finding the ability to focus.

I let his indignity hang for a few moments, our eyes locking. When I was sure he was listening closely, I continued. "The paternity of your son. The paternity of your daughter. Your relationship with Gaston Blanc. That Pierre-Louis, Marianne, and Gaston Blanc all—to a greater or lesser extent—want or wanted something from you. Do you want me to elaborate? Or would you prefer to explain what Gaston Blanc has on you?"

The hint of a sneer ghosted over his face. "So now you're no longer suggesting that I had one hundred thousand reasons to kill my son?" His head moved slowly, as if counting beats. "Between last night and this morning, you've changed your mind, and now it's not my fault? Interesting. But still you're worried about little lies—which, to be frank, Leathan, are white lies of omission."

A gust blew across the large public square; the monochrome ground and surrounding buildings all shivered. His head was still moving.

"Do you want an apology?" I asked. "If you want an apology, of course, you deserve one: I'm sorry that you didn't tell me enough, early enough, to go straight to the guy who could help find the killers of your son."

His head stopped moving—he was listening.

"Did Gaston Blanc kill your son? No. At least, I doubt it. Did he set events in motion that led to the death? Did he set those events in motion in order to increase his leverage over you? Yeah. Would your son be alive if you had told me the truth? Probably not...but we might have found his killers by now."

Every action. Every connection. Everything he had done. Every link. It was all snapping together in his mind. Possibilities and permutations. Decisions not taken. Choices not made. All were weighed. His muscles seemed to contract, and his breathing became heavier.

I continued, my voice soft, little above a whisper. "What does he want?"

Tolomush Okeyev shrugged, shaking his head. A small admission of defeat. "Diplomatic immunity."

It was my turn to be confused. Okeyev gave a small smile, pleased to have suggested something that I clearly hadn't considered and where I would—at best—be sketchy about the details. "It's impractical. Impossible. Illegal under all sorts of international law and centuries-old conventions." He gave a wry smile. "But Gaston Blanc really isn't one to worry about what the law actually says. He's got a friend who's going down for life, and the only way he can find to reverse the sentence is for diplomatic influence to be wielded."

I let him continue.

"And if I wield the influence—vested in me by virtue of my representing the Kyrgyz Republic—then I undermine the Kyrgyz Republic and I undermine myself. Quite literally, it will be the last thing I do as ambassador...as an ambassador anywhere." His voice became soft, almost pleading. "I have much...latitude. But there are lines I cannot cross. There are lines which my country will not allow me to cross."

He raised himself onto his feet slowly—his heavy night still exerting its weight on his shoulders—and stood next to me, blocking any view from behind him, the front view open to Kasym Aitmatov. His hand reached inside his jacket, and he pulled out a stack of bills that he slipped into my hand. "Please find who killed my son, Leathan."

It seemed a bit early to be getting paid, and I didn't feel that I had really earned the money I had already received, but it would be rude to refuse.

forty-six

If you pushed me, I would say the alleyway behind Nico's hotel is less pretty in the daylight than it is at night. At least at night its unattractiveness is hidden by the dark.

I had called Nico from the car using Nesrine Walter's phone. Nico had grumbled—his shift was ending soon—but he had agreed to slip out. I had been waiting outside the door for about five minutes, with Nesrine keeping the engine running so that the car kept warm.

The service door swung open, crashing into the back wall, and Nico rushed out, displaying a level of urgency that I had rarely seen. "Hi Leath." He handed me a bundle. "There. The envelope from the safe and an empty envelope." I took the brown paper. "Oh yeah—and some SIMs." He dug into his vest pocket with his finger and held the excavated contents toward me. "We've got a group of Canadians checking out—total nightmare...who knew?"

And he was gone. I was sure he said he'd be back, but for the moment, I was grateful for the privacy.

There was a green dumpster that offered a useful work surface. I slotted in the first SIM card and turned on my phone, putting it down on the dumpster to give it a few moments to boot and find a signal.

The envelope I had sealed a few days earlier was as I had given it to Nico. I ripped the top and slipped out the contents. They were as I remembered: 3,000 euros, Pierre-Louis' phone with the battery removed, his wallet, and a notebook.

I put the cash, together with a further 12,000 euros that I had collected in two payments of 5,000 euros from the diplomat last night and this morning and with the money under my insoles, into the new envelope.

I opened the wallet. A few bills—old, worn cash that had been in circulation for a while. Some cards, most for college—one for the library, another granting access to something that didn't make sense, and a debit card. Nothing said, "This kid had 100,000 euros." I dropped the wallet into the envelope, thought for a few moments, then threw in the keys I had been carrying around since Monday and sealed the paper container.

The old-fashioned notebook held closed with an elastic loop and with papers sticking out went into my jacket pocket.

When I picked it up, my phone told me it was 20 percent charged and that it indeed had found a service and would let me make calls. I called my answering service. I went through the routine I go through every morning. I got the message I get every morning—disturbing and yet somehow comforting in its infantile ranting. If it ever changes, then I'll be worried. If they ever miss a day, that's the day I'll leave Paris immediately.

I hung up and waited for Nico. The blue sky of the early spring morning was now turning slate gray, mimicking much of the architecture of the city and slipping us back into winter. It took another five minutes and what felt like five degrees of temperature fall before Nico returned.

"Leath, I'm sorry" was all he said.

I gave him the freshly sealed envelope and a €100 bill and shooshed him back inside, then turned and jogged back to the car. It might not have had heated seats like Kasym Aitmatov's Mercedes, but I was grateful for the warmth of the heating system.

"Not that it hasn't been one of the most fun mornings of my life or anything like that, Leathan—you know, driving you around Paris and sitting waiting—but are we going to go now?"

"That's my errands done. Let's go and find a mother."

As Nesrine pulled out, I clicked my phone onto the charger and put the notebook into the glove compartment—I wasn't going to give myself a headache trying to read as we drove.

forty-seven

Giving Seine-Saint-Denis as a direction is imprecise.

It's like saying Manhattan rather than New York. Sure, you're narrowing down the area, but not by much, and Seine-Saint-Denis is still three times the size of Manhattan with a population pushing toward two million, not to mention an airport—Le Bourget—and the Stade de France rugby stadium.

"Apart from Monsieur Corbusier, did anyone ever, ever like this stark modernism?" I asked no one specific, although there was one person listening.

"Because Leathan Wilkey has never made a mistake," Nesrine Walter muttered, replied to no one specific.

"La cité des 4000," I let the inference hang, "is a decision on something of a different scale." It was just one example, but the City of 4,000 was emblematic of the post-war housing outside central Paris. Huge monolithic, brutal, white, featureless blocks all designed with the battle cry: modernism.

The Romans designed every road in the same way: a straight line. The modernists designed every building in the same way: a brutal white block. Paris had swung from one extreme to the other. Inside Boulevard Périphérique, the ring road that follows the path of the old city walls and that now delineates the boundary between city and suburb, Paris had the Haussmann style applied. Broad, sweeping boulevards—bringing air and light—with elegantly constructed buildings, built to a consistent style and incorporating retail spaces and living quarters for all social classes.

But outside the circle, there was bleak modernism. Featureless white boxes designed to house people who, through economic circumstance, could not argue. And not just one or two featureless white boxes—everything was a featureless white box. Some of the featureless white boxes had square footprints; some had oblong footprints—often very long and thin footprints.

But what none of the blocks did was to stand out.

We pulled into the third parking lot at about 10:30. The sky was still gray—somehow the tone made the row of three perfect white blocks, each about ten floors high, starker. The white blocks gleamed against the steel gray sky.

"Is this it?" asked Nesrine Walter.

"I don't know. The address I was given was pretty vague. It was more an aspiration than an actual address... You know, go to the white block, turn right at the white block, when you pass the fifth white block turn between the two white blocks, and..."

"And?"

"And I wish Monsieur Corbusier had designed something that was a bit more distinguishable." I opened the car door.

"Do you want me to help?"

In truth, I wanted all the help I could get. But being realistic, I wasn't sure exactly what I was looking for—I hoped I'd recognize it when I saw it. "You look after the car," I said, pointing around the lot at the burned-out vehicles and others that had been gutted for parts. "It's been disappointing enough today—I don't want to upset myself even more by having to walk home."

"Sure?"

"Really—but don't worry, you will go to the ball one day, Cinderella. But just at the moment, I've got to hope that the elevators in those three blocks are working."

"All three?"

"All three—unless I get lucky before. And even then, I'm trying the seventh, eighth, and ninth floors."

I shut the door on the warmth and traipsed toward the first block.

forty-eight

"Hi," I said, talking to the eyes just visible through the cracked door. "I'm looking for Marianne."

There was something in her hesitation that told me she was going to lie to me. She wouldn't be the first person to lie to me since I started looking for Pierre-Louis. She wouldn't be the first person to lie to me today—and I had hardly come to speak truth.

But I was happy to take a lie. Nesrine Walter and I had spent hours looking for Marianne, driving around La Courneuve, a suburb that seemed to exclusively consist of white apartment blocks. As far as I could tell, the architect had sat down with a box of sugar cubes and had stacked them. Some stacks had formed towers. Some stacks had formed big cubes. Some stacks had formed very, very long, thin blocks set against another block placed a short distance away.

And once the architect had built his sugar cube blocks, he copied the design onto paper and gave it to the construction firm, which had kept pouring concrete until it ran out. The new residents were then pushed into their apartments—which were as healthy as a diet of cubed white sugar—and promptly forgotten about.

At each sugar-cube construction that could, plausibly, possibly, maybe show a resemblance to the one, some, or all of the descriptions given to me by Pierre-Louis' friends, I had knocked on doors, having first got past the simple security for each block—usually achieved by waiting for someone to enter or leave.

Two hours ago, I thought I had found Marianne. I was wrong. But now, at 12:30, for the first time there was recognition in the eyes of someone I was talking to. This wasn't Marianne—she was too old to be a sister—but there was a recognition in her eyes when I said the name Marianne. At a guess, this was a mother or an aunt.

"I don't know Marianne," she said. No hesitation. No pause. And the obvious giveaway: I don't know Marianne...Marianne, a specific person. If she had said "I don't know *anyone called* Marianne" or "there's no one with that name here," then I might have accepted what I was being told.

As it was, she chose to tell a direct lie, and a direct lie has no morals. It will rat on you every time as it slips from your lips.

"That's a shame," I said, reaching into my pocket and pulling out a €100 bill. Her eyes fixed on the bill as I held it in front of me, straightening out the creases.

She shifted her weight, allowing the door to open a bit further. She was puffy, doughy, overweight—at a guess she rarely left the apartment on the eighth floor, and neither fresh air nor exercise figured in her world. Her hair reached between her shoulders and elbows as best I could figure where her shoulders and elbows were under her shapeless white tracksuit. The hair was yellow—not blond, but yellow, bleached cheaply, bleached badly, and the gray roots were showing—not washed recently and with scruffy ringlets.

She didn't take her gaze away from the bill. "Maybe I could help." When she spoke, there was the hint of a German accent. I have trouble with accents. My father was Scottish and my mother French, and I learned English and French at the same time. But living in Scotland and watching British TV, I heard and became accustomed to the nuances and dialects of the English language. The French I heard was from my mother and her family speaking. So while I'm fluent in the language, I don't always get the accent, especially regional accents. But the German accent—the Teutonic precision cutting against the French melody—was clear enough for me. What was less clear to me was how that German accent had been softened.

"Are you her mother?" I asked.

She mumbled. It was neither a yes nor a no.

"That's another shame," I said, pulling out a second €100 bill and slowly flattening out the creases. "It's a shame, because I heard that Marianne's mother would make me a cup of coffee for 100 euros."

I turned away from the door.

"Maybe I can help," she said.

Two hundred euros to get inside and get a cup of coffee seemed a high price to pay, but it was probably a small price if I learned something new and the apartment was heated.

forty-nine

In most living rooms you can make a fair guess about where the head of the household sits. Their place is usually directly in front of the television, and where they sit often shows most signs of wear.

But you can be wrong in this guess—maybe the television points generally into the room, perhaps the seats are equally worn or there are kids who have inflicted disproportionate damage on the furniture.

But here it was obvious. The sofa was like a crime scene, but instead of the body being outlined in chalk, the place where the body usually rested on the sofa in front of the television was outlined in black grease that had been smeared across the fabric. Beyond the comparatively clear area, there was detritus: food scraps, magazines dropped, clothes, and a stack of TV remote controls.

Karen Fischer—200 euros had also bought me her name—put her coffee on the table in front of the seating and let herself fall backward into the clear space on the sofa before rummaging around for a remote control. The table was another old, cheap, battered piece of furniture with a protective layer of dust and food scraps.

She pointed the remote at the large cathode-ray television and silenced the daytime talk show, which seemed to involve people dressed in a similar fashion to her shouting at each other before the studio's security, identifiable because they were dressed in black, pulled them apart.

"I never watch that rubbish," she said. On the scale of lies I suspected she was going to tell me, that one didn't move the needle.

The room was a similar size to the main area of Pierre-Louis' apartment in Belleville, but this apartment seemed to be bigger overall. From what I had seen as I made the trip from the front door, there was a separate kitchen—small but functional, although much less functional than would have been the case if it had been cleaned in the last ten years—and there were three other rooms. At a guess, one bathroom and two bedrooms.

In my short time in the apartment, I had yet to see anything that seemed new. The carpet was old and worn. The kitchen, tatty. This living room hadn't seen a fresh coat of paint in at least twenty-five years, the furniture was probably secondhand twenty years ago, and the photos standing in frames on top of the television were not recent.

I slowed my scan to take in the photos. There was a mother with a baby—I looked to the lump spreading herself on the sofa and back to the photo. "Is this Marianne?" I asked.

The lump on the sofa—the eye of the storm that wreaked havoc on this room on an hourly basis—nodded.

"She was beautiful," I said. And she was a gorgeous kid. Karen Fischer had been a good-looking woman too. I looked at the photos—a mother with her kid, the same woman among a group of men in dinner suits, one of whom could have been a younger Tolomush Okeyev, and one of her on her own. In each she showed a figure, pleasingly curved but not cartoonish—the sort of figure that only comes naturally to nineteen-year-old women. She was always dressed simply—usually in what looked to be one of a number of little black dresses—and her blond curls tumbled over her shoulders.

She looked young. She looked like she was having fun. She looked like she literally had the world at her feet.

"What year was this taken?" I asked, pointing to the picture of the infant Marianne.

She mumbled something—from somewhere she had found food, but clearly it would cost more if I wanted her to share.

"So she'll be twenty-one...twenty-two now?"

"Twenty-one," said Karen Fischer, crumbs spraying.

There was a single-seat chair—with the same level of junk as the rest of the room, but it was outside of the crumb-spraying radius. I pushed back a stack of clothes to reveal the old fabric and perched on the edge, setting my disappointing coffee on the table.

One father, two mothers, two very different lives. I thought back to the story Émilie had told me as I sat in her room listening to her talk. She had spent over ten years making money in the company of men. She had fallen in love several times, but somehow it hadn't worked out. However, all the men she had known had been kind and generous. The generosity had helped her get an apartment—the apartment where she still lived—and furnish the apartment.

She knew back then that there was a limit to her lifestyle—she was reaching thirty, which put her on a par with the dinosaurs in her business. She thought of herself as too old, and so it was a shock when she became pregnant. It seemed to be even more of a shock for the young junior diplomat from Kyrgyzstan who was scheduled to take up another posting in three weeks.

For her, it wasn't a hard decision—she kept the baby. The young diplomat offered some support from a distance, a few men she had known were thrilled for her and offered some help, financial and practical, and she spent ten years bringing up her baby. But by the time she was forty, she had a ten-year-old, no qualifications, no income, and no pension provision. So she went out to work and had spent the majority of the last ten years on the makeup and perfume floor of Galeries Lafayette.

Like my schoolmasters always said: compare and contrast. I looked at the sofa-filler.

Something told me she was younger than Émilie, but the age of Marianne suggested Karen had met Tolomush Okeyev before he met Émilie. A younger woman—maybe nineteen or twenty when she fell pregnant—without the foundation of her own apartment and a range of friends who could offer practical assistance. Maybe the only place she could find to live was in this desolate housing complex, and when you have nothing, there's no incentive to go out to work.

There's no incentive but to spend all day sitting in front of the TV, eating.

And if someone offers you 100 euros, you're going to ask for 200 euros and do whatever it takes to get more cash.

"I need to talk with Marianne," I said.

The shapeless form wobbled. It might have been a shrug. Maybe a grunt. Perhaps wind.

I took out another €100; the eyes within the shape were alert. "Does Marianne live here?"

"Depends what you call living. That's her room," she nodded in the direction of the wall, as if that explained fully what she meant. "Sometimes she stays. More now that shitty boyfriend has started seeing that new whore. The bastard can beat her instead."

"When did you last see her?" I tried.

"Monday...? Tuesday...?"

"A few days ago?"

"No. Tuesday last week."

I rustled the bill. "How do you get hold of her?"

"Phone." She clicked her fingers. "Put it down."

I placed the bill on the table, keeping a finger on it. "What's her number?"

"That'll be another hundred."

fifty

"If I—a complete stranger who offers no identification—come into your apartment," I shut the car door behind me, "and offer you money to talk to your child, what's your reaction?"

Nesrine Walter exhaled slowly, as if thinking. "First, I'd say, 'What child? I don't have a child.'"

I felt a sense of relief wash over me. "Precisely. You deny there is a child or you refuse to talk to this stranger."

"I'm sensing this isn't what happened."

"Correct. I gave her money—she told me about her daughter and gave me her number. So either she's a terrible mother or she's a great liar, and I've just laid down a few hundred euros for nothing."

The car's engine was running, keeping the heater blowing. I reached into my pocket and pulled out two €100 bills and put them on the dashboard. "A small contribution to your fuel."

Nesrine took the cash; there was a slight hesitation in her voice when she began. "You're sure the woman you've just seen is Marianne's mother?"

"There were photos," I said, and then answered the follow-up question she was silently thinking, "which I realize don't prove she's Marianne's mother. But there's something about how Thea described Marianne and how the mother looked that told me I was talking to the right person." I sighed. "And I doubt she's used her brain sufficiently in the last ten years to think quickly enough to scam me to that level of detail."

Two teenagers walked past, both dressed in loose gray sweatpants and with gray hoodies pulled over their heads. Two inhabitants of this alien land. Thankfully, this alien land had cellphone coverage. "Let's see whether she told the truth."

I punched in the number. It answered on the fourth ring.

"Is that Marianne?" I asked. Her hesitation was sufficient confirmation. "My name's Leathan. I need to talk with you."

She mumbled. A habit from her mother.

"It's important—it's not the sort of conversation you can have over the phone."

She didn't hang up.

"I need to talk now. I'm outside your mother's block. I can come to you—just tell me where you want to meet." I scrunched up my face. "I'll pay you 200 euros for five minutes of your time."

"So?" said Nesrine as I hung up.

"We meet in thirty minutes—it's a café that she says is five minutes away." I sighed. "Like mother, like daughter. Wave money and they'll do anything."

"But you're not going to pay?" It was a question, but Nesrine phrased it as a statement.

"I'm paying," I said. "I don't know why, but I need to talk with this woman."

Nesrine Walter waited. She was listening. Expecting.

"Her half-brother died on me. His last words were 'protect Marianne.' He didn't say from whom or how, or even who she was, just protect her. And having met the mother, I'm starting to wonder if it was her that Marianne needs protecting from."

"When did this happen?" asked Nesrine, shock in her voice.

"Monday. Monday as it became Tuesday."

"Why so long—why are you only speaking to her on Thursday?"

I sat back in the seat, staring into the distance across the barren landscape. "He didn't say who Marianne was—I figured she was just a girlfriend...maybe a pregnant girlfriend—and there was no urgency attached. I had to do more important things, like tell the kid's mother and father that their son had been shot."

"He was shot? How terrible."

I continued, "It was only yesterday that I found that Marianne is his sister and she's been a lot harder to find than I expected. You saw how long it took to find the mother's apartment. But now...now I get to meet her."

fifty-one

The coffee was hot, strong, and it had some flavor. The seat was plastic and functional for a short period, and the table was formica-topped for easy wiping. It was a cheap place serving cheap coffee and cheap food.

But this is where Marianne wanted to meet, and it was unlikely that she knew any Bulgarians who wanted me dead and that she would be able to contact those Bulgarians between the time I called her and now.

The door opened, and a young woman entered.

The blond curly locks flowed over a gray shapeless raincoat, which looked more like a poncho designed to hide her pregnancy bump. She could be twenty-one, but those were twenty-one tough years.

I stood. "Marianne?"

She walked over, her heels clipping loudly on the tiled floor. "Are you the one with the funny name?"

"Leathan," I said. She frowned. "It's Scottish."

"Leathan," she whispered. It didn't sit well in her mouth.

I returned to my seat and gestured to her to join me in the seat opposite. "Do you want a coffee?" She looked ready to give birth now. "Perhaps something without caffeine? A bite to eat?"

Her heels clipped as she moved closer. "Where's my money?"

I pulled out two €100 bills, holding one in each hand. I moved my right hand away from her, placing it on the table, and gently slapped my left hand in front of where I wanted her to sit.

She hefted a mid-brown handbag—a huge thing that shone in the way that only fake leather does—onto the second seat and sat across from me, pulling one bill from under my hand. I pointed with my eyes to my right hand and the other bill: "Once we've talked."

She sneered.

Up close, she was clearly her mother's daughter, following down the same tracks twenty years later. Her skin still had some elasticity, but it was weakening, making her face puffy. This wasn't baby weight—this was the peak from which the only direction was downhill.

"I met your brother," I said.

"He's dead."

"I know," I said trying to hide my surprise that she knew about Pierre-Louis. "I'm sorry for your loss."

Another sneer.

"Before he died he asked me to look in on you...to...make sure everything was alright."

A half sneer. "Everything's alright. I just need my money."

"I told you, you can have your money after we've talked." I let my eyes point back at the second bill, still trapped under my right hand.

"Not that money. *My* money. The money that Pierre-Louis had. Did he tell you where that was?"

There was no sadness for her lost brother—there was no common ground I could find with this woman, no basis on which to start a conversation. She felt the silence and reached for the second bill, pulling it from under my hand. "You can call me if you find my money."

Awkwardly she slid out of the seat, dragging her brown bag behind her with her feet clipping on the floor.

"When are you due?" I asked.

"Three weeks," she said, and was gone, the café door swinging closed.

fifty-two

I was aware that I was staring, but I couldn't drag my gaze away. I could drink my coffee, all my motor skills were fine, and, if asked, I could confirm what day of the week it was, who was the president of the republic and the Prime Minister of the United Kingdom, and many other details.

However, I seemed to have lost the power to move my gaze from the place where I had last seen Marianne when she walked out.

Someone came through the door—I couldn't tell whether they were male or female; I was still staring.

"Leath?"

"Yeah." I didn't look; my gaze was fixed.

"Are you alright, Leathan?" There was a hand on my shoulder. I found the power to move my eyes and looked at the hand—it was Nesrine Walter. "I need to pee." And she was gone. I took another sip of coffee, careful not to let my sight wander to the vortex.

Nesrine came back and slipped into the seat where Marianne had been sitting. "Coffee?" I asked. "Something to eat?"

She scanned the room and frowned politely. "Why don't we go somewhere nicer and have some lunch?"

"She knew," I said, then stopped myself and looked directly at Nesrine. "Sorry. Yes. That's a great idea; let's go for lunch."

She smiled. "You were saying—she knew something."

"She knew her brother is dead. As far as I know, no one knows that." I felt the pull of the distance and my gaze defocusing. "Well, I know, the mother knows, the father knows, the people who pulled the trigger know, and some criminal who lives in an Irish bar that you don't want to hear about knows...but apart from that, no one knows he's dead. The cops haven't even figured who he is."

I pulled my gaze back to look at my driver, who was clearly shocked. "That's awful—shouldn't you tell...?"

I shook my head. "Everyone who loved him—apart from some sad ginger-haired girl—knows. That's enough." I finished my coffee. "So who told Marianne?"

"Marianne who's very...pregnant."

I could feel a sly grin creeping across my face. "Yeah, that one. And just so we're clear, it's not mine."

"I didn't think it was, Leathan." It was Nesrine's turn to grin. "But with you we always wonder." She paused, letting out a small sigh. "That was a very expensive bag she was carrying."

"It looked like a piece of shit to me—fake leather."

"Seriously, Leathan, that wasn't fake leather." Her face was stern. "You don't understand fashion, do you?" Her voice was a wave of sympathy sweeping over me. "That bag will have cost over a thousand euros—and they only came into the shops in the last ten days."

For the second time since I had been in the café, I lacked the skill to process what I was hearing.

"Listen to me, Leathan. Listen to me as someone who has looked longingly at those bags. I know for certain that the stock only arrived within the last ten days, and those bags are expensive." She paused. When she continued, she was more matter-of-fact. "That girl wasn't dressed cheaply."

"What do you mean?" I asked. "That tatty old raincoat?"

"Tatty old raincoat?" The question was laced with the venom usually spat by a mother who thinks someone has called her baby ugly. "That coat will have cost about eight hundred euros. The shoes..."

"Why was she wearing heels?" I asked. "I know there are standards...but when you're three weeks away from giving birth..."

"I'm guessing you wear them because they're new and expensive."

"So you're telling me they only came into the stores this week?"

She laughed. "No—I'm saying they looked new. But they probably cost as much as the bag."

I could buy my entire wardrobe three times over for what she had paid for a pair of shoes. And it was only three times over—not more—because leather jackets aren't cheap. "We *are* talking about the same person," I asked.

Nesrine smiled indulgently, her head gently nodding. "It didn't look right to me either. The look didn't fit with the apartment block where the mother lived, and it didn't fit with the car she arrived in."

"You saw the car she arrived in?" It hit me like a jolt of electricity.

"Yeah. Old. Brown. Renault. You know, those wedge-shaped things that were popular before I was born."

fifty-three

I hadn't looked at the menu since we arrived in the bistro. "Do you want to order?" asked the waitress.

"What do you recommend?" I asked.

"It depends..." began the waitress, stopping when she caught my eye.

"If you brought your parents here for lunch," I said, "and you wanted them to have the most...satisfying dish on the menu, what would that be?"

Her answer was immediate, like a child who had done her homework and was ready for the test and knew she had the right answer. "Bœuf bourguignon." Then, almost apologetically: "It really is very good."

I caught Nesrine's eye. She bobbed her head. "Two for the bœuf bourguignon, and..."

"Just water," said Nesrine Walter.

"And some water," I said to the waitress.

"We take our chances," said Nesrine as the waitress left us. "This bistro was close and there were some good reviews." She scrunched up her face. "We can always...if it's not..."

"It's fine," I said. "It's more comfortable than that café, and I'm ready for something to eat."

She went to argue and then stopped herself. "Is that the notebook you got when we stopped at the back of that hotel?"

I nodded, looking at the outside of the black-covered book with the papers spilling from inside. "It's the dead kid's. Marianne's brother."

There was a sadness on Nesrine's face.

"Seems like an intrusion."

Her brow crinkled.

"To look inside."

She winced, but her face stayed in motion as if she was playing each side of the argument. I could understand—I was playing the angles in my head already: Pierre-Louis was dead, so it was hardly a material intrusion. It might give me a clue as to why he was dead, which would excuse any intrusion. Perhaps his mother should be the one to make the call. And the biggest reason—I had stolen the notebook.

Oh yeah, and I had already looked through it on the night I took it.

I flipped off the elastic strap holding the front and back covers together, sandwiching the pages and the papers into one lump.

Nesrine raised her eyebrows. I placed the notebook on the dark wood table between us and turned it so we could both see before gently flipping the front cover, which flopped open.

There was a drawing of a lion. A simple line drawing—the evolutionary pencil first step, which had transformed into paint and onto the wall of the apartment in Belleville. I turned some more pages. The lion evolved—he took different poses, tried different facial expressions, and made friends with a range of animals. I'm not sure the lion and the aardvark was a classic, but it made me smile.

"He could draw well," she said absentmindedly.

"He was planning the nursery for his niece or nephew," I said. "On the night he was shot he'd been painting jungle animals on the walls."

Nesrine's lower lip trembled, her eyes misted, and a tear rolled down the side of her nose. "He was doing that...for her...for some kid that wasn't his?" She wiped the tear away, and a second tear took its place.

"He did that, and the little bitch only wants to know where her money is."

She pulled out a tissue and wiped her nose. "What a sweet guy."

"So everyone says," I said. "He was nineteen and had arranged an apartment for his pregnant half-sister. Ignore what people say—judge him by what he did."

The still between us was broken by the waitress returning with a jug of water and two tumblers.

I turned back to the notebook and flicked forward a few pages. There were sketches—floor plans of the Belleville apartment. The same floor plan repeated, but each time with a different arrangement of furniture.

Nesrine Walter narrowed her brow, looking at the floor plans.

"This is the apartment he took for Marianne," I said. "I think he's trying furniture layouts."

"Is that the nursery?" She put her finger on the small room where the animals were being painted on the wall. I nodded. "He's thinking hard—thinking more than most men would think. Look, that's a changing table."

I flicked forward a few pages and reached the first piece of paper slipped into the notebook. It was part of a page from a magazine. Nesrine picked it up and started studying it as I returned to the notebook, finding calculations over the next few pages. Nothing too hugely complicated—mostly there seemed to be multiplications and divisions by a factor of 48.

"Is Tolomush Okeyev significant?" asked Nesrine Walter.

"The dead kid's father," I said. "Marianne's father, too. Why?"

"He's in this picture. The woman with him is stunning." I lifted my eyes from the notebook—Nesrine had my attention. "Look." She held the picture for me to see.

"That's Émilie, Pierre-Louis' mother."

"She is..."

"She's even more gorgeous now. She's got those eyes that you look into and you fall. You fall hard; you fall deep. You fall and you feel you're never going to stop falling. She's one of those women who somehow gets better looking with a wrinkle or two."

She laughed. "Leathan, that's what all French women do. We somehow found the secret and we're not telling you what it is. We've got enough pretty girls to keep our presidents and our international bankers happy, but beautiful women—who somehow get more beautiful and graceful as they age—are our national specialty."

I flipped a few more pages. There was a photo of Émilie Dubois. A portrait, shot at a studio. I held it for Nesrine to see. "Wow," she whispered, taking the photo and studying it.

Under the photo, there was a newspaper article with a picture to accompany the piece. The photo—as the rest of the newspaper—was in black and white, the grayscale image created with a series of small dots.

The woman was different in this picture. Where Émilie was petite and a brunette, this woman—probably still a teenager—was curvier, with flowing blond curls cascading over her shoulders. I couldn't be certain, but it looked like Karen Fischer had looked in some of the pictures I had seen in her apartment. It looked how Marianne may have looked without the puffiness, without the harshness her face had somehow found in the years since she had been such a cute baby.

Tolomush Okeyev had his arm around the woman—tentative, uncertain, although whether that was because he was unsure of himself or of his partner wasn't clear. He was younger, goofier—still waiting to have to grow up to meet the expectations of a good woman.

Nesrine carefully took the old newspaper cutting. "Oh dear." She laughed guiltily. "He did much better with your woman." My face must have changed. "I mean...the...err..." She held up the photo of Émilie. "The blond is pretty in a plain sort of Northern European way...but she," Nesrine held the photo so it was clear she meant Émilie, "is stunning." Softly, as an afterthought, she added: "I hope she's as beautiful on the inside as she is on the outside."

I was focused on the next few pieces of paper: some preprinted forms and a few pages printed on cheap paper by a laser printer.

"What's that?" she asked.

I flicked through the pages. "Furniture. He ordered...and paid for...furniture for the apartment. It's going to be delivered in three weeks," I said, reading the first sheet. "Ten days," the second sheet. "Three weeks, five weeks..." I stopped the running commentary of delivery dates. "He furnished the whole place—he's even got a TV coming. Look." I passed her the receipts, lifting up the last of the papers.

"Mademoiselle...Monsieur." The waitress had returned with our lunch.

We thanked her, and I returned to my reading, lazily eating with my left hand as I held the pages in my right.

"This is good," said Nesrine. "Eat up, Leathan."

I mumbled.

"Come on, Leathan. You usually enjoy your food, and this is good."

I mumbled again, continuing to read.

"What have you got there?"

"The answer," I said, putting the paper down and taking a proper mouthful. Nesrine sat, expectantly. "It's a rental agreement for the apartment Pierre-Louis took in Belleville. I understand what the kid was trying to do. At least, I think I do."

fifty-four

"What gave you the idea?" asked Nesrine.

"Idea?"

"About the food? I mean sure, ask what's good—but it's pointless, because they're never going to say that anything is bad."

I held the door open, and Nesrine Walter led us back to the cold February afternoon. It was about 3 PM, but a Northern Hemisphere 3 PM in February. The sun had long since dropped behind the skyline of the surrounding buildings on the quiet street, and as it went, any last few hints of warmth in the day had run away. If there was any cheer to be had, the wind had died down, but it was probably readying itself for later in the evening.

"Someone I had dinner with," I said, my mind more focused on the contents of the small notebook that I clutched in my right hand. "He made a point about relying on people who know better than you."

Nesrine seemed to accept the explanation and changed subject. "So what now?"

"Marianne," I said. "I need a proper conversation with Marianne. But first, I need to think how I'm going to approach her. I need to figure what question will elicit an answer—or rather a reaction— that will tell me what I want to know."

"Good luck on that one," said Nesrine, her tone making sure I understood she had little faith.

There were a few people out. A few cars passing, one or two people on the sidewalk, which was narrow by Parisian standards, but probably broad by the standards of the rest of the country. The few people who passed seemed to be older and resigned to the weather, having pulled out scarves and hats to add to the many layers they were already wrapped with. At least, I assumed they were wearing many layers—the other alternative was that there was a highly localized obesity epidemic.

There was one guy who wasn't as tightly wrapped. If I were giving a description to the police, I would describe his clothes in much the same way as mine: leather jacket, jeans, and sneakers. He was probably older, thinner, and with longer hair, which was lank and in need of a wash. I was struggling to pick out details: He just seemed like an unremarkable man.

Unremarkable.

And yet, now that he was getting close, I recognized him. He had a look that said: "Don't run."

"Shit," I muttered under my breath.

Nesrine tilted her head, questioning, ready to ask why I was cursing, when the unremarkable man joined us, forming a triangle. Her head flicked back to him, her shoulder-length hair following— the unasked question was for him now.

"We need a word." His voice was as unremarkable as his appearance. But I remembered yesterday: His ability to hurt was something noteworthy, and the man he worked for was a man who commanded fear more than respect.

I waited a beat, then looked to Nesrine. "There's your notebook. You forgot it, so I picked it up." I pushed the black book with its papers tucked inside toward her. She took it, more as a reflex and less because she understood why she was taking it. I looked back to the unremarkable man and lifted my eyebrows, questioning.

He turned and began walking in the direction from which he had come. I took two paces. "Leathan, should I...?" Nesrine asked behind me.

I shook my head, following the unremarkable man as he led me to his gray Peugeot.

fifty-five

The unremarkable man joined me in the back seat of the Peugeot, and an equally unremarkable man drove us.

I wasn't entirely certain where I had been with Nesrine Walter—she had found somewhere to eat using something on her phone and had then followed the GPS directions to the bistro. The turn-by-turn instructions had been accurate, but looking at a map through a tiny aperture hadn't given me any real sense of where we were, other than still in Seine-Saint-Denis, so trying to figure where we were going was impossible.

"When did you get on my trail?" I asked.

My fellow passenger put his finger to his lips. "Shhhh." Then he reached forward, tapped the driver on his shoulder, and pointed.

The driver grunted before passing something back. The unremarkable man sharing the back seat with me shook open a dark fabric hood, then looked over to me. "It's alright," I said. "I don't know where we are."

He half smiled, grabbing the edges of the hood.

"Do we really have to?" I asked.

He remained quiet, his hands tightening their grip on the hood. I leaned forward, and the last traces of daylight disappeared.

I suspected I was not the first person to wear that hood. "When did this hood last see the insides of a washing machine?" I asked.

The response was swift—a fist unloaded into my gut, bending me over. "Shhh." I tried to sit straight again, but felt a weight across my back, keeping me in place.

From my position being pinned and hooded in the back seat, the journey was unremarkable. Neither man spoke, there was no drama in the driving, and after what I guessed was about ten minutes, we slowed, the road surface changing noticeably. We kept moving slowly, and then the engine sound changed—it was as if we were going into a tunnel, except there were no other cars.

The car stopped. The pressure on my back released. Doors opened. Voices—more than two people. And then I was pulled out and up to a standing position. The hood was tugged off, scraping across my left ear as it went.

I felt the ache as my eyes adjusted to the strip lights. We were in what could have been a warehouse—a small warehouse—or maybe a workshop. The floor was bare concrete—old, dirty, worn, and gouged. The superstructure of the building was concrete pillars. Eight vertical pillars—four on either side—with the main roof framework fashioned from steel. The concrete superstructure had once been painted white, although no fresh paint had been added this century.

A skin of concrete panels had then been slotted between the vertical concrete pillars, with occasional high windows punched to let in light. Or, as was now the case, to let in the closing darkness. This had then been topped with a corrugated roof, seemingly a mix of asbestos and steel panels.

A fist landed in my gut and then a second, taking me down. Two hands grabbed my jacket by the collar and pulled me up before another fist hit me.

My lunch exited. I felt the burn of stomach acid in my throat and the foul taste of vomit in my mouth. What had been a pleasant meal was now a semi-liquidized brown trail across the dirty concrete floor.

The hands gripping my collar moved to my lapels and started to pull my jacket off. I hunched my shoulders forward and felt another blow in my gut; as I doubled over, my jacket was pulled from me, and I felt myself falling to the ground.

There were hands around me, and I was half lifted, half dragged before having my arms released to drop me on my back. I thought my legs were being held—I started struggling when I realized my legs were being tied. One boot to the side of my gut and another in my left arm was enough to still me as I felt my legs being pulled by the rope, lifting them above my head.

As my legs lifted, my back—only protected by a thin cotton Oxford shirt—and my ass dragged across the concrete. My ass lifted off the ground, then my back, and my head hit the solid floor before it too was lifted.

When my eye line reached about knee level, my ascent stopped. There were a few words, a shared chuckle, and I was left swinging by my ankles.

fifty-six

Another car arrived. Bigger. Darker. Cleaner. Good tires—you notice those things when you're upside down and your eye line is low. Better engine. Doors that shut with a reassuring clunk that said, "Made in Germany."

There were voices and footsteps coming toward me. "Leathan, Leathan. You disappoint me." It was too dark—there were strip lights, but once my eyes had become accustomed to the light, I had figured they weren't that bright. It was too cold—I only had a thin cotton shirt, my jacket having been taken. And being hung upside down really didn't put me in the mood for idle chitchat and neighborhood gossip.

Oh yeah. And my lunch had been sprayed across the floor and I would have really liked to clean out my mouth.

"Let him down." It was Gaston Blanc. "And try not to hurt him. If he fucks about when he's down, then you can slap him senseless. But let's try not to break him until after we've asked him some questions."

I was lifted as two of the unremarkable men obediently took the tension in the rope, a third untying the tether before lowering me gently. A hand came out to protect my head as I was delicately placed onto the concrete. The rope around my legs was untied, and a hand offered to help me to me feet.

I shivered and started an inventory of where it hurt. Gut, head, back, legs. My shoulders felt fine—that was the only place without an obvious ache, graze, or cut.

"Speak," said Gaston Blanc.

"Nothing to tell." The fist hit my gut before I could finish the third word, and I fell back. Another stopped my fall, holding me under my arms, readying me for the next blow.

"Really? Do we have to?" asked Gaston Blanc. "Let me give you a taste of how I see things."

I felt my head trying to affirm my agreement, but the muscles in my neck were unwilling to move.

"You went to see Karen Fischer."

I felt my eyes seek out the unremarkable man who had picked me up today. He met my gaze—a slight crinkling of his eyes confirming that was where they had got on my trail. Inwardly I cursed. I had been lax. I wasn't followed when I went to Karen Fischer's apartment so when I left I hadn't checked whether anyone had been waiting for me.

"I'm surprised you didn't get there earlier...although I suppose she doesn't get up much before midday."

"Unfortunately, I didn't have an up-to-date map," I mumbled.

That seemed to amuse him but didn't break his explanation. "After seeing Karen Fischer you then went for a cup of coffee with Marianne. You arrived first, I believe."

I said nothing.

"And let us not forget that you are friendly with—I might even say, *very good friends* with—Émilie, and Tolomush Okeyev would appear to be on your Christmas card list."

The guy behind me moved closer, and another fist landed in my gut.

"Do I need to explain? I'm feeling left out."

Another blow. I doubled over and fell to the floor—the arms holding me had released.

"I thought we had an agreement and now I don't think you're acting in my best interest, Leathan. I think you're more worried about fat man Claude."

I said nothing to Gaston Blanc, the owner of the Irish bar, who stared at me expectantly. The last thing I remember is feeling a boot make contact with my head.

fifty-seven

The line between conscious and unconscious is a fine one.

The journey from one state to the other—particularly from unconscious to conscious—is a strange one. You never know what is real and what isn't. I remember the first time I knew I had been unconscious. I was fifteen and had my wisdom teeth removed. The teeth hadn't come through, but when they had x-rayed my mouth, they found that the wisdom teeth were at an angle and would put out my back teeth when they started moving. This would leave me with a lack of back teeth and with wisdom teeth that were of no use because they were angled.

Hence the surgery—with full anesthetic—to remove the wisdom teeth while I was still a teenager.

A week later, the dental surgeon reviewed his handiwork and took out the stitches. The last words I remembered hearing before I passed out from the pain were, "I'm sorry, I just pulled the knot through your gum."

Consciousness had returned slowly. The surgeon had deputed his assistant to deal with the spotty teenager while he went back to finalizing the arrangements for his weekend, which was clearly a higher priority for him than the welfare of his patient.

Today, consciousness returned quickly. An unconscious awareness of water rapidly turning into a conscious knowledge that a bucket of cold water had been emptied over my head. I felt myself shiver as I tried to sit. "Which one of you pissed in that bucket?" I asked. Some grins, some knowing glances. If they hadn't pissed in that bucket, they were certainly going to piss in the next bucket of water.

I reached a sitting position and pulled my legs up, wrapping my arms around to try to keep some warmth.

Gaston Blanc stood in front of me. Impatient. Waiting.

"Why?" I asked. He seemed confused that I was asking, not answering, questions. "You caused this problem—not me."

He lowered himself to a squatting position and pushed out one leg to steady himself. "I'm down one hundred thousand euros." His eyes bored into me—he could see I had a retort, but he didn't want to hear. "And the best lever I had to control Tolomush Okeyev has gone—he's dead...your friends killed him."

"Not my friends," I said. "Whatever is the complete opposite of friends—that's them."

He snarled and raised himself to his full height, which would have been less impressive if I was standing.

"Do I really need to explain it to you?" I asked.

The snarl softened and a kick didn't follow.

"You knew Pierre-Louis. You had been in contact with him. You told him about his father and what a bad boy his father had been." Gaston Blanc might have shrugged. Maybe it was my imagination. Maybe I was shivering too hard, but I carried on. "You gave the kid information about his father. The unexpected consequence—unexpected from your perspective—was that Pierre-Louis went out and found his sister...his half-sister, Marianne."

The unremarkable men shuffled, readying. Gaston Blanc held up a hand to quiet them. "You also lent Pierre-Louis money. A lot of money. One hundred thousand euros." The hand was still quieting the other men. "The point of giving the kid money was to create an obligation—to create an obligation from Pierre-Louis to you."

He had a look that said "duh—of course, why else would I give a kid money?"

"And with an obligation to you, you would use the son to keep up the pressure on his father so that if, for instance, you wanted a diplomatic favor, then Tolomush Okeyev would be in a much weaker position. Are we agreed so far?"

He shifted slightly. A small movement of his feet, but no attempt to stop me or to rebut the basic thesis.

"You thought you were increasing pressure on Okeyev—you figured Pierre-Louis would be greedy." I snorted. "What you didn't realize was that Pierre-Louis didn't give a shit about the money. When he found Marianne, he saw a sister—the only sister he'd ever known—and he had to do the right thing. She was pregnant, and she was getting no support from her mother or the father, so Pierre-Louis set her up with an apartment and bought furniture for her and his niece or nephew."

The workshop was still.

"And that was your mistake. You can apply pressure to most people, but this kid was far more worried about his sister and her baby than he was about you."

Gaston Blanc squatted again, fixing me with a glare that he had probably practiced over the years. "I'm still down one hundred thousand euros, I've lost my get-out-of-jail-free card, and you keep turning up, fucking things up."

"So why not let me fix things for you?"

He snorted, a grin spreading across his face. The other guys, unremarkable as they were, took their cue and laughed.

"You don't seem to be doing very well so far, Gaston. You seem to be good at finding me—less good at finding you're the root of your own problem." I paused, trying to reason with myself inside my woozy head. The reckless side won. "Let me find your money."

He went to reply but stopped himself, an amused smile forming as if he were dealing with a willful child. He met my eyes, and an unspoken negotiation took place. "Okay, Leathan. You've got twenty-four hours to prove that you're not my problem."

"Car," I said. "I need some transport."

Gaston Blanc snapped his fingers and held out his hand to one of the unremarkable men. There was a shuffling of feet as someone moved closer, and then a car key was dropped next to me. I now had the use of an unremarkable gray Peugeot.

fifty-eight

I turned the heater up to the highest setting and drove the Peugeot hard. When I started to feel some warm air coming, I turned up the fan to blow the warm air faster into the car. It didn't stop me shivering, but I hoped it would dry me out even though when I put my jacket back on all I had done was to create a seal around my wet shirt.

I didn't know where Nesrine and I ate lunch. I didn't know where the workshop I had just been in was. And driving on the right-hand side of the road always disoriented me. I grew up in the UK, I learned to drive in the UK, and I have done most of my driving in the UK. The UK, which—unlike continental Europe—drives on the left. Put me on the right-hand side with a stick shift, and I struggle. My left hand reaches to change. Then I reach a roundabout and want to go left-about rather than right-about, and at the lights, I'm looking for cars filtering left.

And that's before we talk about the wacky new way that traffic is being reflowed around some of the squares, like Place de la République.

After ten minutes driving in the growing early evening traffic, I figured I'd looped around on myself, and the location of the workshop where Gaston Blanc's friends had literally let me hang became clearer.

I had little intention of getting Gaston Blanc's money back—I told him I would get it because that was what he wanted to hear. There was no point in telling him what I knew—the money was spent. But Gaston Blanc was a problem I would have to deal with later. First there was a previous instruction that I still wanted to honor.

I pulled onto a side street and parked, letting the engine run and the heater blow. I wasn't feeling warmer—but I wasn't feeling colder.

I reached for my phone and found my cash. I patted my pockets—my jacket had been emptied and the contents returned to the wrong pocket.

Maybe I was relying on superstition and not science, but I didn't want Gaston Blanc and his friends knowing my number. If anyone was going to have a contact in the phone companies—a contact who would happily disclose my location in exchange for a few bills—it was Gaston Blanc.

The first new SIM card didn't work—I dropped it straight into the gutter. The second new SIM card took a moment or two to find the service. She answered quickly but cautiously, clearly not recognizing the caller.

I told only a small lie.

She said where and when. I plugged the location into the map thing on my phone and propped the handset on the dashboard, then proceeded to follow the instructions coming from the phone, leaning forward and straining to hear the directions while squinting at the small screen.

fifty-nine

The gray Peugeot was warm.

My hair was drying—messy, dirty, but dry enough.

My shirt, under my jacket, was still damp, although with my body warmth, I at least knew that the layer of moisture was warm. Well, warm-ish. Not as cold as it had been.

Me, however. I felt cold.

Not the kind of cold you get in the arctic—there you get cold and die. It's a short, albeit unpleasant process. This cold was different—it was a damp cold, figuratively and literally. It's the kind of cold that gets inside you and nags and nags and nags. Every time you think about it, every time you feel it, your energy saps. Not a huge plunge in energy—just a subtle shaving of one percent of your energy. Enough to get into your muscles. Enough to hurt your bones and joints.

Not enough to kill you, but enough that you will die eventually.

Above the noise of the idling engine keeping the heater blowing, I could hear the clipping of heels. I couldn't see a face, but I could see a body and I could see the brown bag that I now knew was crazily expensive.

She walked past the door and peered through the windshield. Recognizing me, she came back and let herself into the car, cautiously sitting before closing the door behind her.

"That's a nice bag," I said.

"Thank you." Her scowl had been replaced by a look of pride. I hoped she would be equally proud of her baby in three weeks.

"It must be very new—they're only just in the shops, aren't they?"

She was still beaming, but she was able to nod.

"Who bought it for you?"

"My brother."

"So what are you doing hanging out with the people who killed your brother?"

Her face fell. The pride was gone and the scowl was back. "When you called, you said you had my money." And to match the scowl, there was anger in her voice. Anger, or was it desperation?

"No, I said I had a question that might help me find your money."
I counted to three as I let her realize she had been fooled by simple
wordplay. "Why are you with the people who killed your brother?"

"They didn't kill him," she said.

"I was there; I saw them."

"Saw them shoot?" That self-satisfied smirk that we all do from
time to time is never pretty. "They were there for the money."

"What money?" I asked.

"The money from my father."

I could hear my foot tapping—that was me thinking. "So here's
the thing..." I began. "This money. Your father hasn't given you any
money, and he didn't give Pierre-Louis any money."

"But Pierre-Louis had the money." She was indignant. "My
bag." Apparently that was sufficient logic. "Pierre-Louis said there
was money—for the baby—and Nils agreed with me that I should
decide how to spend it. I am the mother."

I tried to ignore the mention of a name. Something in my
subconscious was telling me that all the facts had been presented to
me, but I wasn't putting them together properly.

"So if Pierre-Louis had your money, why did you ask your father
for more money?"

She was indignant, disbelieving I could be so slow. "Because he
should pay. Does he really want everyone at home knowing about
his daughter here?"

"This Nils guy?" I asked. She understood the implication of
those three words and snorted. "How can you be sure it's not just
the money?"

"I'm not stupid," she spat. "I can tell the difference between a
good man and a bad man." She laid a hand under her belly, cradling
her baby as she glared at me.

"Which one is he?" I asked. "The guy with the beard or the other
one?"

She snorted, opened the door, and left.

sixty

I sank down in my seat to get a better view in the side mirror of Marianne walking away, tightly clutching her prized bag, her expensive shoes clipping as she went.

Keeping my eyes focused in the mirror, I let my hand work its way across the underside of the dash, then up the steering column until it found the key. Marianne showed no reaction as I killed the engine.

My eyes dropped their focus and I rolled out of the car, closing the door quietly as I squatted, my eyes just above the bottom of the car's windows. She was still heading away—nothing had broken her concentrated indignation as she clipped up the gentle slope.

I lifted my ass but kept my head down and started to move—following in her direction, passing from car to car, keeping a metal barrier between us.

She didn't look back. She didn't break step. Clip, clip, clip.

I held back as she approached a corner. And then she was gone, but I could still hear: clip, clip, clip.

I straightened and jogged to the corner. Clip, clip, clip.

Slowly, I let my head move out to see more of the street. Clip, clip, clip.

And there she was, approaching a Renault. An old, brown, wedge-shaped Renault. The car that I was kicked out of yesterday. The lights were on, and I guessed they were keeping the engine running too.

She got into the back, shutting the door behind her. The interior light came on. I could make out three figures—her and two others. I knew what she looked like, but I couldn't make out her details in the car, so I stood no chance with the others.

But there was movement. The figures in the car were moving. The lights of the Renault were almost imperceptibly jogging up and down as if the car was bouncing. Later at night, parked in a lovers' lane, and I would have drawn a different conclusion.

Marianne's door opened, and she pulled herself out, shouted back into the car, and slammed the door. Clip, clip, clip. Away from me, away from the car.

There was shouting from the driver. I could see a hand coming out of the window on the far side of the car—the hand was emphasizing the beats of the shouts seemingly directed at Marianne. The engine revved and the tires screeched as the car pulled off, drawing up with Marianne—pacing her as she strode indignantly, occasionally turning back to spit venom at the driver.

The car jerked forward and pulled to a halt, maybe ten yards farther forward of Marianne. Someone got out of the rear passenger door away from me. Maybe female, maybe with scruffy hair, maybe wearing a green jacket—or maybe I was seeing what I expected to see.

She stood, blocking Marianne as Marianne reached the car.

There was a struggle. Green Jacket seemed to have grabbed Marianne's lapels while Marianne was throwing wild but ineffective slaps. Green Jacket moved Marianne toward the open door and pushed her, bundling in after her.

The engine revved. The tires squealed. I stared at the two taillights.

Marianne had made a choice. Maybe not then, but she had made a choice.

sixty-one

Everybody lies.

Everybody.

Not just conmen and crooks. Parents lie to their kids all the time: Yes, Santa Claus exists; of course there's a god, he's an old man with a beard; you're beautiful and clever. The list goes on. Men lie to women—you're beautiful, you're the only one; and women lie to men—where do I begin with that list?

And Claude lies to me consistently. But I lie to him, so in some karmic accounting register, the frequency of lies—if not the mass of lies—balances out. Somehow.

I could have called him. I had basic information that I wished to impart to him: Gaston Blanc has worked out that Claude put me onto him. Simple, straightforward, unambiguous information that I could communicate in a few words. The call would take less than a minute.

But I wanted to see him while I told him.

I wanted to see how he reacted.

I wanted to see the reaction that he couldn't hide. Would he be surprised? Or did he already know? Would he be shocked? Afraid? Relaxed?

And then I could push him. When someone is looking you straight in the eye—when someone is there, in front of you, imposing on your personal space—you react differently. Something primal kicks in—fight or flight. Claude was too fat to run, and he was no good with his fists. But he could talk.

Push him and he talks. Push him harder, and he talks more, talks faster. Push him harder still, and he makes mistakes. Push him even more, and he just says anything—the first thing that comes to his mind.

It had taken an hour for the Peugeot to get me from somewhere north of the Périphérique to the Left Bank. The heater had heated, and I still didn't feel warmer. But it was a preferable way of traveling, and as I opened the trunk and found the toolkit that came with the car, I figured it offered a new range of weaponry.

I took a screwdriver.

Claude was back where I'd last seen him. Same seat, same café, different person, same problem.

I tapped him on the shoulder and looked across to the woman he was talking with. "I'm sorry, Madame, I need him for two minutes."

"Leathan, we're nearly..." Claude spluttered.

"Madame, I'm sorry." I addressed the woman. "Claude."

The fat man followed me to the bar, knocking chairs and customers as he moved his bulk across the room before reaching me. The effort seemed to tire him, and he rested his back against the bar. "What's so urgent, Englishman?"

I moved up close to him—it wasn't hard in the crowded café, filled with the after-work crowd—and stood directly in front of him to shield the sight of the screwdriver I was wielding from the other customers. I let him feel the dull blade of the screwdriver push into his gut. "Did you screw me over, Claude?"

And there it was—the momentary flick across his face. Shock. Surprise. Claude was a master at preparing for confrontation—he had a reaction for every situation. He knew he danced on the edge and he was always ready with a comeback. He had spent so many years telling lies that he was incapable of separating what he had invented from what actually happened.

But every now and then he was presented with something that he hadn't planned for.

And this was something he wasn't ready for. He wasn't expecting me to come here and threaten him. I let the screwdriver release his gut and quickly pocketed it. For perhaps the first time in his adult life, Claude was innocent.

"Shit. I'm sorry, Claude."

"So you should..."

"No, I'm sorry. We've got a problem." I had Claude's attention. "Gaston Blanc knows that we're connected. I'm pretty sure he's figured that you put me onto him."

Claude spat something under his breath. Thought. Then looked up. "How?"

"My guess? Tolomush Okeyev's running out of plays, and we're a way to avoid an awkward conversation." Claude looked puzzled. "I told Gaston Blanc that Pierre-Louis was dead—he didn't know."

Claude's eyes went wide; his lower jaw hung loose—even looser than it usually hung. "That's going to sting—finding out from you that he's not getting information fast enough."

I ignore the insult. "Information about someone he had loaned one hundred thousand euros. Information about someone he was looking for."

"Shit, Leathan."

"What? I didn't tell him—but I didn't deny that I knew your name when he confronted me." Claude's head was slowly shaking— he was disapproving and disagreeing. "They hung me upside down…"

Claude stopped me. His head was still shaking, but there was an indulgent smile spreading across his face. "You might not have noticed, but Gaston Blanc surrounds himself with a bunch of guys who look all meek and mild."

"I am acquainted."

"They're anything but meek and mild."

"I am acquainted, Claude."

Claude sighed. "So why are you making them look stupid in front of their boss? You humiliate these guys…"

"Everyone's allowed a hobby, right?"

"Collect stamps. Look at trains or whatever it is you English do…but don't annoy these men, and don't annoy Gaston Blanc."

"I'll be alright, Claude." Claude seemed unconvinced as I continued. "It's you I'm more worried about."

"Don't worry about me," said Claude. "You're the one in the shit. If they hung you upside down, how did you get away?"

"I said what I had to. Promises were implied, and I think it still stings that I knew more than he did."

Claude straightened himself, pulling his jacket square and making an effort to tuck his shirt into his trousers. "So have you found who killed the kid?"

"Nearly. Probably. But I'm more interested in why he was killed."

Claude chuckled. "A woman?"

I shrugged. "Not in the way you're thinking."

sixty-two

I stepped out of the noisy café.

Noise that was created by people. People who packed out the café. People who gave off warmth and who were also warmed by the café's heating system. Unlike the square, with its sandstone building fronts and its sandstone church standing in the middle of the square.

And while the white noise of people made it hard to hear, it had also given Claude and me some privacy as we talked.

Back on the street, the white noise was gone and the warmth was gone. In their place, the chill of the February evening and the sound of scooters with their revs maxxed out, car horns, people shouting, and sirens—all echoing off the sandstone surfaces of the square.

It took a moment or two to figure my phone was ringing. I'm called so infrequently that I don't expect to be called, and when I hear ringing I always presume it's someone else's phone.

I recognized the number. "Marianne?" I felt the tension in my throat, the tightening of my gut.

"Leathan—you've got to help me." Her voice was a whisper—strained and fast, barely audible over the sound of the city.

I jumped in the car—its nose pointing toward the curb in a row of cars like teeth in the gums of the sidewalk—and shut the door, which barely made a difference to the noise. "Where are you?"

She said something—I couldn't hear what.

"You're going to have to speak up, Marianne. I can't hear. I'll come and get you—where are you?"

The engine of the car moving behind me—a guy desperate for a space—masked Marianne.

"Sorry—where did you say?"

"Near where we met." She sniffed. "And you were right, Nils did kill Pierre-Louis. He says it was an accident when Pierre-Louis wouldn't give him the money."

"I'll call when I get close," I said, firing up the engine of the gray Peugeot.

There was a shriek, and the call ended.

sixty-three

I revved the Peugeot, searching for the light switch—or to be more accurate, searching for the correct light switch.

The car was old enough that there wasn't a sensor to turn on the lights automatically. And it came from a time when no one cared enough to do smart things with the design of switches, so there was something to turn on the lights, something else when I wanted full beam, a switch for the front fog lights, and a separate—different-shaped—switch for the rear fogs. It just wasn't clear which switch controlled which lights.

I revved the car again and threw a few switches, looking at the reflected lights in the café window. I had some light—I wasn't sure whether it was too much or too little, but it was light, so I put the car into reverse and turned to see my path.

The reversing light lit up the car behind me, which was waiting for my space. Waiting, and yet not giving me space to move. Waiting with his front fender about six inches off my rear fender. I hit the horn. It was the third thing I tried after banging the center of the wheel and turning on the windshield wipers—it was the long stalk that also controlled the indicator.

He didn't move.

I hit the horn again and let the car rock backward and forward, balancing its weight on the clutch.

Still no movement.

I got out—the other car's engine was idling—and tapped on the driver's window. The glass slowly lowered, clearing the reflected lights of the small square and reacquainting me with a familiar face. Unremarkable, but familiar. "Get in."

"I'm in a hurry," I said.

He tilted his head back—gesturing that there was something I should see. I put my hands on the car roof, just above his window and leaned forward. I didn't see his hand move, but he grabbed me, pulling me from behind my neck and slamming the top of my chest across the open window.

Something sharp pushed into my throat, finding the soft flesh just beside my windpipe.

"Gaston Blanc has spoken to Mister Okeyev."

I tried to steady myself, placing my hands on the door.

"Mister Okeyev is happy for you to take the fall for his kiddie's death. He says you were there." He paused, the blade making small circles in my throat but not piercing the skin. "You didn't tell us that."

He released me, and I struggled to stand.

"Anyway," said the unremarkable man, "Gaston Blanc just wanted to make sure you're enjoying your first day at school." He threw his car into reverse, skidded as he changed direction, and then drove off. Fast.

sixty-four

For me, driving has always been about getting from one place to another.

Some people take pleasure in the physical sensation and thrill of driving. Others enjoy cars as objects. I'm not one of those people. For me, it's about moving a lump of metal from point A to point B.

Some people can drive fast. I lack that skill. Sure, get me on an open road with no traffic, and I can open up the throttle. There's no skill to that. But put me on a city road rammed with other traffic, and I can move at the average speed that everyone else is moving. I can't do the bob-and-weave in traffic and I'm not one to roar down backstreets—not that I know enough backstreets in Paris from a driver's perspective.

Driving, for me, is a chore, especially in cars with the steering wheel and gear stick on the wrong side, and driving on the right will always feel wrong to me.

I drove as fast as I could—returning from the Left Bank, through the northern half of the city, across the Périphérique, and into Seine-Saint-Denis. A few wrong turns, but eventually I arrived where I had waited for Marianne earlier this evening. I wasn't too worried about the knife that had been held to my throat just over an hour ago, but the driving had wrung me out emotionally.

And that made me feel so pathetic.

"You took your time." It was a male voice when I called Marianne's phone. A male voice—Nils, I guessed.

"Let me speak to Marianne."

"Come and meet her," he said and gave me brief directions. "It'll only take you three minutes."

sixty-five

I did a three-point and drove in the opposite direction, going up the incline where Marianne had walked the last time I saw her. I turned right, mirroring the turn Marianne had made as she went to meet the brown Renault. The brown Renault she had then got out of before being forced back into the car.

Before she disappeared.

Only to make a panicked call to me.

As Nils had told me, the road was straight and was largely residential. After a mile, it kinked left and there were three stores. The shutters down—closed for business, permanently. The corrugated iron fence, with graffiti and posters, was as he had said. I turned right through the gap, catching sight of the poster for the circus he had told me to look for.

The space between two buildings opened into something much wider. Nils had called this a construction site. As a description, that seemed hopeful—sure, there had been a building on this land once, probably a large building—but this seemed like a demolition site, not a construction site. This was more a wasteland littered with old bricks, concrete, and dumped trash—not some beacon of urban renewal.

But however you want to describe it, it was not a place I wanted to be alone.

I tried to convince myself that I was moderately safe—if they killed me, then I was dead; if I was dead, then there was no gain for them. But the logic didn't seem to silence that nagging voice. When you're relying on someone else's greed to stay alive, there's too much room for catastrophic error.

And if I was going to die, then I would really prefer a nobler death—or at least a death not on a piece of wasteland in northern Paris.

As instructed, I drove to the center of the wasteland. As not instructed, I turned the car to face the direction from which I'd come and killed the engine, leaving the lights on.

My phone rang. "Get out of the car—put your hands on the hood." The call ended.

As I hauled myself out of the car, I tried to remind myself: I'm only here because they think there's something I can do for them. I rested my hands on the side wing of the car and waited.

I didn't see anyone, I didn't hear anyone, but I felt my feet being kicked away, and I fell to my knees, my head striking the wing and breaking my fall. Across the hood, I could see enough to know there was a gun pointing at me, and now there was someone frisking me.

"You people enjoy getting your hands all over me. This is the second time in two days."

The snarl close to my ear told me a woman was frisking me. I guessed it was the one with the faded red jeans, but something about the gun unsteadily pointing toward me suggested it was better to focus my attention there and worry less about who was groping me.

"Where's Marianne?" I asked.

"Safe." My eyes were adjusting. I was getting better at recognizing his voice. It was Nils, or at least the man who I thought was Nils.

"Can I see her?"

"Why? Don't you trust us?" The female voice had stepped away. I turned my head and confirmed it was the woman, still in her faded red jeans and green jacket. Her hair no tidier.

I didn't respond.

She continued. "You can see Marianne. You can see her any time you want." She was trying to provoke and was waiting for a reaction.

It was cold, I was kneeling, I had a gun trained on me—loosely trained, by a guy who seemed unable to point straight—and I ached in places I didn't know it was possible to ache. I didn't feel a need to play her game. She blinked first. "It will cost you, of course."

"Of course," I mumbled.

"One hundred thousand euros." She had the tone of someone trying to be casual, but who you know is really desperately excited to reveal a secret. I was disappointed by the lack of imagination.

Nils broke the silence of my not bothering to respond. "This is the car that was outside..." He had recognized the Peugeot I had borrowed.

"I know," she snapped. She had recognized the car too, but seemingly didn't care. "Is she your special lady?" She was trying to taunt. The taunting didn't work. However, the thought that Émilie could be dragged into this was another punch to my gut. No one touched me—but I was winded.

Red Jeans smiled. "It's one hundred thousand for her, too." She paused—the joy on her face, which for once seemed real, wasn't fading. "And if you want them both...well, then it's two hundred and fifty thousand."

She saw the confusion on my face as I did the sums. She knew how my mind was working—buy in bulk, get a discount. She had turned that on its head—pay a premium to get both. At last, someone showed some imagination—just when I didn't need it.

I went to speak, and she stopped me, moving closer and squatting beside me to bring her eyes level with mine. "Grieving mothers—you don't know what she might do; such inconsolable grief makes people do crazy things. Pregnant women—so many complications, so much scope for things to go wrong."

I stopped looking at her. When I looked back, they were gone.

sixty-six

I pushed myself up on the wing of the gray Peugeot, lifting my knees from the hard ground where once a building had stood, but now all that remained was some vague intention to reconstruct something, sometime, somehow.

Away from the river, in a square formed by the faces of buildings never intended to be seen, there was some shelter from the wind, but no protection from the plunging February temperature.

I got back into the Peugeot and turned the key in the ignition, watching the lights flicker as the starter sucked all the energy out of the battery to turn the engine. The reassuring draft of warm air—not as warm as I wanted, not as warm as it would get when the engine had been running for a few minutes—confirmed that the motor was ticking over.

Three rings. Four rings. I waited. Seven rings. Eight rings. I slipped the car into gear and edged it toward the exit, my phone still clamped to my ear. Twelve rings. Thirteen rings. I reached the gate and edged the nose through, careful to avoid any pedestrians. Twenty rings. Twenty-one rings.

I hung up and redialed, letting the car slowly drift along the road I had followed a few minutes ago. At twenty-five rings I hung up, punched Émilie's address into the GPS program, and balanced my phone on the dashboard.

"In seventy-five meters, turn right," said the navigator in my phone. I floored the gas.

It took nearly an hour to reach the green gate. When I pulled up, there was no light at her fourth floor window. I let myself through the green gate, crossed the cobbled courtyard, and slipped through the door that never locks properly.

Two steps at a time left me puffing when I reached the fourth floor.

I dropped to my knees and peered under her door—her door, which must be penetrable because somehow the unremarkable man had managed to penetrate it. There was no light to be seen under the door. I tried sniffing and could make out no new or different smell.

Returning to my feet, I pounded on the door, then waited, pressing my ear to the wood in the hope I could hear something.

All I could hear was the blood pumping in my ears.

I pounded again. Seven rapid impacts between the heel of my hand and the wood.

"Émilie," I called. "Are you in there?" I pounded again.

The door across the hallway, directly mirroring hers, cracked. I turned. Half an eye looked at me through a narrow slit. I tried to calm myself, to let my panic flow out of my body, to appear like a calm and rational person.

"Hi," I said, stepping toward the door. The crack narrowed. I stepped back. The crack returned to its previous width. "Have you seen Émilie this evening?"

When it came, the voice was old and thin. "She left."

"When was this?" I asked.

"When I was coming home." I waited, hoping for elaboration. "They were getting out of the elevator as I got in."

"They?" I asked.

The rising and lowering of the one eye I could see through the slit suggested she was nodding. "Émilie and the girl with red pants."

"Green jacket, frizzy hair?"

"Yes, her."

"When did you get home?" I asked.

"Two, three hours ago." Her voice was apologetic.

"Thank you, Madame." She flinched slightly as I launched myself toward the stairs.

sixty-seven

"I didn't expect to see you again," said the barman. "Didn't they...?"

"They did," I said. "And it was cold and it hurt."

He put a single measure of whisky on the dark wood bar in front of me. "Medicine."

The Shillelagh was more crowded than it had been on my last visit, but as last time, there were no leprechauns dancing and carrying pots of gold, or whatever it is that the small people are meant to do. No one said "top of the morning" or "begorrah" or any other cliché they believe flowed from my Celtic siblings' tongues. No one sung *Danny Boy*, which was a relief.

The barstool was no more comfortable. Indeed, with a few more bruises, it was less so, as I lowered myself and rested on the bar.

"So why are you here?" asked the barman.

"I need to see Gaston."

He paused. "You're sure?" He waited until he had my attention before he continued. "People don't often..." He let the thought hang.

"I'm sure."

He nodded, keeping his eye contact fixed, and briefly raised his right hand. From somewhere out of the gloom in the low light, the dark wood, and traces of green, a man appeared. Dressed in some ways like me—jeans and leather jacket—but otherwise unremarkable.

The barman swiftly slipped away and found another customer. "What do you want?" asked the unremarkable man.

"I need a word with Gaston."

For the first time in my dealings with the man—or the several men who all looked the same—he showed some genuine emotion and laughed at me. Not with, at me. "What? You want to cry because I made you piss your pants."

"When did you do that?" I asked and watched as his joy faded. "I need your help—and I think you might enjoy helping."

He seemed unsure as to whether he should laugh in my face again, get more information, or just throw me out.

"Don't think," I said. "Just go tell him that I want to talk."

The unremarkable man faded back into the gloom and the barman was back by my side, bottle in hand. I put my hand over my glass. "Thanks. One's enough."

"You're still here," he said, as if my continued presence on a barstool in a pub had great significance. "I'm meant to be on their side, but three of them still scare the shit out of me."

"Three?"

"The three brothers," he said. "Joao, Tiago, and Bruno. The Rodrigues brothers if you're looking for the collective term."

Which explained why they looked the same but different and achieved near omnipotent presence. "Their reputation," I began.

"Understates," said the barman. "Offer respect—and if you can't offer respect, then fear."

I nodded slowly. "My problem's more basic. How do you tell the three apart?"

"Smell."

sixty-eight

"I'm cognizant..."

The two unremarkable men—two of three Rodrigues brothers, as I now knew them to be, but I wasn't sure which was Joao, Tiago, or Bruno—stood on either side of the closed door to the windowless room and passed a glance between each other. Unstated, but a sneer. I had tried surreptitiously sniffing them as I entered—they both smelled unpleasant and unwashed. I could discern no notable difference.

I continued, focusing on Gaston Blanc. "I'm cognizant that you've yet to receive a return on one of your investments and you've lost an ongoing source of income."

My somewhat obsequious approach was clearly grating. The small man was probably used to flattery—and probably found that the level of flattery increased with desperation. There were three steel bolts—three inches long, maybe a quarter of an inch thread in diameter—on the table pushed against the once painted white wall, which functioned as his desk. Gaston Blanc shifted impatiently in his chair and picked up one of the bolts, turning it in his fingers.

"I'll get to the point," I said.

"Don't say you'll get to the point," he snapped. "*Get* to the point. Say what you've come to say, then fuck off."

"I'd like to propose a deal," I said.

"I thought," he began.

The side of my mouth twitched.

He dropped the bolt on his table, sat back in his chair, and sighed—the sound of the dropped bolt still echoing in the room. "This deal." He paused, forcing the room silent. "What do you get out of it? No one comes to me with a deal that has nothing for themselves—everyone is a greedy fuck, so what do you want?"

"Nothing," I said.

He snorted.

"I'm asking for nothing for myself. I just hope that maybe one day you..."

He cut across. "You hope that one day we'll be friends."

"I think we're beyond the stage of braiding each other's hair," I said. "In simple terms, I'm asking for an IOU. A possible future favor."

He snorted. "Yeah..." Then he sighed deeply. "Alright... Lay it out for me. What did you come to say?"

"My offer to you comes in two parts: flesh and cash. But there's a third element—time."

Another look passed between the two men at the door.

"First—the flesh. I know who killed Pierre-Louis. I know you don't care about his death—but by killing the kid, they have cut off a source of income for you. There were three people involved in the his death. I will deliver them to you. What happens next is something I'm really not interested in."

Gaston Blanc sat still in his chair, focusing on me.

"The second part—money. You made an investment of one hundred thousand euros."

Gaston Blanc nodded solemnly.

"The value of that investment will be repaid in full." I waited a beat. "I said there was a third element—time. The value of your investment will be repaid within twenty-four hours."

"Last time we spoke you said you were going to find where my money is, but now you're going to give me one hundred thousand euros?" growled Gaston Blanc, unable to keep the incredulity out of his voice.

"No. I said the value of the investment will be repaid." Gaston Blanc's eyes narrowed as I continued. "The kid is dead, which means the investment is worth far less." He twisted his head as if to signal his annoyance, but I continued. "I will repay the value of your investment. I will pay you fifty thousand euros. It's not the full amount lent, but it's more than the current value of your investment. Think of it this way—the money was invested in stocks, and those stocks have gone down, but you get your money before the value falls any further."

He sat silently, his lips tightening as he contemplated.

"As you think about that, let me tell you what you need to do in return."

"I don't need to do anything," he said.

"True. But there's an offer for you to consider—the people who killed Pierre-Louis and a chunk of cash. You need to hear what I want you to do in return for that."

He grunted.

"Émilie..." I waited.

He grunted again.

"Marianne. Tolomush Okeyev's daughter." I waited again.

A small inflection of his head.

"These two ladies are both released from any obligation you may feel they have to you, and will enjoy, shall we call it, *the freedom of the city of Paris*."

The room went quiet, then he let out a mirthless chuckle. "I thought you weren't asking for anything for yourself."

"I'm not. I'm asking for the innocents to be given a free pardon." I fixed his gaze. "It's a small price but a big gain for you."

sixty-nine

"How are you going to lure them?" asked Gaston Blanc, looking at my phone. "They won't be stupid. You can't just call them and say 'meet me here.'"

"They're not stupid," I said. "But they are naïve and greedy. They'll be cautious—but they'll try to double cross me. So far, they've always had an edge on me, and that edge will make them overconfident."

One of the unremarkable brothers grunted.

"They think this is about money. They think I'm playing an angle and will try to steal their money. The idea that someone doesn't really care that much about money is a notion they haven't yet comprehended."

The other unremarkable brother muttered something about me giving him all my money.

"They've asked for money, and Pierre-Louis was killed for money," I said. "They've shown their hand—they've told us what it is they value."

Gaston Blanc sat back in his chair. He looked to the other two men. "He makes a point." He turned back to me. "What have they asked for?"

"They know there's one hundred thousand out there. They know at some point someone had one hundred Ks. That's their starting point. If you'd lent Pierre-Louis a million, that would be their starting point..."

"I thought you said they were greedy," said Gaston Blanc.

"I did—and they are. But they're smart enough to demand a figure that can be met. They could have said one hundred million. They might as well have demanded tickets to Jupiter. Instead, they started at a figure they reckon can be met: one hundred thousand. They think I've got the cash—or I at least know where the cash is and can lay my hands on that much."

"And there is one hundred," said Gaston Blanc. "My one hundred thousand. Why don't you just..."

I held up a hand to slow him. "Because it's gone. It's been spent. There is no money."

His jaw moved, but no words came out.

"And they don't just want one hundred thousand," I said. "It's one hundred for each woman. And two hundred and fifty for them both."

Gaston Blanc threw his head back, laughing. "I like how they think. I like it very much." A look passed between the three men— another line had been added in some unwritten *how to* manual of crime.

"Anything anyone wants to say before I try and set this thing up?" I asked.

Gaston Blanc considered the question. "No." Two-thirds of his cohort of unremarkable brothers followed his lead, acting as if they had made their own reasoned decisions.

I called Marianne's number. "It's Leathan," I said when Nils answered.

He tried to play it cool, but he just ended up sounding like an overexcited kid who was being told he was going to Euro Disney.

"I've got one hundred thousand," I said. "That's all I can lay my hands on at the moment. I'll take Marianne now, and I'll come back for the other one when I've got the rest of the money."

He muttered something.

"Are you changing the deal?" I asked. "You didn't say that I had to pay for them both together."

More muttering—a conversation with a female voice.

"Well, if you don't want the money," I said.

The excitement in his voice had gone. All I could hear was agitation. I looked up at Gaston Blanc—his face showed no emotion.

Nils and his friends had made a decision. "Same place," I agreed. "I'll be there with the money for Marianne—you make sure you bring her. No Marianne, no money. Two hours."

I hung up.

"This is your chance," I said to Gaston Blanc. "This is where you can have a chat with the people who killed Pierre-Louis."

"It's a trap," said what might have been the older of the unremarkable brothers, maybe Joao.

"Of course it's a trap," I said. "For me."

The unremarkable man remained quiet.

"I'm putting myself at risk walking in there. For you, the risk is less. And while they might be considering the notion that I'll be coming with backup, they don't know what you look like or where you're coming from."

"What...?" began the unremarkable brother.

"What if I'm working with them?" I asked, predicting his question.

He half nodded.

"Why?" I asked. "Why go to all this trouble when I could just leave?"

The room stilled. The unremarkable man tilted his head, considering my question.

"Don't you think I could set a better trap?"

The two unremarkable brothers and their employer looked between each other, a conversation continuing by slight eye movements.

"I'm going to need something that looks like one hundred thousand. You must have some cut-up newspaper..."

The second unremarkable brother stood.

"And if you've got a map, then I'll show you where they want to meet."

seventy

I'm not a huge fan of trusting a couple of guys who really don't give a shit about whether I live or die. Expecting them to dash in and save me if things get hairy is maybe not the best way to stay safe when I know I'm walking into a situation where the other guys have guns and have killed an innocent kid. And that's before we talk about the two women they're holding hostage.

If my new BFFs, the two Rodrigues brothers—Joao and Tiago as best I could understand, but one of them might have been Bruno—didn't get there or couldn't be bothered to get there, then the only thing that was going to keep me alive was that I didn't have the money.

It was the second time I'd carried ransom money, and I'd learned from my last experience: People who break the law break the law a lot. They're not amoral in one area but paragons of virtue in another. If they're willing to unleash violence on innocent people, then they'll have no qualms about stealing cash.

And so all I had was some cut-up paper, held together with rubber bands with a few genuine bills on the top and bottom of each of the small stacks.

When I talked with Gaston Blanc and asked for something to look like one hundred thousand cash, I had a vision of waiting a few hours. In reality, he already had a few bundles of fake cash. A bunch of fake bills someone had run off on a colored photocopier. It seemed impolite to ask why he kept so much fake cash, but it seemed to reinforce my view that crime was not a career for honest people.

In the light of his office, the fake bills were obvious. In the dark, hopefully they would be less noticeable, although in my hand, photocopier paper felt different from the paper used for real cash.

If I wasn't thrilled about trusting the unremarkable men to trot in and save me, I was even less enamored with the idea of arriving and just trusting they would know when they were needed. "No need to call," said the slightly shorter brother. "We'll be there." Then there was a vague confirmation—more of an understanding or a suggestion—that there would be no killing while I was around.

Which was as good as saying they intended to kill.

My squeamishness was nothing more than a weakness as far as they were concerned. In fact, it was worse than that—it was stupid. Death was a natural consequence. If you have a shit, then you wipe your ass. Pleasant? Enjoyable? No. But the alternative...?

I didn't want to say that I'd already been present at one death that week, and being present at a second, third, and fourth wasn't something I was keen to do. They shrugged and sent me off in the gray Peugeot.

I pulled the car to a halt on the so-called construction site where I'd stopped it several hours earlier and killed the engine but left the lights. After five or so minutes, there were car headlights coming through the gate. The brown, wedge-shaped Renault lumbered across the wasteland.

The descriptions I gave back in Gaston Blanc's office had been weak—a brown Renault, old style, the model was a 12, I thought. I wasn't sure what else I could add. Looking at the car, I still wasn't sure what else I could add.

The Renault drew up to the side and out of my headlight beam, angled with its lights pointing toward me. The lights flicked, and I got out of the Peugeot, closing the door behind me and keeping the car between me and the Renault.

A light came on in the Renault as the passenger door opened. Nils stepped out. The frizzy-haired woman was at the wheel.

No Marianne.

No guy with a beard.

Their show of good faith was as hollow as my show of good faith.

"Where's Marianne?" I asked as Nils moved toward me.

"Where's the money?" he retorted.

"If you haven't got her, then I'm going. No Marianne, no money."

"Stop." His voice was calm. The gun—which he'd probably been holding since before he got out of the car—was now visible. He wasn't pointing it at me, but he made sure that the headlights from the Renault caught it. With his other hand he indicated I should come around to his side of the car. "Hands on the roof."

I hadn't been aware of the driver coming out of the car, but I was being frisked, again, by someone standing behind me, and Nils had moved to the edge of my vision so that I wouldn't forget there was a gun trained on me.

Having checked my legs and jeans pockets, she moved to my torso and my jacket pockets, pulling out the bundles of cash and laying them on the car roof along with my phone and the few loose bills that I still had in my pockets.

I looked at the bundles. Something in their uniformity and consistency screamed photocopying paper. Even in the dark with only the light from the Renault's headlights, they looked fake.

Satisfied that I had been sufficiently frisked, she moved on to the car, opening the trunk, which was more than I had done in the few hours that I'd had the car in my possession. "You do keep a clean car," she said. Then she moved to the other side of the car, opening the rear door. She looked, then leaned in, letting her hand run over the seats, between the seats and into any nooks, and then along the floor before she opened the driver's door and followed a similar procedure. The glove compartment opened, a hand ran inside to add a touch inspection to the visual inspection she had already carried out.

She looked to Nils. Something passed between them, and he relaxed—the tension dropping from his shoulders, his weight dropping from the balls of his feet and onto his heels—and moved in closer.

"Money," she said, looking at the four stacks on the car roof, reaching for the closest bundle.

"It's what they gave me," I said weakly.

"Are you trying to...?" There was anger in her voice. Nils straightened, lifting the gun to point directly at me, seemingly not seeing that any bullet would likely pass straight through me, killing his compatriot with the same shot. "You think we're that stupid," she spat.

I turned my head to face the woman and waited for my breathing to still, willing my heart to beat more slowly. "This was meant to be an exchange. You've come to the wife-swapping party without a wife...and now you're upset that they won't let you throw your keys in the bowl."

She looked confused.

"It seems I made the right choice—if I'd brought cash, you would have robbed me. And you're getting offended because I wouldn't let you rob me." The confusion was turning to anger.

"Where's our money?" The man with the gun took a step closer.

"Where's Marianne?"

"Just give us our money," he said.

"Or?" I looked back to the woman.

Nils made an odd noise—a slightly strangled, muffled groan. The woman let out a stifled yelp. To my right—near to Nils—a metal object hit the ground.

I looked from left to right and back, then relaxed, releasing my hands from the car roof and exhaling. "Good evening, gentlemen." I would have liked them to appear earlier, but there was something reassuring about seeing the two unremarkable brothers, each with a knife held to the throat of my two interrogators.

The woman moaned. "Stop," I said to the brother. "We need to know where Marianne and Émilie are."

The man with his knife to Nils' throat looked back at me. "You might, we don't." He pushed the point of his blade deeper into the Nils' throat, pulling the skin tighter.

"We all need to know," I said.

"They're not going to tell us," said the man holding the woman. "Are you?" he asked his victim.

"Fuck you," said the woman.

There was a spray of liquid—fluid squirted across the car. Instinctively I jumped away, shielding myself even though my brain had yet to process why I was jumping away.

There was a soft sound, like a pile of laundry being dropped. Not a singular sound like a gunshot, but a number of smaller sounds making up one big sound, and the woman's body fell to the ground at the feet of one of the unremarkable men.

He stood, holding his knife and looking toward the rear window of the car, which was splattered with a dark liquid.

"Stop." I held up a hand to the other man, his knife boring into Nils' throat. It was dark, but it was still clear that the color had dropped from Nils' face as he stared at the lifeless body of the woman. Unbelieving. Uncomprehending. "Really... Just, just, just..." I held up a hand to the other man, hoping for a pause.

I stepped forward and felt myself restrained by a hand on my shoulder. I spun, holding up my hands in an attempt to show I was surrendering. "Please," I said, looking between the two unremarkable brothers. "I've got a question."

The brother who had just dispatched the woman looked back to the corpse as if to say, "These people don't answer questions."

"I need the gun and his phone," I said. The blade cleaner was confused. "The job isn't done with these two—there's a third person. Give me this one's gun and phone, and I'll bring the third one to you."

The brothers looked between each other, and the one who had just murdered the woman walked to the gun, picking it up and casually throwing it to me. Nils looked down, as if indicating where the phone might be. The unremarkable man's hand went into the other man's front pocket and pulled out a phone, which he tossed to me with a vague shrug.

"One question," I said, looking toward Nils. "Are you the father of Marianne's kid?"

A sneer spread across his face, and he made a small movement to shake his head.

"Then there's nothing I can do for you," I said and looked between the two unremarkable brothers. "Give me five minutes before..." Somehow I felt happier not specifying what was going to happen after I drove off.

seventy-one

The car seemed to drive itself for five minutes, pulling its way through the indistinguishable streets of Seine-Saint-Denis, past faceless stores and interchangeable blocks of apartments.

Then the car pulled over. I had my hands at the wheel and my feet at the pedals, but the car made the decision to still itself. The road was quiet—there were a few parked cars outside closed stores. A single car passed and then the road fell quiet again—it wasn't the time or the place for crowds of people to be out on the streets.

I looked down into the foot well in front of my seat. A gun—a pistol. Dark metal, probably forged in Northern Europe. Quite possibly the weapon that ended Pierre-Louis' teenage life, and now it had my fingerprints over it. I didn't like guns, I didn't carry a gun, and yet this could be forensically connected to me.

My impulse was to wipe it clean and throw it.

Something else told me I had taken it for a more important reason.

I pulled out the phone I had taken from the man who had brought the gun—the man who I had left with the two unremarkable brothers who seemed to be taking great joy in their use of knives. A quick scan through the logs confirmed this was Marianne's phone—she had received and made calls to a number that seemed like my number at around the times I had spoken with her. Not that I could remember today's number with any precision.

Since my last exchange with the phone, when I spoke to Nils, the phone had only communicated with one number. I hit the call button and waited as the phone rang.

"Thank fuck, man. You took your time."

What to say?

"Nils, man?"

I sighed audibly. "It's Leathan."

"I'll fucking shoot them." In the background, I heard women squealing.

"Are you the leak?" I asked. "Someone grassed—I know I didn't grass on myself."

"What the fuck are you talking about?"

"You need to take a deep breath," I said. "You're sounding far too agitated and you're going to start upsetting the ladies with you."

"Fuck off. Put me on to Nils."

An old guy with a walking stick—out of place at this time of night—passed me. I pulled the phone tighter and waited for him to pass.

"Your guys were picked up by the cops," I said.

"Bullshit."

I waited, listening to the heavy breathing on the other end of the phone, hoping the adrenalin kick would soon pass.

"Do you hear me? Bull. Shit."

"I'm sorry," I said softly. "I wish I was lying to you. But if you don't want to believe me, by all means go down to the station and ask."

"Bullshit." The confidence in his voice was fading. Had faded. There was now a tremble as he spoke.

"I was there—I saw what happened. Your guys got picked up, but not before they took forty thousand euros."

He made an indistinct sound—the sound you make when you're really not sure about the information that's flowing into your head.

"I gave Nils forty thousand; he gave me his phone in return so I could call and make sure the women are alright. He stepped away to count the cash, and that was when the cops busted in. I ran, but the woman tripped and he went back to help her."

"Fucking Inaya," I heard him mutter. She was dead, but now I had a name. "It's always fucking Inaya fucking up."

"They created a distraction. I got away. They got caught."

I could hear his breathing at the end of the phone. Heavy but regular, and slower than it had been. His heart was beating less fast. He would be less impulsive...more ready to deal.

"I've still got sixty thousand," I said. "Sixty thousand, just for you—sixty thousand for the two women. That's nearly twice what you would have got if there were three of you."

"The deal was two-fifty."

"The deal was no cops and Marianne would be at the exchange—Marianne for the money." I let him think for a moment before I continued. "But things change. Think about it. Sixty thousand, cash. Tonight. As soon as I can get to you. You can leave—you can have this car. You can get out of Paris—avoid the cops, avoid the mess the other two created."

He was breathing—I could hear his exhalation like a heavy wind.

"Come on," I said. "I'm on my own. It's just me...me and sixty thousand. We can do this, can't we?"

Still just breathing.

"Put the phone on speaker so I can make sure the women are alright, and then you can tell me where you are."

seventy-two

Maybe I should have guessed. But I probably would have guessed a lot of other places first and would have tried to find somewhere closer to the café and the street corner where I talked with Marianne.

I got out of the Peugeot, scanned the parking lot, which had many more cars than it did when I had visited that morning, and looked up at the white tower block. He answered on the first ring. "It's Leathan. Do you want to come down and get your money?"

"What? And leave them here?"

"I'll come up," I said, tucking the black pistol into the back of my jeans' waistband, feeling the cold steel against my spine. "But first, let me hear that they're still alive."

"Say hello to Leathan," he said. In the background, three female voices—hesitant, unsure—said, "Hello, Leathan."

Throughout the elevator journey, I kept patting my jacket pockets and the back of my jeans, confirming that the fake cash and the gun hadn't somehow disappeared when I hadn't been paying attention. Left pocket, right pocket, gun. Left pocket, right pocket, gun.

The elevator doors groaned open at the ninth floor, and I stepped out—left pocket, right pocket, gun—following the narrow passage to the front door.

Left pocket, right pocket, gun.

I stood in the place I had stood earlier, ready to knock, then moved to the side. When I had first knocked, I was an innocent. Now I knew there was a man inside with a gun, and the light wood of the door wouldn't do much to protect me.

Left pocket, right pocket, gun.

I stood to the side of the door and reached out my arm to firmly rap on the wood, swiftly withdrawing the limb.

Left pocket, right pocket, gun.

I knocked again. The voice responded quickly, close to the door. "Yeah?"

"It's Leathan." I tried to keep my voice quiet as it echoed in the empty hallway.

The door cracked open. A body keeping its weight behind the door, and clearly less worried about bullets coming in than I was about bullets coming out.

I reached into my pocket and pulled out a stack of cash—the genuine bill clearly visible on the top. He opened the door further—from somewhere under the beard a hand reached out, grabbing for the money. The knock of metal on wood told me his gun was in his other hand.

I pulled the stack away. He glanced behind, then looked back to me. "Just give me the fucking money." And again, a glance behind before looking back at me.

"Do you want the car?" I asked, returning the stack of fake cash to my pocket. I put my hand in my pocket and felt the key for the gray Peugeot.

"Easy," he said, opening the door far enough that I could see the gun in his other hand.

I lifted my hand slowly, pulling the car key, and held it up, rattling it as if that would encourage him. "If you don't..." I shrugged, returning the key to my pocket. Something in his face—as best I could make out under that mass of beard—said that he did want the car, or at least a car.

His looking behind was becoming like a tic. Each time he glanced back, he seemed to be more agitated. I kept my voice low, talking slowly. "I've got something you want. You've got two things I want. Why don't you invite me in and we can sort ourselves out?"

He held my gaze—breaking as he looked back and then refixing—his body motionless in the half-open door. He exhaled slowly and stood straight—spreading his weight between his feet as he let the door swing open. "Come in." He flattened himself against the hall wall to indicate I should pass. His left hand was empty, but his right hand gripped a pistol—similar to the one I had, but I was no expert. All guns look pretty similar to me.

His gaze focused into the apartment, with the occasional flick back to me. I rocked forward as if to enter, then stopped. "You're not going to pinch my bum as I go past, are you?"

"What?" He looked back to me. As his brain processed the question, the center of the beard cracked, revealing yellowed teeth. "I might. But you're not really pretty enough for me."

"Oh sir, you do flatter," I said, turning so I looked at him across my shoulder. I fluttered my eyelashes badly and drew my hands to clasp my heart. I held my hands over my heart, keeping my elbows raised. "It's a very nice bum," I said, stepping forward and over the threshold, looking back at my ass.

His eyes looked down.

I lifted my right elbow and jabbed, making contact with his throat while my left hand reached for the pistol in my waistband.

He wasn't to know that I was right-handed. That said, I was pretty much ambidextrous when it came to guns—I couldn't shoot straight with either hand. But I can punch, and with the weight of the gun in my left hand, I let the grip of the weapon slam into his temple before reloading my right elbow and launching it into his solar plexus.

There was the sound of air rushing from his lungs as he bent forward. I aided his journey, pushing him to the ground, and closed the front door behind us. I stamped on the hand that was loosely clutching his gun, then picked up the weapon and slipped it into my pocket.

"Good evening, ladies," I called. "Could I have a bit of help?"

Émilie was first to reach the doorway, just as my foot was making contact with their fallen captor's gut. He had moaned; my response seemed the only sensible course. Émilie was soon followed by Marianne, standing behind her and looking over the shorter woman. In the background, Karen Fischer was making sounds that might have been whale music, but could have been her complaints as she tried to stand to come and see what the fuss was.

"I'll need something to tie him up," I said to the two women who were likely to offer some practical help. "String, cord, old sheet cut into strips—something like that."

Marianne tapped Émilie on the shoulder and whispered something to her, pointing as she talked. Émilie dashed down the passage, away from us, her slender frame moving with its customary grace.

She was back in a few moments—a sheet in one hand and a kitchen knife in the other. She held the sheet up; her eyes said, "Really?"

"That'll do," said Marianne. "Cut it."

Émilie shook out the sheet and started at it with the knife. Marianne stepped forward, coming close to the bearded man on the floor. "Asshole," she said, kicking him in the side of the head. "You mess up everything."

"What do you want me to do with these?" asked Émilie, holding up the strips of shredded bed sheet.

"You're pregnant," I said to Marianne. "Go and sit down." She looked reluctant. "Keep your mother in there," I added quietly, and Marianne retreated.

"Swap," I said to Émilie, holding the gun by its barrel, the grip toward her. There was a look of confusion...repulsion...on her face. I pointed with my eyes to the man on the floor, then to the sheet, then to the weapon.

And waited.

Her eyes followed the path I suggested, and her brain undertook the same calculation mine had performed. She reached forward slowly for the gun, touching it as if she were stroking a big hairy spider. Her small hand reached around the grip, her slender fingers looking too delicate to be grasping a piece of machinery like this.

When she pulled the gun away, her grip was firm. There was no hesitation. No wobble. She held the gun securely, bringing up her other hand to support her grip, and lowered the barrel to point at the man on the floor.

"Did he kill my son?" she asked.

The man on the floor whimpered.

"No." I pulled the man away from the wall, rolling him onto his chest and straddled him, dropping my weight onto him. "But he was probably involved."

Her foot made contact with his temple, and his head jerked back.

"Not now. Not here," I said. "There will be time." I turned my attention to tying up the man under me.

seventy-three

I dragged the bearded man into the doorway between the lounge and the hallway, then released him. He struggled against the cotton strips holding his arms behind his back and binding his legs together. As he struggled, he rolled, knocking himself on one side and then the other side of the doorframe.

He tried to argue against his predicament, but the gag—fashioned from a leftover piece of sheet—militated against him being able to communicate clearly. Not that I really cared how upset he was.

"Are you alright?" I asked Émilie Dubois as we stood in the hallway, looking down at the trussed-up man. "You, personally; and you, all three of you?"

"I feel sorry for the girl," she said, drawing me into her deep brown eyes, her voice reminding me of what calmness sounds like. "We've had him waving his gun around, and Karen has spent the whole time telling Marianne what a spoiled and selfish child she is. Then when she's not telling her daughter what a little bitch she is—and while I don't love her, in the few hours I've been with her, Marianne has been anything but a bitch—Karen has been demanding money from the girl. She wants what's owed to her, apparently."

"I got the impression she was money focused," I said. "But I didn't see any evidence that she was prepared to earn it."

Émilie shook her head, the dark waves of her shoulder-length hair silently vibrating. "I think the last work she did was when Marianne was born. Even then..." She stopped, pulling her hand over her mouth. "No. That's too uncharitable to say out loud."

"Even then, she shouted at someone else to push for her," I offered.

Émilie blushed and wouldn't meet my gaze. "Perhaps."

"We need to get him out of here," I said.

Her attention was back on me. Alert, but clearly seeing many problems. She was thinking about the challenges of getting a trussed-up man out of an apartment when you've got a fat woman who does no work, a highly pregnant woman who's not really suited for manual labor, and her—who may be willing, but who was built as the complete antithesis to a weightlifter.

"We'll need to untie his legs," I said. She looked sharply at me. "We can't lift him."

She went to speak. Then paused, her eyes suggesting she was running through scenarios in her head. She sighed—the tension seemed to fall from her shoulders. "We can't lift him," she agreed softly.

"Can you hold a gun again?" I asked.

Those calm pools of tranquility that I wanted to dive into registered discomfort again.

"With two of us, he's not going to get away." She still wasn't agreeing. "Just until we get him into the car."

She stared at me silently. There was a noise of uncomfortable shuffling, and Karen Fischer appeared inside the room, examining the trussed-up man who was blocking her doorway. She looked up at me and grunted an acknowledgement. "That sheet," she said.

I reached into my pocket and pulled out a €100 bill, offering it to her. "For your inconvenience," I said. She grunted again, squirreling the bill away.

Émilie looked up at me, her eyes saying, "Like that."

"We're going to take him out of here," I said to Karen. "Can you look after Marianne for five more minutes?"

There was a pause. I guessed Karen was looking for an angle—another way to cast herself as the financial victim who should receive financial recompense...for sitting with her daughter for five minutes.

I stepped forward, resting my foot on the bearded man's arms—which were tied behind his back—and leaned into the room. Marianne sat on the chair I had sat on during my last visit. She looked different—smaller, diminished. She wasn't the independent adult anymore—she was now the child. But the hard shell seemed to have cracked, letting the person underneath look out.

"We're going to take him down, then we'll come back for you," I said. "We'll be back in about five minutes."

She smiled without saying anything. Her mother muttered as she began her shuffle back toward her seat.

"Ready," I said to Émilie.

Her face wrinkled—a noncommittal affirmation. I reached into my pocket and pulled out a gun. She took it, cautiously wrapping her fingers around the lump of metal. Not entirely alien—it was the second time she had handled a gun in a short period of time—but equally, clearly not an experience she was enjoying.

She weighed the gun in her hand, then looked up at me. When she spoke, her voice was firm. "Ready."

I dropped down onto the man lying in the doorway. He groaned as my weight fell on him, expelling the air from his lungs.

"Shhh," I said. "We really don't care."

He tried to speak, but the lump of cloth stuffed into his mouth didn't aid his diction.

"Seriously, shhh," I said. "We don't care what you've got to say— you can tell us when we get to where you're going."

His muscles tightened, and he tried to struggle. I raised a hand and let it lazily fall to slam into his temple. He tried to complain, but slowly became aware of his helplessness and relaxed.

He tried to say something. The sound was still muffled, but the inflections were questioning.

"We're getting you out of here," I said. "That means we're going to loosen your legs so you can walk, but your hands will still be tied." His head moved as if to acknowledge. "And you do understand that we've got guns and we're up high, so if you struggle, either we'll shoot you or we'll open a window and push you out."

He nodded. I didn't believe him, but he was making an effort to appear compliant.

"You're sure you're going to behave?"

The nodding was more vigorous.

I reached and loosened the ties around his legs—enough that he could waddle, but not enough that he could stride. "Remember," I said. "We've got guns—you haven't."

We might have guns. What I didn't know was whether we had bullets, or whether either of us would want to actually shoot the guy. I was happy to tie him up. I was happy to knock him about. But shoot him? That's a different story.

I got off the bearded guy and stood, pointing with my eyes, suggesting Émilie should move away from us and toward the front door. She positioned herself, her gun held tightly in both hands.

"Does he have a name?" I asked as I took my gun from the waistband of my jeans.

"Léo," said Émilie, then smirked. "Not very lion-like."

I pulled Léo to his feet and turned him in the doorway, resting my non-gun-holding hand on the side of his head as I fixed my eyes on his.

"Remember," I said. "One wrong move by you, and..." And I slammed his head into the doorframe.

There was a sound behind me. I looked back at Émilie—there was a pained look on her face, but the gun was held firmly in her hands. When she saw me looking, she pointed back to Léo.

"One wrong move," I said.

He flinched, pulling his head back, and when he saw I wasn't moving toward him, he nodded his affirmation of the conditions.

"Go call the elevator," I said to Émilie. She nodded, looked down to her gun, then back up to me, questioning with her eyes. "Of all people, I don't need to explain discretion to you."

She half-smiled, holding the chunk of weaponry that looked to be about three times the size of one of her delicate hands. I returned my eyes to the bearded man, listening as the door opened and footsteps—light, precise, regular short steps—moved along the hallway outside.

I moved the bearded Léo toward the front door, which had been left ajar, then stopped him, resting my free arm across his throat as I leaned in to whisper in his ear. "Do I need to explain that the only reason that I haven't put a bullet into your skull is because I've got a few questions I want you to answer?"

He frowned. It wasn't disagreement—it was more that he wasn't expecting the approach.

I continued. "You understand what I'm saying—there's a chance for you to get out of this alive." He nodded, but with little sign that he believed me. "But if I need to..." I let him see the gun in my other hand. "If I need to...then all I lose is the answer to a few questions."

There was more nodding.

"In other words," I said. "One of us has got a lot more to lose than the other." I released his throat, looked back toward the living room, and called out. "I'll be back for you in five, Marianne."

I didn't hear the response as I pushed Léo into the corridor, gently shutting the door behind us.

I shoved him toward the elevator. Each pace a tiny step with his half-bound legs, more like a constipated penguin waddling. We found Émilie standing half in, half out of an elevator, keeping it for us. I pushed the bearded man, letting him stumble into the metal box—the wall on the far side stopping him from falling.

He righted himself and fidgeted as we descended. The cage bumped to a halt at the ground floor; Émilie and I both shielded our guns as the doors opened. She stepped into the white lobby first, quickly scanning. "It's clear."

I shoved Léo, who began his penguin waddle again.

Émilie held the front door open, letting the evening chill chew into us. This seemed to invigorate the penguin, who was picking up speed, which made him rock from side to side with greater vigor and increased the distance between him and me.

As he rocked through the exit, he slammed into the door, knocking Émilie, who staggered backward. Still taking short steps, his speed increased as he reached the top of five stairs down from the block.

The penguin was jumping down the steps as I exited. Émilie was sitting on the ground. I offered her a hand up, but she angrily pointed toward the penguin, who was nearing the bottom of the steps.

He stepped off the bottom stair as I reached the top.

I learned the other night—it was a lesson that Nils had taught me—he who has gravity on his side wins.

I jumped, launching myself forward, letting momentum and gravity move my mass on top of the escaping penguin.

As I had done the other night, the penguin collapsed and provided a soft landing. I grabbed his hair, pulling up his head. "Were you not paying attention?" I slammed his head down, feeling the fight under me relax, but the breathing continued.

There was a sound of footsteps at the top of the stairs. Small, delicate, precise. She glided down the stairs and stood looking at us. "Are you alright?" I asked.

She nodded without saying anything.

I slipped my gun into my pocket. "I think Mister Penguin needs his legs tightened."

She frowned.

"The car's just over there. He can bounce."

Her face softened, and I reached over to tighten the bindings around the bearded man's legs before dragging him up to the vertical.

I escorted him to the car—a mixture of bounces and tiny steps—with Émilie keeping a distance, gun discreetly in her hands as she scanned. We reached the parking lot, and I pushed the penguin toward the Peugeot, watching as he looked at each car in turn.

As we reached the gray Peugeot, there was a realization, a double-take.

Then there was panic. He tried to shout. He tried to run. He pleaded. He begged. He dropped to his knees, making strange noises behind his gag and shaking his head.

I looked back to the Peugeot and the realization hit me. "Yeah," I said. "That blood was the last one of your friends who argued."

The noises continued. The head shook. I opened the trunk and turned back to him, slapping his face. Hard. His head still shook.

I stood behind him and pulled him to the vertical. The noise started again, and he tried to run. I pulled him back and landed a single blow in his gut. As he doubled over, I moved to place him between me and the trunk, and pushed him.

He tilted and fell against the car. I pushed harder, flipping him into the trunk, and folded his legs in after him before slamming the lid shut.

"Do you want to wait here?" I said to Émilie. "I'll go and get Marianne."

seventy-four

When I returned with Marianne, I stood between her and the car, blocking her view of the blood spray over the vehicle. I still wasn't certain how close she was to the three who had been responsible for Pierre-Louis' death and didn't feel a need to let her find that they were dead.

"Everything alright?" I asked Émilie as I fired up the engine.

She nodded without elaborating.

"Shall I take the gun?"

Again another nod.

"Will you be okay to look after Marianne for a few hours?"

Her eyes widened; she half-looked to the back seat where Marianne sat, then met my eyes again and nodded.

"Only a few hours," I said.

The nodding was more confident.

There was little traffic as we traversed Seine-Saint-Denis. When we crossed the old city walls ringed by the Périphérique, the city changed. The stark modernism—unyielding white blocks—gave way to Haussmannian consistency: six floors on either side of broad boulevards. The barren emptiness of the outer suburbs was replaced with humanity. While quieter than it would be during the daytime, there were still people around—cars driving, the odd person walking, and municipal crews out cleaning the streets.

We pulled up outside the green gate, and I helped Marianne out of the back seat.

"I'm going to look after you for a while," said Émilie, leading Marianne away.

The younger woman looked to me, her eyes pleading. "It's just a few hours, then I'll explain." Reluctantly she turned, following Émilie. I was moving again before they reached the green portal.

One of the cleanup crews had opened the gate to flush through a gutter. I pulled the car into the side of the road and got out, watching the slow-flowing water divert itself around the near-side tire.

The guys of the cleaning crew—two men with brooms and a third driving the bug-like vehicle—were at the far end of the street.

The two with brooms were a mass of Day-Glo and fluorescence. I cupped my hands and ducked them into the flowing stream, then roughly sloshed water over the rear quarter of the gray Peugeot. A few more sloshes, and then I loosely rubbed at the blood with my hands. I didn't want a clean car, but I didn't need a beacon screaming, "Blood! Blood! Blood!"

I sloshed some more water, rubbed a bit more, and felt my feet getting damp as I paddled in the stream.

Back in the car I looked at my hands—two lumps of a glowing pink at the end of my arms. Two lumps of throbbing, glowing pink, which felt incapable of gripping a steering wheel. I shook them vigorously, willing some sort of life back into the ends of my arms, and tried to grip the steering wheel, which now felt oddly outsized.

I let the car pull off slowly, steering with the heels of my hands while I tried to accustom myself to the sensation of my throbbing hands. By the time I had reached Albert's café, some feeling had returned, and the glowing pink had been replaced by the more conventional yellow and pinky splotches.

The café was closed. The doors locked. A few lights glowed in the kitchen—probably from the fridge and freezer, and maybe a clock. But there were no lights in the living quarters. I tapped on the glass and rapped on the wooden frame of the doors as loud as I dared—at street level, there were stores; the other five floors were all residential.

There was no response.

I scanned, looking for a menu—there was always a menu outside cafés, bistros, and restaurants. I found it next to the door—a typed sheet on Café Albert writing paper. Café Albert writing paper with the address and the phone number.

"You sound rough," I said when Albert finally answered. "Was there alcohol involved?" My voice had a cheeriness I didn't really feel.

Albert grunted and then muttered, "And then her boyfriend arrived." A tragedy of epic proportions in the world of Albert.

I ignored his plight. "I'm outside—are you going to make me wait here all night?"

"Sorry, Leathan, I didn't realize." He hung up.

It took a minute or so before he reached the door. He was dressed in gray sweatpants and a sweatshirt. From the way the shirt was tucked into the pants, I guessed he had slipped these on without thinking before he came to the door.

"I thought you'd be coming," he said as he opened the door, inviting me in. It was warmer inside than it was outside, but it wasn't a comfortable temperature. "Coffee? Something to eat? Come into the kitchen; it's warmer in there."

"Why were you expecting me?" I asked.

"That woman—the one you were with this morning..."

"Nesrine," I offered.

"Tall, a bit flat," said Albert. "She dropped off something for you." He opened the fridge door and scanned—looking left to right, dropping a row with each pass.

"There," he said. "Tarte au citron. It's good—try it." He passed me a plate and scrabbled in a dark recess, producing a fork, then disappeared for a moment. "Coffee's on," he said as he reappeared, the sweatshirt now having been removed from his waistband. He dropped a white envelope in front of me that looked as if it contained a paperback book. "From the woman."

"This is good," I said, indicating the lemon tart and ignoring the envelope. "I should drop in when you're closed more often."

He half smiled. "Yeah...that being closed...how can I help you, Leathan?"

"I wouldn't inconvenience you if it didn't matter—especially not in the middle of the night—but I need my money," I said.

"Okay," he said. There was a hesitancy in his voice. He saw my concern. "Most of it is easy, but I might be getting down to small bills if you want it all now. I can go to the bank as soon as it opens and get some larger denominations."

"Time, unfortunately," I said.

"Right," he said. "Wait here, and I'll see what's in the safe."

I finished the tart and opened the envelope. Nesrine was a mind reader—it was Pierre-Louis' notebook. I pocketed it and pulled out my phone.

"Kasym, it's Leathan." If he had been asleep, he gave no indication. "I need to see Tolomush. Now. And I need some cash."

He muttered something. I checked the time on my phone and calculated. "That's about ninety minutes. Can we meet sooner?"

He demurred and suggested a meeting point.

"That's near Place de la Bastille, right?" He confirmed. "I'll see you there."

As I hung up, Albert walked into the kitchen. "Two thousand," he said, putting a stack of bills on the counter. "The rest is going to be in much smaller denominations." He wandered out of the kitchen again.

"Claude?" I had woken him. "Leathan." He was too tired to swear at me or to try to get a rise out of me by calling me Englishman. "I need money—all of the money you're holding for me."

He tried to argue.

"I need it now. All of it." I was firm and unimpressed as he tried to explain. "Four AM, your place," I said.

He said something that wasn't a no and hung up.

"It's going to be five hundred in fives and tens," said Albert, returning with a stack of bills, counting them into piles of one hundred euros. When he had counted out the fifth pile, he looked up. "Do you want to check?"

"No."

I wasn't sure whether the look Albert gave me was pleasure that he had been trusted, pleasure that he had shortchanged me, or a thought that he could shortchange me in the future if he needed.

"What do you need the money for?" he asked.

"A debt."

Albert nodded knowingly. "You've got to pay."

I didn't want to tell him that I didn't have to pay—it wasn't my debt. In reality, it wasn't even a debt—it was extortion by another name, and this money wasn't about settling the extortion, this was about making a show. This was about offering respect.

"Do you want me to come with you?" asked Albert.

I contemplated telling him why I didn't. I contemplated telling him about the man in the trunk of the car parked outside his café. I contemplated many things, but in the end I just said, "No, I'll be fine. Thanks."

Albert nodded knowingly, even though he didn't have a clue what he was agreeing with.

"One small favor," I said.

"Sure." Albert brightened.

"Cleaning stuff. Can you let me have a cleaning spray and some paper towels...and maybe a trash bag or two?"

"Sure," said Albert, shrugging. "But first you need some more food."

seventy-five

Nico was out within ten minutes of my call. "Hey, Leathan." It was the same courtesy that he probably extended to the guests of the hotel. Some might find his approach to be false, over cheerful, but so often the pleasure of meeting a fellow human was a matter of joy for my Italian friend.

His tightly curled hair wobbled as he shivered, feeling the chill of the February night. "Will summer ever come back?" he asked.

"Yup," I said. "And then we'll bitch about how sweltering it is. All the Paris residents will shut up their homes and go south, and you'll just be left with a whole bunch of idiot tourists who are happy to drink unpleasant beer."

Nico nodded. "Yeah, you're right." Then he had a thought. "Do you want a beer?"

"I've just had enough coffee to float a battleship, so no thanks."

Nico was continuing to nod. A slow forward and back tilt of his head. I suspected this was a habit he had developed in the hotel. If he kept moving like this, then the guests he interacted with would assume he was agreeing with them. Even if the words coming out of his mouth were not what they wanted to hear, his body language would still be saying yes.

The Italian handed me the envelope I had left with him that morning, when Nesrine Walter had been driving me.

"Thank you," I said, taking the envelope.

Nico frowned. "You're not leaving anything?"

"I am leaving one thing," I said. Nico relaxed in the comfort of having successfully predicted someone else's needs. "I'm leaving a debt."

Nico was confused.

"I am in your debt and I'm out of cash."

Nico's face fell. This was preferable to explaining how much cash was in the envelope and my reasons for not slipping him a bill or two.

"And that debt will accrue interest," I said. Nico's face brightened.

I returned to the gray Peugeot and paused, looking at the trunk. I thought about going back and asking Nico for some water for

Léo. Then I felt the guns in my jacket pocket—one that had been pointed at me, and the other that had been pointed at Émilie and Marianne.

I'm all in favor of kindness and the whole do-as-you-would-be-done-by thing, but I think that once the waving-guns-at-you line has been crossed, then it becomes acceptable to be less worried about the welfare of someone in the trunk of your car.

I fired up the engine and felt the heaters wheezily blow out near-warm air.

I scanned the road, looking for anyone watching me. In front, behind, double-checked the mirrors—there was no one. I tore open the envelope and, without checking, transferred the bundles of cash directly to my jacket pockets.

I slipped the keys into an outside pocket and then removed them, searching for one particular key, which I slipped off the ring. The ring of keys went back to my pocket, and the individual key slipped into my jeans.

Finally, I pulled out Pierre-Louis' phone—an old-style brick with its battery that I had detached. I couldn't figure a use for the phone, so I dropped it back into the envelope, rolled over the top, and dropped the envelope into the first dumpster I passed.

seventy-six

The Marais district, close to Place de la Bastille. A small side road, off the road that was already off the main route through the district.

I checked my phone again. Five minutes had passed. No missed calls. Five minutes, which was five minutes after the previous five minutes, after the previous five minutes.

Somewhere behind me, headlights. Bright. Cutting. German efficiency to bring light to the back streets of Paris. The Mercedes drew level. Kasym Aitmatov looked across, recognized me, and backed his car into the space behind me.

The big Kyrgyz and I got out of our cars at the same time, synchronizing the closing of doors. He raised his eyebrows. I wasn't sure whether that was an acknowledgement of the lateness or his amusement at the battered Peugeot I was driving. He put his hand to the handle of the rear door and waited as I walked over.

"You can get into my car if you want to stay warm," I said, offering him the key. "Fire up the engine to keep the heater running."

Aitmatov seemed amused. "My job is to look after the diplomat, not to protect your car." He opened the door, and I slipped into the rear of the Mercedes, which was warmer than the Peugeot. Indeed, it was probably warmer than the Peugeot had ever been.

"Mister Wilkey," said Tolomush Okeyev, his voice slightly slurred. He was lounging back in his seat, seemingly unable to focus with his eyes in constant, albeit slow, motion.

"Good dinner?"

"Mmm. Very."

"Wine?"

"I only carry spirits in the car," he said. Something told me he had used that line before and would use it again. I wondered whether I should tell him it wasn't funny.

"No. I meant, did you have some wine with your dinner?"

"Very good wine," he said, almost stammering on the V of very. "But then..." He seemed to will himself to be less affected by the alcohol, and became more alert. His eyes—fresh and clear—locked on me. His voice regained something, but not all of its normal abruptness. "While I'm grateful for the feedback—and it is true that I did ask for regular reports of your progress—it's starting to feel a bit like you think I work for you, and not the other way round."

"I'm sorry if I've let you feel that way," I said. "But this is important, and I didn't think you'd want me to make the decision about when it would be an appropriate time to tell you."

"Appropriate time?"

"To tell you what happened to Pierre-Louis," I said. "We knew when and how he died. I now know why he died." I paused, watching as he took in what he was about to hear. "If you want me to come back tomorrow morning...to tell you in somewhere that isn't...well, isn't a car parked on a side street in the Marais...at three-thirty in the morning."

When he spoke, his voice was soft. "Just tell me."

I sat up straighter and turned to face him. "Pierre-Louis found he had a sister—Marianne. Gaston Blanc led him there."

The diplomat listened. He had the look of someone who wanted to ask questions, but who knew that asking questions would just delay hearing what he wanted to hear.

"Gaston Blanc's intention was not to introduce Pierre-Louis to Marianne. He just wanted to cause some trouble for you and to find a new way to apply pressure to you. Blanc figured that if he could get Pierre-Louis into a position that he had an obligation to Blanc, then Blanc would have another way to encourage you to help him."

Tolomush Okeyev's face darkened.

"So Gaston Blanc stumbles in and tries to cause you trouble by telling your son about your past—and the consequence was that Pierre-Louis found his half-sister, Marianne. But Pierre-Louis didn't just find Marianne, he found that she was pregnant and alone."

The diplomat frowned.

"Marianne's mother would happily suck the life out of her own daughter. She expects Marianne to provide for her. There is no maternal instinct there."

The diplomat bit his lower lip. "I'm sorry."

"Gaston Blanc gave Pierre-Louis newspaper clippings and photos. He told him about his sister. He gave him money, too. What better way to influence the kid to turn on you—give me dirt on your father, and I, Gaston, will release you from your debt." The diplomat nodded slowly as I continued. "But Pierre-Louis wasn't thinking that far ahead—he just saw a sister who was pregnant and needed help. He was being offered money, and he could see where the money was needed."

A scooter fizzed past the car. I looked out at Kasym Aitmatov, who was totally focused on the potential threat as its noisy buzz of an engine echoed along the narrow street.

"Trouble was—if I'm being charitable—Marianne had been conditioned to grab any money that was on offer without thinking. And with money, she found new friends—she felt like the ugly kid at school who had just been let into the cool kids' gang. But..."

The diplomat talked across me—his voice barely above a whisper. "But the cool kids were only interested in her money. And it was those cool kids who came to me demanding more."

He paused, letting the interior of the car fall silent.

"They didn't just try to get money from you," I said. "They tried to get money from Pierre-Louis. They figured there was one hundred thousand euros out there..."

"One hundred thousand?" His voice louder than he intended. The surprise revealed more than he wanted to reveal.

"That's how much Gaston Blanc gave Pierre-Louis."

The diplomat slumped back into his seat.

"Marianne's new friends knew there was a sum of cash worth having, and Pierre-Louis soon understood that these people were after the cash for themselves. He twigged long before Marianne did. And once he twigged, he put the money beyond everyone's reach." I paused, waiting for Tolomush Okeyev to take in the details and meet my gaze. "Pierre-Louis put the money in a place that even he couldn't get to it."

There was movement on the diplomat's face—a look of something between admiration and pride.

"You will understand this led to a situation where Marianne's vultures became more frustrated. When they couldn't get money in other ways, they started to demand it directly from Pierre-Louis. Pierre-Louis wouldn't—couldn't—hand over the money. That money was to provide for his unborn niece or nephew. On Monday night, Marianne's so-called friends went to confront Pierre-Louis. They took a gun, and there was an argument. The gun went off, and Pierre-Louis died shortly after I arrived."

The car was silent again. A tear had formed in the diplomat's eye. When he spoke, his voice was trembling. "I want justice... I want justice for my son. He was trying... No, he was *doing* a good thing, and they killed him for that."

"Justice is coming," I whispered.

He looked up, questioning.

"There were three so-called friends who attached themselves to Marianne. One is dead—I saw her killed tonight. A second... He's probably dead by now—or if he isn't, then he'll be pretty close to death."

The diplomat leaned forward, as if he wanted to hear more.

"What you don't know..." I said.

He understood. A single bob of his head in confirmation.

"The third person is in the trunk of that car," I said, pointing to the gray Peugeot in front of the Mercedes. The diplomat raised himself to look through the front windshield. "You can have a go if you want, but I suggest you don't. Your hands are clean, and what I think's going to happen to him will probably hurt a lot more than anything you can devise."

He released himself from looking at the Peugeot and relaxed back into his seat. "And Marianne? Was she to blame?"

"She was guilty of stupidity. Greed. Poor judgment. Wanting friends. Having a bad mother—although that may be rather harsh. Perhaps it might be more appropriate to say she's guilty of having a mother who was herself a kid when she became a parent, and was left alone not knowing how to look after a kid."

Tolomush Okeyev stared at me. He understood the implication of what I said and was calculating his share of the blame.

"We make choices—things happen that we don't expect," I said. "And now you're going to be a grandfather."

He seemed to be about to tell me I was wrong, then paused, processing the new information, as if making the link between his unacknowledged daughter's pregnancy and his status.

"You need to get past the problems Marianne has caused and behave like a grandfather. The kid—your grandchild, who by the way is due in three weeks—will need some stability and support. You might need to spend a bit of cash here or there. Not big lumps, but small drips, directly for the child until Marianne and her mother can be trusted. But that's not a conversation for today—and that's not a decision for me."

I watched—Tolomush Okeyev sat in silence, still processing the fact that he was going to become a grandfather in three weeks.

"I've got a few last expenses that I need to meet," I said.

"Yes, yes," he said, breaking away from his daydream. "Kasym Aitmatov said you needed money—he's got all we had in the safe. Twenty-something and change. He can get you more after the banks open."

"It'll do," I said, putting my hand on the door handle.

He reached out, resting his hand on my arm. "My son is dead, Leathan. I want more than just three stupid kids dead."

"You've got a grandchild—that's more," I said. "Beyond that, unless you want to burn down Paris, there's not much more to be had. However, I think your relationship with Gaston Blanc needs to end tonight."

"Then I don't think you know Gaston Blanc."

"I think we will find that he is a gentleman with whom we can reason," I said, letting myself out of the car.

seventy-seven

The Mercedes pulled off as I checked through the cash the diplomat's aide had given me. It wasn't that I didn't trust Tolomush Okeyev—I wanted to know what I had. Adding what I had retrieved from Albert and Nico, I was just shy of 35,000 euros. Claude was holding more than enough of my money to get me to 50,000 euros.

At nearly 4 AM, the drive to Claude's was uneventful. From the side street it took me less than a minute to reach Place de la Bastille, from where it was a short trip to the river. I crossed la Seine at Pont de Sully touching Île Saint-Louis, and as I reached the Left Bank I was at the edge of the Latin Quarter, Claude's home territory.

I parked the Peugeot half a block from the fat man's apartment and killed the engine, then waited, listening to whether the passenger in the trunk was going to start wriggling. And if he wasn't going to start wriggling, then I wondered why he was being so quiet.

Both details I could check at my next stop. For now, I needed to get the balance of the cash to fulfill my deal with Gaston Blanc.

The keypad for the door onto the street was pretty much like every other keypad in Paris. I'm sure there are new ones, but every one I have encountered seems old, with a tarnished back plate and sticking buttons. And of course, the advantage of keypads is that you don't need keys—you just need to know the number.

Or wait until someone else passes.

Claude had told me the number, and as I walked under the arch and into the courtyard, the similarity between his apartment and Émilie's struck me. Then again, it was probably similar to every other apartment built in Paris during Baron Haussmann's time.

I let myself into the stairwell off the courtyard. Unlike Émilie's apartment, this door did close properly, but again, it was protected by a keycode, so I was able to pass.

I rapped on Claude's door, quietly so as not to wake the neighbors.

No response.

No response and no light under the door.

The fat man had probably fallen asleep again.

Claude might be a bachelor, but he had a cleaner who visited regularly. And cleaners need access. Access to an apartment requires a key, and to get a key to the cleaner there are two options: Give the cleaner a key or leave a key for the cleaner.

I looked to the side of the door. Claude had taken the sensible option. Rather than expect a cleaner to carry bunches of keys—all individually labeled for each client—Claude had fitted a small key safe, big enough for two or three keys and no more. You could find these key safes outside apartments all over Paris, and they all worked the same way: a four-digit combination lock.

Ten thousand different combinations: 0000 through to 9999.

Not a huge impediment to a determined burglar, but sufficient enough of a pain to distract a casual thief and send them looking for an easy window to scramble through. Sufficient enough of a pain to annoy me. I didn't want to spend the next hour trying the combinations because the fat man had fallen asleep and I was too polite to wake his neighbors with my banging.

I offered a silent prayer to the gods of key safes and lockboxes that Claude's cleaner did what most other cleaners did and hadn't jumbled up the numbers.

3847.

I moved the four tumblers down one: 4958. No luck. I moved them up one: 2736. No luck. Each digit up one. Each digit down one. One digit up, one down. One digit down, one digit up: 2938. The key safe opened.

Claude is a bachelor. Claude is a bachelor with many faults. But one fault I don't expect is an unpleasant smell—especially since he has a cleaner.

It wasn't an all-pervasive smell, more the lingering hint that a bad smell had passed through.

The kind of smell that would be hidden if Claude kept flowers or used scented candles in the bath. The kind of smell that would probably be hidden by tomorrow's aftershave, and in any case would have dissipated before it was time to shave.

But the odor was here, now, and out of place.

I reached inside the door, feeling for the light switch, and shielded my eyes as they became accustomed to the glare.

The bathroom door was open, so I started there. As expected, Claude was not present. There was evidence that he had been through—a damp towel on the floor and a small heap of dirty clothes, but nothing else. The kitchen was equally empty of Claude, but also showed that he may have passed: a dirty coffee cup.

I reached into the bedroom and turned on the light, pausing for a few moments to allow Claude to compose himself.

The room was comparatively fresh and tidy, with no unpleasant smells and no heaps of clothes. The bed had been slept in, and someone had got out of bed, leaving the top cover turned back exposing the under sheet, which was crisp and white.

Still no Claude.

There was one room left: the lounge. I turned on the light and stepped in. The smell—oily, musky, dirty—was strongest here, but I was still left with the feeling that the source had gone, leaving the memory of the smell.

I scanned the room, looking for the source. It felt like a double take as my eyes were drawn back to Claude. He was sitting in round-backed leather chair—one of four that were probably intended as dining chairs, not that he dined in his apartment. He was wearing a robe, but the robe was open to reveal an expansive and hairy gut flopping over his underwear.

His head lolled forward and under his throat, streaking down the loose skin on his chest, was a broad river of blood, which seemed to have stopped flowing and might be drying around the edge.

"Shit," I muttered, pulling out my phone and dialing. "Can I speak to Gaston Blanc?"

I wandered back to the bathroom, kicked the pile of discarded clothes, and picked up a shirt.

The guy on the other end of the phone came back to me. "He's not here."

"You can pass a message," I said, moving into Claude's bedroom and wiping the light switch, looking for anywhere else I might have touched. "This is Leathan Wilkey. Tell Gaston Blanc I've received his message, not that it was necessary. I've got his third package for him. I'll meet him at the workshop as soon as he can get there."

I hung up and continued to wipe the surfaces I had touched before letting myself out.

seventy-eight

I killed the speed of the gray Peugeot and let it crawl along the loose gravel. The track looked familiar, but I'd only been there once, and for my arrival I was hooded, while when I left I didn't expect to be back.

There were several industrial buildings. All old and twenty or thirty years away from their last coat of paint. All disused—or apparently disused—and all of a similar cheap construction with a concrete skeleton. However, one showed signs of life, with a weak light pushing out from under the roll-down shutters. The collection of cars on the narrow strip seemed to congregate around this workshop.

The Peugeot skidded as I pulled it to a stop.

The workshop door wasn't properly shut. It creaked as I pushed it, stepping into the space that might have looked more familiar if I was upside down.

"Did you forget your needlework?" The strip lights hadn't been switched on, but there was light in the space. The voice had come from a gloomy corner with three men warming themselves around a brazier.

One moved away from the heat source, allowing me a better view. An unremarkable man, although which of the three unremarkable siblings, I wasn't sure. He didn't say anything more; he just looked slightly surprised to see me. Or maybe he was disappointed to see me.

"I'm meeting Gaston Blanc," I said. "He's expecting me."

The unremarkable brother looked behind him. One of his siblings pulled out a phone and made a call, talking in a low voice. The caller returned his phone to his pocket, then nodded to his brother. The sibling in front of me returned his stare to me, wordlessly questioning.

"I've got a present for him. It's in the trunk," I said. "I should probably roll the car in." The other man stared. "It would ruin the surprise to look at it out there."

He sighed and turned away from me, moving toward the central shutter. There was a rattling of chains and then a metallic ripping sound—a low-pitched saw echoing inside the hard surfaces of the workshop—as he tugged the chains. Slowly the shutter began to move, squealing with every millimeter it moved.

When the shutter had raised to about my waist, I ducked under and fired up the Peugeot. I eased the car back and forward to get a better angle, then swung it into the workshop, bringing it to a halt in the middle of the open space. The shutter was nearly closed when I got out of the car.

I pointed to the trunk. "Do you want to see?" I asked, my voice barely audible above the squeal of the door and the buzz of the chains.

The unremarkable man by the shutter ignored me, finishing his task. As the shutter banged to the concrete floor, he turned to me and pointed to an old wooden chair by the wall. I hesitated for a moment. He wordlessly repeated his instruction, pointing from me to the chair, and at the chair, his finger motioned down.

I went to the chair and sat. And waited.

The unremarkable brothers returned to the warm brazier.

After about fifteen minutes, one of the unremarkable men twitched, like a dog hearing a distant whistle.

I could hear nothing.

But the other two agreed with their brother's assessment. Like athletes readying themselves for a race they started moving, stretching, and shaking out muscles. One of the brothers went to the door—from the sound of footsteps crunching gravel, he was shuffling just outside the entrance.

Slowly, the sound of a car became audible. A low engine rumble and big tires on the loose gravel until the engine drew level and closed off. A car door opened and closed, and there were footsteps over the loose surface.

Gaston Blanc looked tired as he stepped through the door. I stood—I figured I should make a show of offering respect. All it did was remind me that he was shorter than me.

"I've come to conclude our business," I said, moving toward him. He met me at the rear of the Peugeot and looked up at me, waiting. "He's in there." I pointed to the trunk. "Do you want to see?"

He shook his head, then looked around. One of the unremarkable siblings, who were now standing in a semicircle around us, stood forward, holding out his hand. I dropped the Peugeot key into the moist palm.

"Any relationship you feel you may have had with Marianne is now concluded," I said.

Gaston Blanc nodded.

I reached into my jacket pockets and pulled out the cash—legal tender, not the photocopies he had given me—laying the bills in small stacks on the flat trunk of the gray Peugeot.

Gaston Blanc surveyed the piles. "That doesn't look like fifty."

"It's not," I said. "It's thirty-five...thirty-six..."

"We...you said fifty."

"Yeah. And Claude had fifteen of mine, which added to this makes fifty." He frowned slightly. I continued. "It's not on me if you chose not to take the money from Claude."

A look passed between Gaston Blanc and one of the siblings. The sibling turned and left. There was the sound of footsteps outside, and then a car started. It moved over the gravel swiftly.

"You didn't need to do that to Claude," I said as the sound of the high revving engine faded.

"I did. His tongue was too loose."

We stood in silence, staring at each other. He spoke first. "Are we finished?"

"Nearly," I said. "Any debt or obligation you may feel that Émilie had to you has now been settled in full."

He grimaced, his chin pushed forward—I guessed he was running his tongue inside his teeth—and then he nodded.

I reached into my pocket and lifted out a gun. There was a scrape as a foot slipped, trying to get some traction. I felt an arm around my neck, a blade at my throat. Another sibling took the weapon, and the tension around my neck diminished.

"There's another after this," I said and waited before going for the second gun. The constriction around my throat tightened, and a hand went into my pocket to take the second weapon. "No more guns."

Gaston Blanc looked past me, across my shoulder—a dismissive sneer—and the tension on my throat released. From the breathing and the sour smell, I knew the sibling was still close, and if he was close, then he was sure to have a blade in his hand.

"The larger of the guns is the one that killed Pierre-Louis. I figured it might be of some use for you one day. The other is the weapon our friend in the trunk was waving around last night."

Gaston Blanc stared at me, questioning.

"They're no use to me," I said. "And if you can't find a use for them, then I'm sure you know of a suitable charitable institution that would be pleased to receive a donation."

The hint of a smile crossed his face. As the smile faded, I continued. "Tolomush Okeyev. His son was killed. His son was killed because of something you started."

The workshop was silent. The oxygen seemed to have been sucked out, and the temperature—a little over freezing when I arrived—had dropped by several hundred degrees, freezing the features of the other men.

"I think your business with him is also concluded. Permanently."

He went to speak.

I cut across him, speaking slowly, making sure each word had resonance. "His son was killed." I watched his breathing and continued. "There's not a price you can put on that. The boy is dead. You didn't kill him, but you need to accept your role in his death."

He went to speak again. I held up a finger. He looked at the finger as if ready to rip it off, but then relaxed and nodded, seemingly accepting my assessment of the situation.

"And now I need something from you," I said.

He looked annoyed, as if a pesky gnat were buzzing him.

"Furniture," I said.

"Furniture?"

"A sofa. A bed—with bedding. A TV."

"Yeah," he said, not sure where I was going with the conversation.

"I need some furniture—it doesn't have to be new, but it has to be reasonable. It has to be clean. I need it for a few weeks."

"Then go to Ikea," he said.

"I need it in the next two hours." I said. "You're not telling me that you had Claude killed because he blabbed your name, but that you don't have the resources and organizational skills to get some very basic furniture delivered to an apartment in the next two hours."

Blanc grunted.

I turned to the unremarkable sibling behind me. "Get me a piece of paper; I'll give you the address." A small pad and stubby pencil were thrust into my hand. As I handed it back, I said, "Get the key from the guy next door—his name's Bastien, I think, it's all down there—and once you're finished, give the key back to him."

I looked back to Gaston Blanc; he seemed to be readying himself to leave.

"One last thing," I said. "I need to borrow your car for a few hours."

He laughed. "You think..."

"I don't think. I just need to borrow your car." I let the request linger. "What I know is that I've shown I am sufficiently reliable that you can trust me with a lump of metal for a few hours." I held out my hand. "You'll have it back before lunchtime."

He shrugged, pulling out his key. "Lunchtime today?"

"Yeah. I can drop it here or at the Shillelagh."

He pointed to the ground.

"It will be here by lunchtime. In fact, let's be more precise. Before midday."

seventy-nine

Blanc's Mercedes didn't feel as impressive as Tolomush Okeyev's Mercedes, but the car was still a far more pleasant vehicle to drive around Paris that the old Peugeot, although it took a while to accustom myself to the additional girth.

I found a space outside the apartment block in Belleville. To me, it still looked like a huge white lump at the top of a hill, but now I could see how Pierre-Louis had come to his decision, and it did seem a good choice.

I carried the cleaning spray and other pieces that Albert had given me, and which I remembered to recover from the gray Peugeot just before I left the workshop. The workshop where I had left the man with the beard who I first saw sitting across the street from where Gaston Blanc's Mercedes was now parked.

The elevator pinged as it discharged me onto the fourth floor.

It was early, and clearly too early for Bastien as I let myself into the apartment, dumping the cleaning materials on the kitchenette counter before closing the door.

The dried blood was as I had last seen it. I tore off a few sheets from the roll of paper towels, dampened them in the sink, and placed the wet mush on top of the dried blood, leaving it to soak before I set to work with the spray cleaner.

I began just inside the front door, working from left to right, spraying every black streak where fingerprints had been lifted before cautiously wiping away the black residue. Black grit seemed to embed itself where the paint strokes hadn't been smoothed and needed extra spray to flood out the last few specks.

By the time I returned to the dried blood, it had been moistened sufficiently to lift off the flooring, although the trace in between the laminate boards seemed impossible to move, even with Albert's magic spray.

I spent another thirty minutes filling trash bags with paper towels and then admired my work. A career as a cleaner didn't beckon for me, but if you didn't know better, then the place probably looked alright, and by the time there was some furniture, the last few traces of black powder wouldn't be noticeable.

I was stuffing the trash sacks into the rubbish chute when I heard Bastien's door open.

There was a brief look of confusion on his face—he recognized me but couldn't place me. There had probably been many people passing over the last few days; he was unlikely to be able to remember them all.

"Morning," I said. "It's Bastien, isn't it?" He seemed confused to have his name known, but didn't demur. I continued before he could respond. "Bastien, you're getting a new neighbor."

His face brightened.

"A young lady."

There was something approaching excitement in his face. "Are you saying I should put on my best suit?" he asked, not entirely joking.

I shoved the final sack and closed the chute, turning my full attention to the old man. "We're going to need your help," I said. For some reason that line works—especially with older people. The need to be useful is probably buried deep in our psyche.

"Certainly," he said, puffing up his chest.

I moved closer, casting a glance over my shoulder. I wasn't expecting to see anyone, but everyone wants to think they're hearing a secret, and this guy seemed no different. When I spoke, I kept my voice low. "Look. She's been through a bit of a rough time—she needs someone to look out for her."

"Of course, of course."

I reached into my pocket and pulled out my last few bills. I counted 110 euros, then passed the bundle to the neighbor. "Just in case. If she ever needs anything—spend the money."

He nodded seriously.

I pulled out the key I had removed from Pierre-Louis' key ring and held it for him to see. "Some furniture should be delivered—hopefully in the next hour. Can you let them in?"

"Most certainly. Do I need to...?"

"Just let them in and take the key back when they leave," I said, turning toward the elevator. "I'll be back soon with your new neighbor."

eighty

The traffic had picked up.

When I had driven to the apartment in Belleville, the pre-dawn traffic had been minimal. Now the sun still hadn't risen, but Parisians had taken to their vehicles and were driving fast. As the traffic signals flicked from red to green, the routine was familiar. First, all the scooters—a range of small fizzy machines and expensive three-wheeled vehicles—that had worked their way through the stacked-up cars would take off with a buzzing cacophony. The advantage of their power-to-weight ratios gave them a fast time off the line, which seemed designed to catch out the ambitious and lazy pedestrians who disobeyed their signals.

When the signal turned, the cars would hit the power too, but the weight of the huge lump of metal giving a comfortable shell of protection for the driver and any passenger meant that the cars moved far more slowly off the line. But after ten seconds or so, the situation changed—strengths became weaknesses, and the disadvantaged found advantage.

The scooters—lightweight with their small engines—lost the power to keep accelerating, and the cars with their heavy engines found their momentum and were able to apply power through their tires on the blacktop. Some scooters thought they could stay ahead—and some could—but for most, it was time to gracefully give in and let the cars pass.

Not that the cars were going far. On the broad boulevards laid around Paris by Baron Haussmann, the city powers had later decided to bring traffic lights, giving the assurance that motorists would never be more than a few hundred yards away from another stop/start. The cars would stack up, and the scooters that had been passed would thread through the gaps between the cars, working their way to the head of the queue and readying themselves for the next green light, when they would again take off, being pursued by the cars that would inevitably pass them but would inevitably be stopped at the next junction.

My concern was less about how quickly I could reach the next set of traffic lights, but more about keeping the Mercedes I had borrowed from Gaston Blanc free from scratches. I slowed toward the next set of lights and cautiously moved away from the guy in the next lane who had already pulled to a halt: There was enough space for a scooter to get through. Any less space, and the scooter would still get through—they *always* got through—but one of our cars would likely pay the price for the scooter rider's impatience.

I felt relief when I reached the familiar green gate without damage to the vehicle. I gently tapped on Émilie's front door. "Hi." She smiled, opening the door as if indicating I should come in.

"How is she?" I asked.

"She's a kid...alone. Scared, unsure, brave..." She shrugged.

"And you?"

"I was worried about you," she said.

"Me?"

She nodded—an imperceptible bob of her head. "You were gone a long time."

"A lot of people to see, but now..." I sighed, thinking. "Do you want to come along?"

"Where?"

"To see what Pierre-Louis was planning...was working on...for Marianne."

A range of emotions passed across her face—there was joy, sadness, confusion, curiosity. "I don't think I..." She was hesitant.

"I think it would help make sense of one small part of Pierre-Louis' last few days," I said. "I'd like you to see what he was trying to do."

She remained quiet, focusing on me as a conversation passed across our locked gaze. She asked for reassurance; I gave it. Was I kidding? No. Would it be upsetting? Probably. What would she see? Well, come and see what you'll see. How...? What...? Why...?

She stepped back. "Okay," she whispered.

I waited a moment or two. She tilted her head, pointing to her lounge. As we entered, Marianne was sitting where I had sat on the night I told Émilie that Pierre-Louis had been killed. She had a blanket wrapped around her—a blanket that was familiar to me—and her shoes were lying about four feet away, their heels looking even higher than they did when she was wearing them.

"Hi," I said softly. "How are you?"

Her face seemed to have aged. She might only be twenty-one or twenty-two, but the worry etched on her face suggested she was a generation older and a generation wiser. The protective shell had cracked and fallen away.

"Have you slept?" I asked.

She nodded. "A few hours. Émilie offered her bed, but I was happy here."

I looked to the facing sofa. A blanket had been folded and neatly laid over the back.

"Have you eaten?"

She nodded, again. This time more enthusiastically, as if she had enjoyed the experience.

"Are you ready for a short journey?" I asked.

"Where to?" Her question was asked simply. There was no anger, no aggression, no presumption that this was a trick.

"I'm going to show you what Pierre-Louis had planned for you and the little one."

Marianne instinctively reached for her stomach, cradling the unborn lump. Émilie sniffed—she had been standing so quietly that I had nearly forgotten she was in the room. Marianne looked around. "I won't if..."

"No. No, my dear," said Émilie wiping her eyes. "You must go."

"Will you...?"

"I'm coming too," said Émilie.

Slowly we made our way down to the car. Marianne wrapped the blanket around her shoulders, and Émilie carried the big brown bag. She seemed more respectful of the fashion than I could ever be.

Both women sat in the backseat of the Mercedes, making me feel—even if I wasn't dressed that way—like a chauffeur. A chauffeur whose mission was to transport two-and-a-half delicate packages across Paris.

We arrived in Belleville, and the car pulled us steadily up the hill. "Do you know this place?" I asked Marianne.

She shook her head. "Think of it as a vertical village," I said, holding the entrance gate for the two women. "Everything you need is here. Shops, childcare, friends—all here."

There was an excitement on Marianne's face as she seemed to contemplate the reality of existence as a mother with a child for the first time.

The elevator pinged as we reached the fourth floor. Bastien had his front door open before I was out of the metal box.

"Greetings, greetings, greetings," he said, his attention focused solely on the women. He had a dilemma—I had told him that there was a young lady, singular, who would be his new neighbor. I had then returned with two women, both of whom were young in comparison to him.

"Bastien," I said. "This is Marianne, your new neighbor."

"Mademoiselle," said the neighbor. "Anything you need, I'm here to help." He turned to me, holding out the key. "They left ten minutes ago." I took the key. He took the hint and scuttled back into his apartment.

"They?" asked Émilie.

"A temporary loan," I said, opening the door. "Welcome to your new home, Marianne."

"But…"

"Step inside," I said, following the two women through the hall, past the bathroom and into the main room with the kitchenette. A large leather sofa, disproportionately large for the room, had been placed against the wall where Pierre-Louis lay as he died. If there were any last bloodstains caught in the gaps between the laminate boards, then they were covered by the sofa. On the opposite wall, an equally bombastically sized television stood on a small table.

"What do you mean, *my new home*?" asked Marianne.

"This is your new home." I eased her down onto the sofa, the blanket still around her shoulders. Émilie's heels clipped softly as she went to explore the apartment while I tried to explain the situation to Marianne. "Pierre-Louis wanted this for you—for you and the baby. He knew that everybody else wanted whatever they could get out of you. No one had your interests—or your baby's interests—at heart."

"But…"

"You might have thought Nils and the other two were your friends. In the end, they wanted money and they held you hostage. Pierre-Louis saw them for what they were. He wanted you to have this apartment—a place where you could be safe and could look after your baby."

The still of Marianne reassessing her situation was broken by a gentle sob coming from the smaller bedroom. I helped Marianne to her feet. As we entered the small room, Émilie was standing, her hands to her face, half as in prayer, half as if in shock. Tears rolling down her cheeks. Her gaze was fixed on the crudely painted animals on the walls. "A nursery," was all she could say.

Marianne took a moment or two to comprehend the significance of the room. Her initial look told of the disappointment of someone who realized the room was too small to work as a regular bedroom. Then she silently wondered whether this could be a walk-in wardrobe. And finally, she caught up with how Pierre-Louis had seen the room, as the perfect size for a nursery. She walked over to Émilie and embraced her.

I left the two and checked out the main bedroom.

As Gaston Blanc had agreed, a bed had also been delivered. Like the sofa, it was huge in comparison to the size of the room, and a heap of linen had been placed at one end. Not perfect, but it would suffice until the furniture Pierre-Louis had ordered could be delivered, and today was not the day to explain to Marianne the arrangements Pierre-Louis had put in place for her.

eighty-one

"That's where he died," said Émilie, a question phrased as a statement.

I nodded. "But Marianne doesn't have to make that connection." The elevator reached the ground floor and we stepped through the lobby, out onto the path winding around the block.

"It's a nice apartment," she said. "Clean, fresh, good view—it'll be nice for her when the baby comes. I can see why Pierre-Louis chose it." We walked in silence for a few paces. "You've got something you want to say to me, haven't you, Leathan?"

"Not here," I said. "Let's go...somewhere else."

I held the front gate for her. "Whose car?" she asked as we reached the Mercedes.

"I think you know."

"So you work for him now?"

"No," I said. "But I had to deal with him. If I didn't, well... Marianne, you, me..."

We drove in silence. The car seemed to know better than I did where we were going. It found its way to Île Saint-Louis—the smaller of the two islands in the middle of la Seine—and led us toward its west tip. The café looked over the other main island in the middle of the river: Île de la Cité.

A pedestrian footbridge linked our island to the island that had once been the entirety of Paris. That island with its cathedral, police station, law courts, and apartments.

We sat within the plastic awning protecting us from the cold, made worse by the wind driving along la Seine, and stared out across the six-floor residences ringing the other island. The tower of Notre-Dame de Paris peeking above the roofline. Two cups of coffee and some croissants arrived at our table; then the waiter left us to our silence.

I reached into my pocket and pulled out Pierre-Louis' notebook and his keys, placing them on her side of the table. She looked but said nothing.

"The money," I said. Her head moved slightly, as if she were moving her ears to better listen while she allowed her eyes to continue to stare into the distance. "One hundred thousand euros that Gaston Blanc gave to Pierre-Louis. I know what happened to it. Or at least, I know what happened to most of it."

Her eyes left the distance and turned to meet mine.

"The apartment—Marianne's apartment."

"Rent would never be that much," she said, a hint of confusion in her voice.

"He paid for four years," I said. "A four-year lease cost him eighty thousand. The paperwork's in there." I tapped the notebook. "The whole legal agreement—Marianne's apartment is guaranteed for four years. That's why the money seemed to be gone—that's why he wouldn't or couldn't give anything when the leeches who were sucking Marianne dry came calling. And I'm guessing he knew that Marianne was so lonely that she would give whatever she had to anyone who would offer her comfort and tell her they would take her away from the grind."

Émilie pulled at the end of the croissant's claw. "What about the other twenty thousand?"

"Furniture, mostly. The receipts are in there," I pointed to the notebook. "He's got it all—a sofa, chairs, a bed, a crib, a changing table. Anything you can think of, he's ordered and paid for. I'm sure the paint cost something and he spent money here and there—he bought that bag Marianne seems to love so much but that just looks like fake leather to me."

She smiled. "You don't understand fashion, do you, Leathan?"

"You're not the first person to tell me that. And yes, I do know that those bags have only arrived very recently and that they cost a lot…like enough to feed a baby for a year."

I sipped my coffee. "Everything he ordered will get delivered in two or three weeks—that's why I had to ask Gaston to sort Marianne with something for the next few days, hence the rather overly large furniture."

"You seem very friendly with him—borrowing furniture, borrowing his car." She tilted her head from side to side. "Seems more than a passing acquaintance."

"No. We're done. I've got to return his car before lunchtime, and once it's back, then we're finished."

It was as if an unpleasant smell had caught her nose. Not enough to revolt her, but enough to irritate. "You're never done with Gaston Blanc. Ever."

I let the thought hang for a moment or two before I replied. "Maybe. Maybe not. But he has given me his word, for what that's worth."

She snorted. "You think you've done a deal with Gaston and he's given his word."

"It was more of a transaction." I paused. "I gave him some money and helped him with…"

"Please tell me you didn't give him one hundred thousand euros."

"I didn't," I said.

"But."

"But I had an opportunity," I said. "Marianne and the baby… Tolomush Okeyev…you… You're all clear of Gaston. Debts paid in full, no future obligation to him."

"You're telling me you've paid for me." Her voice was calm, but suddenly as cold of the day outside.

"I made an exchange for a number of things," I said, "for a number of people."

Her face lost its color. She seemed frozen. Slowly, softly, she began to speak, her voice weak. "I thought you got it, Leathan. I thought you understood. You pay for me, and you make me something I never was."

I went to reply. A small shake of her head silenced me as she stared straight into my eyes. "I've spent the last twenty years trying to be free from men doing things *for me* and expecting me to be grateful when really what they've done is something that was easy for them to do but which created some sort of unspoken obligation on me."

She stood. I went to speak. Another small shake of her head held me silent.

"I thought you understood." She looked at me, her eyes reddening. "Goodbye, Leathan."

I watched her walk out of the café. Her small, precise steps following the road along the edge of the island. I finished my coffee and followed her outside. She was gone.

I sat on the concrete wall designed to keep cars out of la Seine and pulled out my phone. The SIM card landed in the river, and when the new card had contacted the service, I called the number I call every morning.

Note from the author

If you enjoyed this book please consider writing a short review. Reader reviews help me, and more significantly, they help other readers find books they will enjoy. The best place to post your review is where you bought the book, but you might also want to consider posting on Goodreads, Facebook, or any of the other social networks.

I'd also like to invite you to join my readers' group. If you sign up I'll send you my introductory library for free. And of course, as a member of my readers' group, I'll let you know about my new releases and any special offers.

Join my readers' group and get your free books at: simoncann.com/readers.

Other books by the author

Be sure to check out Simon's latest books at: simoncann.com.

The Leathan Wilkey series

Clementina

Leathan Wilkey faces up to the man who is menacing Clementina as a threat against her father.

The Camera

The only way for Leathan Wilkey to bring about justice for his murdered friend, is to track down the cause and ensure it is eliminated, permanently.

The Boniface series

The Murder of Henry VIII

When the author he is representing is murdered, Boniface realizes the job demands more than he expected. And when the man he is talking with is shot, Boniface runs.

Pollute the Poor

The first Boniface knows about the dead body in the next room is when he is arrested for murder.

Tattoo Your Name on My Heart

When his client's wife disappears, Boniface uncovers the secret she has been keeping from her husband.

About the Author

Simon Cann is the author of the Boniface, Montbretia Armstrong, and Leathan Wilkey books.

In addition to his fiction, Simon has written a range of music-related and business-related books, including the *How to Make a Noise* series, the most widely ready series about synthesizer sound programming, and *Made it in China*, about entrepreneurs building businesses in China. He has also worked as a ghostwriter on a number of books.

Before turning full-time to writing, Simon worked as a management consultant, where his clients included aeronautical, pharmaceutical, defense, financial services, chemical, entertainment, and broadcasting companies.

He lives in London.

You can find more about Simon and his other books at his website: simoncann.com.

You can also find him at:

- Facebook: simoncann.com/facebook (simoncannauthor)
- Twitter: simoncann.com/twitter (@simonpcann)
- YouTube: simoncann.com/youtube